the s
secret
©o de
r
e
t

the secret
secret ©ode
a *novel*

by paul meier & robert wise

A JANET THOMA BOOK

THOMAS NELSON PUBLISHERS
Nashville

Published in Nashville, Tennessee, by
Thomas Nelson, Inc.

The Bible version used in this publication is THE NEW KING JAMES
VERSION. Copyright © 1979, 1980, 1982, 1990,
Thomas Nelson, Inc.

Library of Congress Cataloging-in-Publication Data

Meier, Paul D.
The secret code : a novel / Paul Meier and Robert Wise.

ISBN 0-7852-7090-6 (pbk.)

I. Wise, Robert L. II. Title.
PS3563.E3457S33   1998   98-38983
813'.54–dc21   CIP

Printed in the United States of America
1 2 3 4 5 6 7 QPK 03 02 01 00 99 98

FICTION
3/99

DEDICATION

For Michael Lawrence Wise

Number eleven and holding

ACKNOWLEDGMENTS

The authors wish to thank

Janet Thoma for her skillful and faithful editing.

Always the best.

And we thank Todd Ross

for excellent insight and suggestions in shaping the manuscript.

Such good friends are hard to find!

DAY ONE
AV 5 5766

"Tell us, when will these things be?

And what will be the sign of Your coming,

and of the end of the age?"

Matthew 24:3

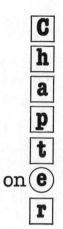

Chapter one

Tel Aviv
July 30, 2006

SHE STOPPED AND WATCHED her fellow passengers hurrying out of the El Al 747 and into the shuttle bus waiting to take them to Tel Aviv's Ben Gurion Airport. Clutching her brother's hand, she muttered a prayer under her breath. "God help us. If they identify me, I'm dead for sure." The brother and sister climbed into the blue bus and clung to the overhead straps as the bus sped away. Within minutes the large vehicle pulled to a stop in front of the entryway.

Hordes of tourists streamed into the terminal, pushing, jostling, jockeying for the quickest route through passport control. American pilgrims to the Holy Land blurred into a collage of nationalities. Jews of diverse backgrounds surged onward, making *aliya,* the return to their homeland. The air was hot and stale, smelling of unwashed bodies. The irritated mob lacked any sense of humor, lumbering forward like captives in a human zoo seeking shelter from the hot sun.

"These people in line behind me are in my tour group," a

rotund, perspiring American explained to the attractive Jewish immigration official. "I'm a minister of the gospel," he beamed. "These are all good southern church folks." He pointed over his shoulder.

The young woman looked up from her computer and glared. "We put people in jail for proselytizing."

"Oh, my, didn't mean any harm, miss." The bowling-ball-shaped preacher mopped his forehead. "I just wanted you to know we *really* love Israel."

"Next," the passport control agent called out, stamping the man's passport. *"Ba'ruch ha'ba* to Israel."

Before the next lady in the minister's group could respond, a slender woman barged in front of the line, pulling a younger man behind her. "I'm with the reverend." She grinned innocently and thrust two passports in the agent's hands.

The immigration officer glanced quickly at their faces and read the passport names aloud. "Mary and Alvin Smith. Married?"

"No-o-o," the woman scoffed. "Alvin is my younger brother." She smiled infectiously into the deadpan gaze of the Israeli, who appeared to be twenty-eight, about her own age—though she hoped she didn't look twenty-eight now. "It's been my lifetime dream to come to Israel. You must have a very fascinating job, seeing so many different kinds of people pass through," the American chattered. "And you're *so* young."

"Both born in the United States?" The government official reached for her stamp. She didn't look up again. *"Ba'ruch ha'ba,"* she recited.

Still smiling, the American quickly dragged her brother

4

toward the luggage carousels, hustling after the minister as if she might lose her tour leader in the crowd. When he turned and looked blankly at her, she stopped, smiled as if greeting an old friend, and then slowly slipped past, walking toward the belt delivering luggage from the United States.

"Those two are the rudest people I ever saw," a woman complained to the minister. "Did you see that smart-aleck couple push right in front of me? Line jumpers and all. Said their name was Smith."

The Smith woman ignored the complaint and pulled her brother to the other side of the conveyer belt away from the minister and his travel club. She carefully looked around the room, watching for any sign of recognition. Police seemed oblivious to her presence. For the first time since the El Al 747 hit the ground, she relaxed.

"We did it," Judy Bithell whispered to her younger brother. "Rabbi Shiloh was right. Blending into a tour group caused the agent not to check our passports carefully. I can't believe it! We slipped into Israel on fake passports and got away with it."

Jim Bithell stopped staring at the endless stream of bags and slowly turned toward his sister. Although taller and much heavier than she, he appeared dependent and childlike. His eyes moved back and forth as if a nerve was stuck in repeat mode. "I am named Jim. Why did you call me Smith? Have . . . I . . . been . . . a bad boy?"

"No, no, of course not." Judy gave him a little hug. "We just had to use those names for a little while. Remember how much you wanted to come here with me? The message you are bringing to our friends?" She looked into his blank eyes.

"The only way I could come back to Israel was with a forged passport because they deported me last time I was here."

Jim tilted his head slightly and frowned. "We haven't been naughty, have we?"

"Absolutely not." Judy patted his hand. "Just look for our bags. Everything is fine." Again she watched the police and immigration officials working their way through the hordes of tourists. No one appeared to have the slightest interest in the Bithells.

Jimmy's brown eyes stared aimlessly at the luggage lumbering past him. His striking resemblance to Judy marked him with handsome features. The stylish cut of his light brown hair and his fashionable clothes identified him as an American. Yet his rumpled shirt and disheveled look gave him the demeanor of a person totally indifferent to his appearance.

In a few minutes Jim mechanically pulled two bags from the line. "These are ours." His voice was flat. Without looking at the tag, he repeated, "Numbers 45827318 and 45827319 accounted for. We are ready."

"Yes, dear." Judy put her arm in his. "Let's just casually stroll into this new batch of tourists getting ready to pass through the baggage check area. We'll blend in with them as well as we did with the reverend's flock." Judy turned and smiled enthusiastically at the new faces around her. "Where you all from?" Judy drawled to an elderly lady in a faded dress.

"Kansas," the little woman replied. "We own a farm up near Topeka."

"Really?" Judy beamed. "Kansas is one of my favorite places in the whole world. Awfully hot today, isn't it? Come along now, Jim."

The tour leader was at the front of the line talking to the customs agent. He waved for the group to follow him and to crowd together.

"Just awful." The old woman fanned herself with her passport. "It feels like Kansas in August."

Judy pulled Jim closer and put her arm in the elderly woman's. "I think the Menninger Clinic in Topeka is a national treasure." Judy spoke to the lady as if confiding a secret. "It's a marvelous institution."

"So many people are helped by their work," the Kansas woman agreed. "Never been there myself, you understand, but I know some people who have."

Judy smiled to the dark-skinned Israeli at the customs inspection desk as the group breezed past. The man winked back.

Seconds later she and Jim burst through the swinging doors and were on the street in front of the airport, confronted with an even larger and more unruly throng. Locals milled about, looking for family members coming out of customs. Tour guides frantically tried to usher their new groups into the large buses in the adjacent lot. Vendors spaced along the wall offered ice cream and cold Cokes. Taxi drivers hawked their services from the edge of the street. The sickening smell of roasting meat drifted through the air. Tourists looked frazzled and slightly terrified.

Judy broke ranks with the Kansas crowd and barged into the masses, blending into the mob like a native. Without breaking stride, she pulled Jim through the throng until she found the familiar bus stop that offered rides into downtown Tel Aviv and further.

"The bus to Jerusalem should be here any minute," she told Jim. "We want to catch this one or we've got a long wait. Good thing Keith got the tickets for us before we left California. That makes everything so much simpler."

Judy searched the large signs on the front of the passing buses. "Ah!" She pointed just ahead. "That's it!" She jerked Jim behind her and onto the bus as soon as it stopped.

The bus driver quickly stowed their bags underneath; Judy and Jim hustled to two vacant seats in the middle of the bus. Jim looked out the window in his trancelike stare. Judy glanced to see if anyone was watching them. Her sweep ended at the large driver's mirror with its panoramic view of the bus occupants. She gaped at the image reflected back to her.

Yes, that's me but . . . oh my! The black dye in my hair is just awful . . . and these black eyebrows make me feel like Groucho Marx. She felt her usually full, light brown hair pulled back in a severe knot at the back of her head. *The aging makeup under my eyes worked. I look fifty years old . . . and like an escapee from the Menninger Clinic. That poor woman from Kansas probably wasn't surprised I knew something about that hospital.*

The bus pulled away, taking the express highway out of Tel Aviv toward Jerusalem. Judy watched the flat plains disappear as they sped toward the high hills that would become the mountains around Jerusalem. As usual, Jim said nothing, just stared out the window.

Today is Av 5, Judy reflected. *We have less than four days to do our job. We must have everything accomplished before Av 9 or there is no second chance for any of us.*

"When do I talk?" Jim suddenly asked.

"Not until we find our friends. I will tell you."

"What I'm going to say is important?"

"Very important." Judy patted his hand.

"We are going to keep Ramallah from fulfilling the prophecy?"

Judy gritted her teeth and rolled her eyes. "We're going to do the best we can."

Jim turned back to the window.

The bus began the winding journey up through the pine forests. Old hulls of tanks and troop carriers had been left as reminders and monuments to past wars. Stark, ugly rusting metal carcasses stood against the backdrop of the lush forest, as if to remind even the most casual tourist that no amount of beauty could conceal the ever-present possibility of violence.

The air became much cooler than it had been in Tel Aviv. White limestone buildings loomed ahead. "Ah." Judy squeezed Jim's hand. "We are entering Jerusalem."

The bus wound its way into Jerusalem's main thorough-fares and down into the central area near Hebrew University, stopping at the Shrine of the Book to pick up passengers. Young men in civilian clothes carrying Uzis and machine guns got on. Old ladies lugged groceries in plastic bags. People seemed uptight and wary of each other.

"That's where the Dead Sea Scrolls are kept," Judy said, pointing to a strange spiral-shaped building. "We're not too far from our stop. When we get to Ben Yehuda Street, we'll get off. Be ready."

Jim's nervous eye movements started again; they always did when he was agitated. He folded his hands together tightly and looked straight ahead.

The old street broadened, the buildings changed, and the avenue took on a more modern look. New architecture did not clash with the ancient edifices, but the nuances in design were recent, subtle in ways the eye didn't immediately catch. Modern businesses lined the streets.

Ben Yehuda Street was clearly the uptown center of things. A large sign above a restaurant advertised Russian cuisine in both Hebrew and English. The bus pulled to the curb next to a sheltered stop, and the driver rattled off something in Hebrew. Judy immediately grabbed Jim's arm and rushed to the front door. She gestured toward the bus's baggage compartment. The driver nodded and went for their bags.

Once Jim and the luggage were parked on a bench under the shelter, Judy went to a pay phone a few feet away. Within minutes, she was back at her brother's side. Jim rigidly clutched both bags and stared straight ahead as if something blocks away had captured his imagination.

"Don't worry," Judy soothed him. "Everything is okay. No one is going to hurt us now. Our friends will be here in a few minutes."

Her words did not appear to register. The wind picked up and swept refreshing coolness over them. Judy breathed deeply and tried to relax, but her body refused to cooperate. Within five minutes a red Chevrolet van pulled up to the curb and two men jumped out.

"Shalom!" A small wiry man opened his arms, offering an embrace. "Welcome home!" A receding hairline and a jet-black beard gave his thin face balance. "Your ol' rabbi is here to offer you wheels!"

"Keith Yaakov!" Judy leaped to her feet. "Is it ever good to see you." She rushed forward.

The young man hugged her tightly, putting his mouth next to her ear. "Say nothing," he whispered. "Nothing. The enemy is in our midst."

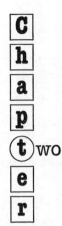

Chapter Two

KEITH YAAKOV'S ASSOCIATE hustled Jim and the luggage into the van. Judy piled into the backseat. In a matter of seconds, the vehicle pulled away from the curb into the fast-moving traffic. Keith spoke but watched the traffic. "You may have met Liat Collins the last time you were here."

Dressed in an Izod shirt, the redheaded, blue-eyed young man extended his hand. "Good to see you again. Glad you got back in the country."

"Yes, I remember you." Judy smiled politely and shook his hand. "Meet my brother. Jim, say hello to Liat."

"Good to meet you." Liat reached out farther.

Jim stared straight ahead but said nothing.

"I'm Jewish but originally from the Bronx." Liat smiled but received no encouragement from Jim. Collins looked puzzled. "Hey, I'm one of you guys."

"Jim's a person of few words," Judy apologized. "It takes awhile for him to warm up."

"Our congregation is gathering right now in anticipation of your arrival," Keith explained as he drove. "We estimated your landing just about right. After you called, I had some of our people contact the rest of the members and let them know you were actually here. By the time we get to the meeting hall, everyone should be there." He shot her a hard look in the rearview mirror.

Something's going on. Judy looked out the side window, pretending to survey the sights. *Keith is trying to telegraph a warning of some sort. Is Collins "the enemy"?*

"You'll be here long?" Liat smiled.

"It depends," Judy answered evasively.

"I understand you have a special message for us," Liat persisted.

Judy studied his face for a moment. *Sure, I remember him. He kept interrupting all the time. Lots of American Jews don't look Semitic, but he definitely doesn't fit the image.* She noticed that his constant smile seemed insincere, his eyes cold. *Something's not right about this man.*

"I don't think we should discuss any details until the meeting," Keith interjected. "Best let the whole group hear at one time so we don't risk misinterpretation."

Liat's smile turned into a frown.

"Sure," Judy said. "Good idea."

No one spoke for the next mile. Judy studied the embroidered yarmulke on the back of Keith's head and thought about the tremendous sacrifice he had made to leave America and come to Israel as a messianic rabbi. He had traded in his very secure life in Philadelphia for a tenuous existence as a leader of a persecuted congregation of survivors. Jewish believers were the constant targets of the Hasidic and Orthodox Jews, who were trying to run them out of Jerusalem. Keith looked thin. His wife, Ann, and their three children had also paid a significant price.

A faithful man, Judy concluded. *Keith survives on a pittance but never complains. I must do everything I can to help him and Ann.*

Heavy traffic made progress slow. Eventually Keith pulled into an alley and parked in a small space between two old office buildings.

Keith pointed to the top of a fire escape stairway. "Liat, why don't you take the luggage up, and I'll follow with our guests." He spoke to Judy. "We've been meeting here for a couple of months to avoid detractors. No one would suspect that a church is located upstairs."

Collins nodded but said nothing. He took the two suitcases up the narrow stairs. When Jim started to follow, Keith grabbed the back of his belt and held him in place. Jim stiffened like a robot. Only after Liat disappeared into the second-story entrance did Keith speak.

"We've got a problem," he said under his breath. "I don't know what's going on, but I suspect Liat is trying to wrestle control of the congregation away from me."

"Why?" Judy puzzled.

"I'm not sure, but I fear there's more here than just a power play. He may be an informer for the government."

"Why?" Judy's mouth dropped.

"I don't know. We thought he was truly one of us."

Judy took a deep breath. "That's *all* I need, someone to tip off the police that I've slipped into the country. This could be big, big trouble."

"Yes," Keith said slowly. "I've already thought about the implications. We must be very circumspect."

"I can't tell the group my message and exclude Collins?"

"Right," Keith agreed. "Still, I want you to be ready for anything."

Judy nodded. "Do they know about Jim? That he has a problem?"

"No."

Judy put her arm around her brother. "Well, Jimmy, you'll certainly give them something to think about."

"Now?" Jim asked.

"Wait until I tell you."

"We'd best hurry upstairs." Keith beckoned for them to follow. "The group's probably waiting. Watch your step."

Judy pushed Jim behind Keith, and they hurried up the rickety metal fire escape, down a narrow hall, and through a double doorway at the other end. A small fellowship hall was filled with Jewish believers, crowding around a table covered with assorted cookies and a coffeepot on one end. Looking around, Judy guessed that maybe forty or fifty people had gathered to hear what she and Jimmy had to say. The room was old and badly needed paint. A slightly musty smell hung in the air. Large chunks of paint dangled precariously from the ceiling.

"Welcome! *Shalom!*" someone called out of the crowd. Others applauded and waved. An older lady shoved a cup of coffee into Judy's hands. "Refresh yourself, dear."

Judy smiled and quickly sipped the bitter brew. Trying not to grimace, she could feel Jim pressing next to her. "It's okay," she assured him. "Everything is fine." He didn't relax.

Keith made some preliminary remarks, giving Judy a moment to catch her breath. *Oh, Benjamin,* she thought, *I wish you were here. You always know just the right thing to say, the right thing to do. I pray you are all right and safe out in that strange wilderness.* She remembered how the hidden desert center in the Petra-Bozrah area was so very hot in the summer. And even though Petra wasn't *that* far away by car, Benjamin Meridor seemed an eternity removed from her.

Keith held up his hands, signaling for complete quiet. "We know you have a very important message for us, Judy. I was grateful when my friend, Rabbi Reuven Shiloh, e-mailed me about your coming." Keith motioned for her to come to the front of the room. "Please tell us what you have discovered."

Judy walked confidently to the center of the group, leading Jim by the hand. She looked across the smiling faces and nodded pleasantly. *"Shalom,"* she began and waited for the group to echo back the greeting. "I have gone through considerable difficulties to be here today. Reentering Israel was dangerous."

Judy cleared her throat. "But peril is no stranger to any of you. We all know the many painful experiences Jewish people have lived through in past decades. Many of you or your parents barely survived unimaginably terrible things. Now, I come with more frightening, difficult news. Unfortunately, another baptism of fire lies ahead for us. The time is short, but we can still escape the catastrophe."

The room became intensely quiet. Old women stared with mouths open, and mothers pulled their children close. Men stiffened.

Judy continued. "My friend Benjamin Meridor and I came to Israel sometime ago to warn your government." She looked carefully around the room, trying to determine how the members were receiving her. "These efforts were rewarded by expulsion from the country. Our sudden ejection prevented us from speaking to your congregation. I am back because the issue is critical and time is running out." She pointed to the chairs, feeling the anxiety build. "Please sit down."

People reluctantly filled the available chairs. Liat Collins merged with a group of young men standing against the back wall.

"Some time ago, Ben and I discovered that an atomic bomb is going to explode in Jerusalem on Av 9, 2006 . . . Four days from today."

Cries of alarm burst from the group. Husbands clutched the hands of their wives. Agitated chatter echoed throughout the room. The men at the back crowded together.

"Please." Keith motioned for the group to be silent. "Listen carefully to the details. Our lives depend on it." He nodded for Judy to continue. "Forgive us for interrupting you."

"We don't know the exact time of day when the detonation will occur," Judy went on, trying to sound calm, "but we have no doubt Av 9 will be a day of destiny. The prediction is in the Bible."

The congregation erupted in more commotion. Fear spread over the room. People began weeping.

"Anticipating extreme difficulties," Judy talked over the uproar, "even now Ben and a group of concerned friends are making preparations for you to find shelter and safety in the one place the Bible says Jews can survive the attack. Water and supplies have been stockpiled in a secret location so you will be able to survive both the explosion and radioactive fall-out that will follow."

"Where is this place?" Liat Collins shouted.

Judy looked at Keith. He shook his head slightly.

"We must keep this information confidential until we are on the road out of Jerusalem. Security will be important."

"You don't trust us," Collins shot back.

"I don't know who's listening." Judy's voice was resolute.

Collins looked at his friends and shook his head.

"Since we have not been able to spread the warning in the secular community," Judy continued, "at least we can save you. As Jewish believers survived the Roman attack on Jerusalem two thousand years ago by fleeing to the cities of refuge, you will be able to avoid the impending disaster."

"Four days from now?" Collins again broke in. "How do you know such a thing?"

"I can answer that question, but it will take a few minutes. Perhaps many of you are unfamiliar with the history of what happened to Jewish people through the centuries on this par-ticular day. My brother has an unusual memory for facts. Let me ask him to tell you about Av 9."

Because he was standing behind her, Judy had not looked at Jimmy for several minutes. His eyes quivered as they always did when he was nervous. Judy squeezed his hand and pulled him forward. "Now, Jimmy. Talk now."

Staring at some point far out beyond the back wall, Jim began a rapid-fire recitation of facts. "Five hundred eighty-seven years before the Common Era, Babylonians invaded and defeated the Jewish people. On Av 9, the first Temple was destroyed. The same destruction reoccurred in A.D. 70, when the Romans tore down the entire Temple on an Av 9." Jim caught his breath and his face reddened. "Sixty-five years later, Simeon bar Kochba led the last uprising against Rome, but he and a million Jews were crushed on Av 9." Jim's voice sounded increasingly mechanical as his unemotional staccato progressed. "In 1096, the Crusades began on Av 9 and many Jews were killed by the Crusaders. The expulsion of the Jews from England and France in 1290 and 1306 both happened on Av 9. All Jews were expelled from Spain in 1492 on Av 9." He drew a deep breath. "The Holocaust officially began on Av 9, 1942, when Hitler began loading crematoriums at Auschwitz and—"

Judy put her arm around her brother's shoulders. "Stop now, Jimmy," she interrupted. "You did very well."

"I have more." His voice sounded like an answering machine. "I . . . I must tell them how Ramallah will fulfill a prophecy."

"They've got the idea." Judy looked carefully at the astonished congregation. "Do I need to argue further about the seriousness of this day for Jewish people?"

"Nonsense," Liat Collins scoffed. "I've heard this fear mongering before, but I'm not buying the idea of a bomb going off this year just because you've got some harebrained premonition. Look at our congregation! You've scared the old people nearly to death." He looked at the man next to him. "Harrison? Are you going to tolerate this manipulation?" He pointed at Yaakov. "Keith, you're responsible. What sort of nonsense are you foisting on us?"

"Please." Keith looked nervously around the room. "I know Judy Bithell and Benjamin Meridor. They are people of integrity. She wouldn't be here if this wasn't—"

"I want to know more about her sources," Liat interrupted. "I'm not about to listen to some cock-and-bull story on the basis of a so-called prophecy in the Bible she dug up somewhere. People try to prove all kinds of things from Scripture." He pointed at Jimmy. "Then, we next get the automated printout from this anthropoid. He's *really* weird."

Another uproar followed.

Judy hugged Jimmy and looked at the floor for a moment. "It's okay," she assured her brother. "Let's be honest with these people." Judy looked hard at Collins. "Jim has an affliction that makes it hard for him to relate to people . . . sometimes. He doesn't think in the same way most of you do, but he does have a phenomenal memory for facts and figures. He forgets nothing. Jim is a walking encyclopedia. Underneath his problem is an amazing mind. What he's telling you is completely trustworthy."

"Look, Keith—" Harrison Levy gestured menacingly. "You call us together with this end-of-the-world story and drag in some chick we know nothing about—"

"Then you try to substantiate the nonsense by turning a mental retard loose whose sister says he is really a genius in disguise," Liat continued. "You really think we're *that* gullible? I think your credibility and leadership need to be questioned."

Keith stood next to Judy. "She is talking about life and death."

"Listen," Liat said, "the time has come for us to make some changes in what happens around here. I think we need to send you *and* them packing before you frighten these good people any further."

"I second the motion," Harrison Levy jeered.

"Here! Here!" the young men around Collins shouted.

"Listen to me!" A bent old woman stepped out of the crowd. "Don't you talk to my rabbi in that tone of voice!" She shook her fat finger at Collins. "Mr. Skypanksi, God rest his soul, and I grew up in Poland and lived through the terrible times." The heavyset woman's pudgy face grimaced. "We didn't pay attention when the warnings came, and I watched my family perish. I know Keith well. Listen to what he says."

"Yes. Exactly," people around her chimed in.

"Trouble is, you're afraid to think for yourself," Collins answered. "Well, some of us aren't! We've lost all respect for Yaakov. I say that if he wants to run off to some hideaway with the mystery woman and the freak with the automated voice, let him hit the street." He crossed his arms over his chest defiantly. "If the rest of you want to continue being a responsible presence in Jerusalem, I suggest you stand with us. Let's stop all this doomsday talk and go back to the way things used to be."

The men around Collins applauded vigorously.

"Why don't you resign, Keith?" Liat taunted. "We need new blood, new leadership." He paused and let the threat sink in. "And take those two screwballs with you!"

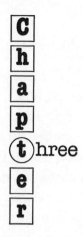

chapter three

THE MEETING EXPLODED in pandemonium. Children cowered next to their agitated mothers. Keith Yaakov's supporters shouted for Collins and his cohorts to leave. No one listened to Yaakov as he tried to restore order. Jimmy steadily retreated until he pressed against the room's front wall. Judy cringed, putting her hands against her cheeks.

"All right," Collins yelled over the hubbub. "You want me to leave. Done." He stepped toward the door. "See what it gets you. Come on, everybody who's sick of this nonsense follow me."

Harrison Levy and a dozen young men fell in behind the American. A few women joined them. Liat looked angrily around the room. "Well, are the rest of you going to stay here with the nut fringe?"

People froze in place. Keith said nothing.

"So be it!" Liat backed through the door. "Hang around these crazies and see what price you pay." He paused one last time. "You'll be sorry. You had your chance to get out." Liat slammed the door behind him.

Silence settled over the room. Finally an older man asked, "What in the world was that all about?"

"It's been coming for a long time," Keith answered. "Liat and his friends have fomented dissension for months. I'm a little worried about what he's up to."

People drifted back to their chairs. The elderly looked shaken, the young angry. Keith nervously ran his hands through his hair and beckoned for Judy to continue. "We must listen carefully to our friends from America. Judy, tell us the rest of your message."

Judy cleared her throat and tried to look composed. "Right now, I don't have time to tell you the details of how we made our discoveries, but my friend Ben and I stumbled across amazing information that we completely trust. Jimmy's unusual ability to assimilate facts and figures helped us put the implications together. Please believe me. An atomic attack is just days away."

"What shall we do?" Mrs. Skypanski pleaded.

"We have carefully researched the alternatives," Judy continued, "and I am here to lead you to the only place in the region that will be secure. Some of you may want to leave the country another way, but since time is so short, other routes may prove to be impossible. You sure won't get any help from the government."

Keith held up his hand. "I already had a hint of what Judy just told you. My old friend Rabbi Reuven Shiloh gave me a few clues. He couldn't say much for fear of discovery, but Reuven instructed me to prepare for a quick departure. That's why we sent our three children out of the country two weeks ago. And that's also why I've been urging you to get your houses in order."

A murmur of agreement buzzed around the room.

"What's next?" Keith asked Judy.

"We must maintain tight security. I suggest you quickly return to your homes and gather up only what you can carry or put in a car. We can rendezvous back here and leave as a group, traveling in a caravan."

"I'm not trying to create problems like Liat did, but what if you're wrong?" Danny Rubenstein asked from the back of the room. "Maybe Miss Bithell's information isn't accurate."

"Then in five days we come back home and everything is fine," Keith answered. "We were wrong, and we all had a little vacation. I'll submit my resignation if you wish. On the other hand, if Judy's right, we'll be in the ark and not the flood."

"Amen!" someone shouted.

The old Polish woman held up her hands and smiled. "A very Jewish thing to do—take a quick trip to somewhere else and wait for another disaster." She laughed and her large stomach shook.

A ripple of giggles went across the room.

"Only Jews laugh in the face of danger." Keith smiled. "Now, can we go to our homes and be back here in two hours?"

"Three hours!" several people insisted.

"Three hours it is," Keith agreed. "Be ready to be on the road out of town when you get here."

"No." Jimmy held up his hand slowly. "Ruppin Street

winds across Hakriya and then runs into Ben Zvi Street before becoming Yehuda Halevi. The alleyway runs into Ussichkine, which intersects with Bezald Way after twisting through the city. On the other hand, Nablus Road meanders into the Via Dolorosa through the heart of the old city, crossing the old Jericho Road and coming out on the valley road to Bethany."

Judy shook Jimmy's shoulder slightly. "What are you saying? I don't understand."

"Crooked roads and crooked people. Hard to travel safely."

"You're telling us something important." Judy watched his eyes jerking back and forth. "You want us to think about where we are going . . . or be on guard as we travel?"

"Or make sure we're not *followed!*" Keith exclaimed.

Jim nodded his head mechanically.

"If Liat is truly against us, returning here could be a big mistake," Keith concluded. "Jim is trying to protect us." He paused. "We need to congregate somewhere else."

"How about gathering in the parking lot at the Shrine of the Book?" Judy ventured. "Tourists pull in there all the time, and we wouldn't be obvious."

"Excellent," Keith agreed. "In three hours we'll meet in the tourist parking lot . . . Let's go."

The younger members hurried down the back stairs while the older people went out through the front entrance, leaving in small groups to appear inconspicuous. Keith and the Bithells left with Ann in the family van. Silence fell across the meeting hall.

Thirty minutes later a man slipped out of an office door at the end of the hall. He hurried down the corridor and into the back of the empty meeting room. The tall redhead reached under one of the wooden chairs and pulled out a small battery operated tape recorder. He flipped a switch and let the machine rewind briefly. Holding the recorder next to his ear, he hit the play button.

A familiar voice said, "—go to our homes and be back here in two hours." Other voices echoed back, "Three hours."

The young man hit the stop button and smiled. After peering out the second-story window, he dropped the recorder into his pocket and scurried down the back stairs.

JUDY WAITED IN THE RED VAN with Jim while Keith and Ann Yaakov hurried to collect the last of their possessions in their apartment. The one-bedroom flat in a new housing development in the Talpiot area was several blocks from the edge of Jerusalem on the Hebron Road to Bethlehem. The last Jewish outpost in the Six-Day War, Kibbutz Ramat Rachael, lay straight ahead, a reminder of perpetual strife. Judy watched traffic come and go into the city.

A red van the same make and model as Keith's, though considerably more battered and dirty, pulled to a stop at the intersection next to them. Judy could see the Arab driver and two other men.

Jim pointed at the dirty red vehicle. From the front passenger seat a European in a black mock-turtleneck pullover turned and looked at them. The thin man's completely bald head made his narrow, bony face seem even longer. Without hair or eyebrows, the face had the appearance of a vast plain of skin interrupted by two sinkhole eye sockets; murky blue eyes disappeared in the shadows, and his black sweater gave him the look of a mob executioner. The man stared intensely at Jimmy.

Jimmy immediately reached for his sister's hand and jerked her arm, watching as the bald man put on sunglasses. Behind him, a fat Caucasian with graying blond hair abruptly pressed his face to the window and then quickly looked away. The man's pudgy, fiftyish face sagged at the jaws and neck. Small round glasses made his features seem even larger. The hairless man said something to the driver, and the van shot away from the stoplight.

"What a strange man!" Judy strained to watch the van as it sped down the street. "But then again everything here looks strange to me." She watched a Palestinian in a checkered headdress and a long white robe cross the street, passing a bent old woman who looked like a character straight out of a 1940 European movie. "Jerusalem certainly is a long way from our world," Judy told Jimmy. "How did we ever get here?"

The question took Judy's thoughts back eight years to 1998 and the high-tech world of the University of California at Davis.

❑ ○ ❑

PREPARING TO FINISH HER DEGREE in mathematics, even the toughest studies at the highly demanding college had not been difficult. With time on her hands, Judy joined a weekly Bible study held in a nearby Presbyterian church.

During her sophomore year, Judy had bought into the usual agnosticism expected of science and math majors at Davis. She remained indifferent to religion until her senior year, when a friend challenged Judy to look into the meaning of numbers in Bible prophecy. The idea had intrigued her, as solving any puzzle did. The more Judy heard, the more interested she became. Eventually, the Wednesday night study in the Presbyterian church became the most exciting hour in her busy week.

The group of young women gathered in the fellowship hall and sat around a large table as they always did. Each of the participants laid notepads and Bibles on the table. Mariam Yates, a staff member of the church, always called the study together with a prayer for wisdom.

"We're going to look further into Matthew twenty-four tonight," Mariam began. "The 'little apocalypse' is one of the most intriguing chapters in the New Testament. Important clues are hidden between the lines! Studying these clues will help us understand what lies ahead for the nation of Israel."

"You are into prophecy?" Janice Norris asked.

"Absolutely," Mariam answered. "God left us important messages so we would be prepared for what the future brings."

"Far out!" Janice rolled her eyes.

"I've got one better for you!" Rachel Conrad plunked a new book on the table in the middle of the six young women. "Here's some spice for our Bible study—a real challenge for the skeptics."

"What is it?" Jane Conroy picked up the large book.

"That is the biggest thing on today's *New York Times* best-seller list." Rachel opened the book. "That book will make you think twice about all this prophecy jazz. It really blows my mind."

Mariam read the title aloud. "*The Eternal Code* by Rabbi Edlow Moses? Hey, this book was featured on *Good Morning, America* last week. This book has the big predictions on what is going to happen *right now.*"

"You won't believe it." Rachel opened the book to the middle. "It details and explains a secret code embedded in the Hebrew version of the Old Testament. When Moses received the inspired word, God put in disguised messages that can only *now* be deciphered with a modern computer."

"You've got to be kidding!" Judy looked at a page of Hebrew text with strings of letters circled up, down, and across the page. "This looks like a giant puzzle—a crossword or an acrostic."

"Thousands of years ago," Rachel explained, "God hid instruction for our time. The next ten years of Israel's future are revealed in these pages."

"What you're talking about is mathematically impossible," Judy scoffed. "The odds of this happening are off the chart."

"For us," Rachel answered, "but not for God. Before the beginning of time He apparently set up a little joke on our pretentiousness."

"Wow!" Judy stared at the page. "Who knows where this could take us."

"Let's get some New Testament perspective." Opening her Bible, Mariam Yates read a verse from the twenty-fourth chapter of Matthew's gospel: "'Tell us, when will these things be? And what will be the sign of Your coming, and of the end of the age?'" She laid the Bible on the table. "Rachel, you really think the messages are connected?"

"That's what many Hebrew scholars and mathematicians are saying, Mariam. The code says the hidden information is for what the Bible calls the 'end of days.' Rabbi Moses started working years ago but only figured this thing out around 1993. He discovered a prediction concerning the assassination of the prime minister of Israel. Moses was able to warn Rabin but no one listened. When Rabin was shot, important people started paying attention to the code."

Judy thumbed through the pages. "The book says the code even predicted the Oklahoma City bombing and Oswald killing Kennedy. That's a little hard to believe."

"Look at this." Rachel pointed to a line in the fourth chapter. "Not only is the Holocaust in the Bible, but the gas used to kill Jews, Zyklon B, is encoded next to the name of Eichmann. The hidden acrostic predicted two world wars and suggested a coming nuclear attack on Israel."

"The code was written into the Bible at least three thousand years before these events," Mariam explained.

"Look at this!" Jennifer Whimple pointed to another page. "The date for Neil Armstrong's landing on the moon is encoded next to the word moon. The hidden prophecy also says, 'Done by mankind, done by a man,' almost exactly what Armstrong said when he walked on the moon's surface."

"That's not all." Mariam checked the exact chapter and verse in the Hebrew version and then flipped back to her English Bible. "This moon landing message is hidden in Genesis where God tells Abraham to look at heaven and count the stars. Apparently, the messages are also somehow correlated to the more general biblical themes."

Judy scratched her head. "The possibility of finding hidden information even one time on the basis of random chance has to be 1 in 10 or 20 million. The probability of this whole system occurring randomly is virtually incalculable."

"But why?" Jennifer puzzled. "Why would God put together such a strange way of telling us something?"

"Well," Mariam thought aloud, "maybe this was always how Jesus intended us to find the answer to the questions in Matthew twenty-four concerning His coming and the end of the age."

"Exactly," Rachel answered. "From what I've read in the book, God gave us this system especially to prepare His people for the terrible things that are ahead between the years 2000 and 2010. No one could find the directives until the computer age. Of course, we've just touched the tip of the iceberg."

"What do you mean?" Judy asked.

"The complete meaning of the code isn't entirely clear, nor are all the insights worked out yet. Further decoding is necessary. This whole thing is like some enormous puzzle that is only partially solved."

"Really?" Judy's eyes sparkled. She smiled broadly. "I wonder if this Hebrew text is available on software?"

Rachel turned to the back of the book. "The appendix says that the original research is in the scholarly journal *Statistical Science*, and that the Hebrew text without any spaces between the words is easily obtained."

"Wow," Judy mused. "What a fascinating project. This sort of thing is right up my alley. I'd love to play with the code."

"I don't know," Mariam hesitated. *"Play* is not really the right word. Finding messages from God sounds like very serious business."

Judy picked up the book. "Best-seller at all the local stores, huh? Well, I've got a friend who's a computer whiz. I'm going to see what the two of us can squeeze out of this puzzle."

Mariam shot her a doubtful look. "Judy, be careful. No telling what you might get into."

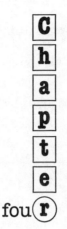

Chapter four

Davis, California
October 28, 1998

SWINGING A BRIEFCASE at her side, Judy Bithell hurried through the crowded student center and into the popular snack bar on the second floor. She looked carefully around the packed room until a young man at a table in the back motioned. Judy waved back and edged through the students milling around the cafe.

"Benjamin Meridor," Judy slipped into the booth across from the black-haired collegian, "the hero of the computer department and my old lab partner in first-year chemistry." She looked into his black eyes. "Look at the Ralph Lauren shirt, the Lands' End pants, the Gucci shoes. Mirror, mirror on the wall, who's the most GQ of them all?"

"What is that supposed to mean?"

"Oh, take it easy. I meant it as a compliment."

"It didn't sound like a compliment. Listen, Judy—" Benjamin cocked his head sideways and squinted as if barely awake. "You woke me up at midnight last night to tell me some wild story about, of all things, the *Bible*. Give me a break."

"Well, this all came up at my Bible study group, and when our meeting was over I had to find a bookstore before I could call you," she explained. "I had to call you. I knew you were the guy to help with the project I have in mind. You'll love this."

"People who party all night and call me at four o'clock in the morning to haul them home from a bar, I understand. A girl waking me up in the middle of the night because she thinks she's found a secret message in the Bible, I don't understand. If you weren't the best-looking brain in the math department, I would have made several suggestions about what you could do with your little idea. Really, Judy."

"Come on, Ben. You're supposed to be a man of science. What I've found out couldn't be a coincidence—the chances against it are twenty million to one. Aren't you at least a little intrigued?"

Ben looked at the date on his wristwatch. "Okay, Judy, let's see. October 28. Hmmm. You've found Freddie Krueger's story in the Bible. Or maybe your friends discovered the plot of Stephen King's next big thriller."

Judy didn't respond; instead, she studied his face for a moment. Ben's eyes were different from hers. Their almond shape hinted of Mediterranean origins. His unblemished olive skin was naturally darker than Judy's. From the cleft in his chin to the fashionable sweep of his hair, Judy liked everything she saw.

"Speak up, Miss Math Major. Since when did you get into this religion thing, anyway?"

"Hey, religion might do you some good." She poked her finger at his nose. "Where do you go to church?"

"Bedside Baptist. I just hit the TV remote on Sunday morning and wander from service to service." Ben laughed.

"Very funny." Judy pulled *The Eternal Code* out of her briefcase. "Look, this is the book I told you about last night. You won't believe it."

"I already don't."

"I know. You told me last night you're an atheist."

"To the core. My God is the latest computer on the third floor lab of the math building."

"Right." Judy opened the book and pushed it in front of Ben. "Get a load of this." She put her fingers on the uninterrupted string of Hebrew letters. "When sequences of numbers are entered in a computer to establish combinations, words pop up at intervals in the Hebrew Torah. For example, if we count every fifty letters and encircle the Hebrew character, the outcome spells *Torah*. Get this. This system works and produces the same result in Genesis, in Exodus, in Numbers, and in Deuteronomy."

"You're kidding." Ben frowned.

"No." Judy turned another page. "I've been up all night studying this thing. It's like the Bible contains one gigantic cryptogram invented by God."

"This sounds like something some screwball televangelist would come up with."

"The search started with Sir Isaac Newton way back in 1700. Believe it or not, Newton not only believed in the idea but spent half his life trying to prove it. He wrote more about esoteric theology than math or astronomy, and his mathematical calculations led him to believe that Jesus would probably return shortly *after* the year A.D. 2000."

"Come on, Judy. Newton was one of the greatest mathematicians and scientific theorists who ever lived. I find it hard to believe that he wasted his time predicting when Jesus would return."

"Well, he did. The next step happened in Prague, Czechoslovakia. A rabbi named Weissmardel was the first to find the word *Torah* in every fifty characters."

Ben squinted and looked skeptically out of the corner of his eye. "Mirror, mirror on the wall, who's become the weirdest of them all?"

Judy ignored him. "A major code breaker for the National Security Agency worked on this material and came away a believer."

Ben shrugged. "Okay. How does this thing work again?"

Judy pointed to the line of continuous Hebrew letters in Moses' book. "The code is found by skipping letters, like skipping every fifth or tenth or twelfth letter." She traced across the page. "Rabbi Moses simply removed all the spaces between the words until the Torah was one continuous strand 304,805 letters long. You can go up, down, or across the lines and then words and phrases emerge just like working a crossword puzzle."

Ben stared at the page and frowned. "According to legend, Moses received the Bible on Mount Sinai in a continuous flow without any breaks." He bent closer to the page.

"Really? I never heard that before."

"Supposedly God dictated the material exactly the way He wanted it recorded by Moses."

"Ben, for an atheist, you're not doing badly."

Ben traced the letters circled on the Hebrew text and carefully read aloud Edlow Moses' notations at the bottom. "Shoemaker-Levy . . . found Jupiter . . . eighth Av. Oh my gosh, that comet passed by on July 16, 1994!"

"Get the picture?" Judy pushed. "Of course, you have to read Hebrew to really be in on the big secrets."

Ben pulled the book closer and began reading the encircled letters.

"Daled . . . lameth . . . tet . . . yod . . . hay . . ." His eyes widened. "Why, that spells *Hitler!*" Ben started again. *"Mem . . . tet . . . vet . . . hay* spells *slaughter.* I can't believe my eyes."

"Ben, you read Hebrew?"

He shrugged and kept following the text.

"Wait a minute." Judy put her hand on the page. "You know exactly what that says. Quit blowing smoke. What's going on here, Sherlock?"

Ben puckered his lips and took a deep breath. "I'm Jewish, Judy. Been bar mitzvahed, the works. I've read Hebrew since I was a child."

"Benjamin, the atheist?"

"Nobody's perfect."

"Come on, level with me."

"My family is secular. We didn't ever go to the synagogue. I gave up God entirely in Science 101 when I hit the University of California. That's the truth."

"Okay, Friedrich Nietzsche. Explain what you've just read in the Bible if there's no God."

"I don't know." Benjamin shook his head. "I'm really baffled." He slumped back in the booth. "Judy, I'll be honest.

You've caught me at a strange time. That's why I'm listening even though this sounds crazy to me. Recently, some of my suppositions have been rather shaken by a new project I'm doing."

"How?" Judy leaned on the table and looked directly into Ben's black eyes.

"I've been thinking about going to work for NASA, so I did a little boning up on space work and astrometric projections. I got off on a side project with satellite data, charting the continental drift."

"My, you certainly live an exciting life, Ben."

Ben ignored her comment. "Using my computer, I've discovered that I can actually piece all the continents together in a solid land mass. I am projecting that the constant whirling of the earth pulled the land apart and started continental drift."

Judy blinked her eyes several times. "Ben, that's amazing. Especially for a senior in college."

"I've come up with two distinct scenarios from my study of the satellite data. I can demonstrate that the drift occurred over millions of years, which is a commonly accepted view." He paused and looked down at the table for a moment. "Then again, I can also demonstrate that the whole thing might have happened in a very short period of time . . . like the Genesis account."

"Ben, you've really been holding out on your old lab partner. This is amazing."

"Such a potentiality is a little hard for an atheist to digest." Ben rubbed his cheek. "Sort of shook me when I came up with a God possibility. Pretty weird, huh?"

"Why not? You're Jewish. That ought to give you a clue."

"Being Jewish doesn't guarantee anything." Ben squirmed. "We lost some close relatives in the Holocaust. The whole episode really made my family cynical. I couldn't grasp how a good God or a providential Protector of Israel could let it happen . . . if there is a God."

Judy looked into Ben's pain-filled eyes. "I understand."

"Actually, that's where my atheism really started." Tears welled up in the corners of his eyes. "As a boy I saw many pictures of piles of bodies at Auschwitz." He looked down again. "I never quite got over the sight."

Judy took his hand. "Ben, you're one of the best and brightest people I know, but as good as your mind is, you can't explain everything. Computers won't ever make sense out of tragedy. We've got to reach out in trust to the mystery that surrounds our universe. Don't be afraid to accept something that math won't explain." She squeezed his hand. "I've found that God is bigger than any of our questions."

Ben picked up the book. "And God is the genius behind this three-thousand-year-old cryptogram?" He flipped through the pages. "Judy, I don't know what I think about all this religion stuff, much less this book. I admit you've stumbled across some rather confounding material in the code book, but I'm too confused these days to be of much help to you."

"Far from it." Judy shook her head. "I'd rather work with an honest skeptic than an enthusiastic true-believer type who avoids the hard questions. And I need your talent."

"Why? Just exactly what are you looking for?"

Judy smiled. "This book is filled with staggering insights, but one prediction is paramount. I've got to figure out when the most important event in the next ten years will happen, and you can help me do it."

"What is it?"

"I want you to help me figure out exactly when an atomic bomb is going to explode in Jerusalem."

❑ ○ ❑

A TAXI DRIVER HONKED at a pedestrian and jarred Judy. Noise filled the air. Judy watched the stoplight change at the street crossing on Hebron Road. One string of cars left for Bethlehem. Another started toward downtown Jerusalem. Jim stared up the street toward the old city.

I can still see that look on Ben's face when I first mentioned the atomic bomb, Judy recollected. *You'd have thought I asked him to help me rob Fort Knox. He never knew what hit him. That one little question changed both our lives.*

Judy opened her purse and found a picture of Ben she kept in her billfold. She smiled. *Well, that was one way to get his attention,* she thought.

Jimmy grabbed Judy's hand and pointed up the street. The battered red van they had seen minutes before was returning. The man in the front seat appeared to be studying a map while the driver strained to see the street sign. When they passed, Judy noticed that the van's back windows were covered or painted black.

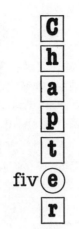

Chapter five

THE VAN PULLED TO A HALT at the stoplight on Hebron Road. Dietrich Heinz leaned over the seat and spoke German to Orlaf Pimen. "Are you sure this idiot knows what he's doing?"

The Russian eyed the Arab driver. "I don't know," Pimen answered in German. "The Hamas big shot, Adbel Rantisi, said he's an expert, but I don't think the man knows anything. We seem to be going in a circle."

"Mohammed," Heinz said to the driver in English, "have you ever been in Jerusalem?"

The unshaven Arab looked angrily out of the corner of his eye. "The street signs are confusing."

"But have you been in this section before?" Pimen pushed.

"No."

Heinz and Pimen exchanged glances. The Russian held the map closer to the Egyptian. "I think we're back in the Talpiot area," Pimen spoke in slow English. "We are traveling in the opposite direction from where we need to go."

Mohammed Bitawi abruptly cut across the intersection and sped down the side street, past an identical van in much better shape. A man and woman watched them pass.

Orlaf patted the Arab on the shoulder. "Please, I need not remind you that we must not be stopped by the police."

Bitawi shouted something in Arabic to the teenage boy sitting in the backseat next to Heinz and pulled over to the curb. "Want to drive?" he asked the Russian.

Pimen took off his sunglasses. "I can." His voice was flat. "But your assignment is to stay behind the wheel. If this proves to be too difficult, I'm sure Mr. Rantisi can find another Hamas member to replace you." Pimen forced a smile.

Mohammed Bitawi glared at the German and the Russian. "I know what I'm doing," he said firmly. "You have the map and must tell me where to turn several blocks before we get to the street. Agreed?"

"Certainly." Pimen sounded condescending.

The Arab slowly pulled away from the curb and made a U-turn in the center of the street. The dirty van swung back on Hebron Road. As they retraced their route, Pimen noticed the young couple he had seen staring at them earlier.

"I don't like anyone noticing us," Pimen said in German. "We can't afford a single screwup."

"The quicker this guy gets blown to pieces, the better I'll like it," Heinz growled, rolling his eyes in the direction of their driver. "No wonder Hamas considers him expendable."

Pimen looked out the window. "At least in getting rid of him, we'll also go down in history as the two people who cleared Jerusalem's Jewish blight off the face of the earth in one single stroke."

Heinz nodded. "My father would be extremely pleased to think his son was a part of such a noble achievement. He always believed the Jews had to be eradicated or they would multiply like rats until they overran the world. The vermin should never have been allowed to get a toehold in Palestine."

"Agreed. Are you satisfied with how the Hamas people assembled the shell of the bomb in Hebron?"

"They did a surprisingly good job," the German answered. "I found everything met our specifications."

"Excellent." Pimen pointed straight ahead. "Ah, the walls of the Old City. In four days, they will be nothing but powdered limestone."

The van rumbled through increasing traffic, turning east alongside the walls of the Old City. A continuous stream of tour buses rolled along in the opposite lane. The terrorists turned north on the Jericho Road and crossed the large plaza in front of St. Stephen's Gate that leads into the Via Dolorosa. Speeding along the northern corner of the ancient walls, Pimen traced with his finger their progress on his worn map.

"Turn into Port Said Street." He pointed to the left. "We will pass the Rockefeller Museum just before we hit Salah E-Din Boulevard."

Bitawi grunted and glared straight ahead.

"The church is our benchmark, no?" Heinz asked in German.

"Ya, ya," Orlaf Pimen said. "We are in the Palestinian section now and among friends." He pointed at St. George's Anglican Church. "The garage should be in the next block." Orlaf spoke to the Arab driver in English. "Slow down and watch for a car repair shop. Pull in the driveway. They are expecting us."

Bitawi pulled close to the curb. Straight ahead a sign in Arabic promised excellent transmission service and repair. In front of the garage, transmission parts and pieces of motors littered the area. Black grease and motor oil covered the ground. He pulled into a small driveway and tapped the horn. Several workmen in dirty clothes quickly pushed a large battered tin door open.

Bitawi eased inside the messy shop, barely clearing the entrance. A lift rack dominated the center of the floor. Standing in front of a wall covered with belts, hoses, and tools, a dark-skinned mechanic beckoned him forward. The workers closed the front door.

"Wait," Pimen commanded, "we have a little surprise today."

The wall behind the mechanic began to move. The numerous objects on the partition didn't shake, as if each were wired or nailed in place. Within seconds, a much larger and cleaner workroom opened before the van, the walls lined with electronic equipment. "We are here," Pimen announced. "Go on in," he said to the driver. Bitawi rolled in.

Mohammed Bitawi stopped and got out. He walked around to the center of the van and stood with arms crossed over his chest, glaring at Heinz and Pimen. The two men immediately began inspecting the room. A fourth person, no more than sixteen years old, got out of the back of the van and stood beside Mohammed. As if totally overwhelmed, the Palestinian boy looked at the cement floor and nervously shifted his weight from one foot to the other.

Heinz watched the youth for a moment before asking Orlaf in German, "You think this kid is capable of handling this assignment?"

Pimen scrutinized the boy for a moment and commanded suspiciously, "Get my map out of the van."

The Palestinian immediately rushed to the passenger seat and brought the map to the Russian, bowed politely, then returned to the side of his sullen counterpart.

"He follows orders to a tee," Pimen said in German. "That's the only thing that counts.

Dietrich shrugged. "Okay."

The Arab mechanic offered his hand to the two scientists. "I am Abdul. Here at your service."

Pimen nodded perfunctorily but didn't shake the man's hand. "Are all the supplies here?"

"The first shipment awaits your attention." Abdul pointed toward a back storage room. "I have arranged the devices for your immediate inspection."

"When does the rest arrive?" Pimen folded up the map.

"The electronic equipment will be in the city by tomorrow morning."

"Good, good." Pimen smiled at the Arab for the first time. "Excellent. We will begin assembly in a few moments." He gestured toward Bitawi and the boy. "They don't set foot outside this building without an escort until the moment they drive the van out. See to it that they are well fed and cared for, but they must not leave this place unaccompanied."

Bitawi grunted a sullen acknowledgment and patted the boy on the shoulder.

"Everything appears to be in order, as Amr promised." Orlaf again spoke in German. "No one but us and the generals in Baghdad know that the detonator will not be here until the last moment."

Dietrich Heinz looked at his watch. "It should take us about five or six hours to get the first pieces assembled. Perhaps we should go to work immediately."

"Agreed." Orlaf abruptly spoke in Arabic. "Abdul, get the back of the van open so we can begin."

Mohammed Bitawi blinked in surprise. "You speak our language?"

"I miss nothing." Orlaf glared menacingly at the startled Arab. "Never doubt for a moment that I understand every word that comes out of your mouth." Speaking to the mechanic, Pimen barked in Arabic, "Abdul, take the back seat out and rip out the interior padding. We will begin the installation immediately."

The two scientists watched the men rip apart the back of the van. The Arabs pushed the rear seat against a wall and quickly pulled down the vinyl covering on the ceiling and sides as the German and Russian sauntered into the storage room.

Orlaf Pimen looked around the work area. "The basic equipment appears ready. Abdul seems fairly competent."

Heinz sneered. "I don't trust Arabs much more than Jews. They're all inferior."

"We're working with Semites. Can't expect much," Pimen acknowledged. "But we have no choice; we need these inferiors in order to achieve our objectives."

"To return our great peoples to the place they should have in history," Heinz added. "Once these fool Arabs serve our purposes, we will return them to their correct status as desert rats."

"We must make sure Mohammed knows exactly where to drive the van." Pimen looked at the map in his hand.

"Shouldn't be a problem for someone with half a brain, but it will challenge Bitawi."

"Orlaf, instruct the boy carefully. He will be the map reader. We may have to make several trial runs."

"And we must make it simple. I suggest we send them back down the street we came. In fact, we could have them pull off the Jericho Road at St. Stephen's Gate and park in the plaza. That's the perfect place to set it off."

"Yes." Heinz chuckled. "The bomb would literally be only a few feet away from the site of the old Temple. Everyone in the Temple Mount area would go up in fire and smoke. Would that not be a desolating sacrilege of magnificent proportions?"

Pimen chuckled. "We would be clearing the mount so the Jews can rebuild their ancient Temple someday—" Pimen feigned sincerity. "If any are left."

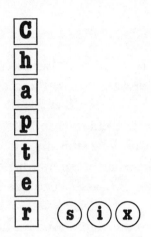

Chapter six

KEITH YAAKOV put the last box of his family's personal effects in the back of the red van and opened the door for Ann. A tiny woman, Ann slid in the front seat and smiled bravely at Jim and Judy. Keith slammed the side door and hurried around to the driver's seat.

"We will never see this place again." Ann looked at the plain, stone apartment building and adjusted the scarf tied over her forehead and back behind her neck. "Talpiot was originally developed as a sort of artist colony," she explained. "We've had so many good times here."

Judy studied Ann. Her Philadelphia look had been clearly left on the other side of the Atlantic Ocean. The young woman blended into the world of refugees and immigrants as though she had always been one of them.

"Soon only a memory will remain," Ann concluded. "And even that won't last very long."

Judy watched Ann fight back tears. She was reminded that

in small villages all over Europe, Ann's ancestors had fled impending disasters across the centuries. Ann's narrow face was resolute, her thin lips tightly set. Black ringlets hung down under the head scarf and circled her high forehead. The young woman's long, thin fingers interlaced like those of a supplicant kneeling at a prayer bench.

"To think . . . after centuries of persecution, and then resettling in our homeland, we would see the final blow come like a thief in the night." Ann bit her lip. She looked at Judy. "And so few listened to your warning."

Keith stopped the van at the traffic light. "We don't have much time left." He looked at his watch. "It's 4:45. I am sure most of the group is already in the parking lot at the Shrine of the Book."

"On the way to your apartment I saw a van pass by here twice." Judy watched a vendor selling vegetables by the curb. "It looked exactly like your van but in much worse shape."

"Vans are pretty common." Keith watched pedestrians hurry across the street in front of him. "Lots of people in the West Bank use them to haul merchandise into the city. Palestinians pack 'em out bringing commuters into Jerusalem."

"PO 636 701," Jim recited in staccato fashion.

"What?" Ann looked over her shoulder, and Jimmy repeated the numbers.

"The license tag on that other van," Judy answered. "Jimmy never misses a number."

"PO 636 701," he said again. "Will it go to Ramallah?"

"Thanks, Jimmy." His sister patted his hand. "We've got the message. The men in the van were really strange looking. Guess you get all kinds around here."

Little more was said as the Yaakov's vehicle pulled into the heavy traffic and entered the business district west of the Old City. Keith followed Ramban Street until it turned into Ruppin. At the intersection, he turned away from the Knesset, winding instead toward the Israel Museum and the Shrine of the Book.

Tourists were coming and going from the vast complex. Flower gardens lined the walks. Huge statues in the Billy Rose Sculpture Garden loomed in the background. Keith and Ann immediately recognized their friends parked together at the end of the lot. Church members milled around cars, talking to each other. Keith drove into the middle of the gathering and got out of the van. His congregation crowded around.

"We are going to form a caravan," he explained. "I count an even dozen cars. Periodically, we'll pull over and make sure no one gets lost. Okay?"

A murmur of approval arose from the group.

"Danny Rubenstein?" Keith called. "Would you bring up the rear with your white VW? The drivers can make sure they stay between my red van and your white car."

"Sure," the young man in a gray yarmulke agreed. "I'll watch for problems."

"I don't think we ought to talk over our cellular phones," Keith continued. "The calls could be intercepted. Let's just look and sound like typical Jerusalemites out for a ride. We will leave on Ruppin Street and take the long way up to Herzl Street. Eventually, I'll get us back on the Jericho Road. Beyond that, you'll be better off not knowing information the police could pry out of you."

Mrs. Skypanski interrupted. "We should pray. When we

fled Krakow, we prayed Kaddish for those left behind. If the disaster occurs, we will be praying the mourner's prayer forever. I have said those words so many times they are engraved on my heart."

"Thank you, Mrs. Skypanski." Keith looked around the group. "We must not be conspicuous, but please pray aloud on our behalf, and we will repeat the words silently."

The bent old woman bowed her head; her worn woolen sweater looked like the relic of another era. Mrs. Skypanski's lips began moving and tears ran down her cheeks. She kept rubbing her hands together, massaging her arthritic knuckles. The refugee's long shadow stretched across the cement like a jagged broken spike.

As the prayer ended, a man in the back sang softly, *"Shalom a-lay-kem maly-a-khay ha-sha-rayt."* Others hummed and then let the melody fade. Then they slowly got into their cars and waited for their leader to guide them.

Keith squeezed Ann's hand, then put the gearshift in drive. He stopped at the edge of the street to make sure he could see Danny's white VW in the rear. As he eased into the street, a 1972 Mercedes roared from a parking place next to the curb and pulled in front of the van. The blue car's fenders were dented and a taillight was broken. A burnoose, the one-piece hooded cloak often worn by Arabs, was tied over the driver's face, concealing everything but his eyes. The driver leaned out of the car and frantically motioned for Keith to follow.

"What's going on? Looks like an Arab flagging us down."

"We can't drive around him," Ann fretted. "He's blocking us so we have no choice but to follow."

Keith inched forward. "I don't like it." He pointed at the

black-and-white checkered head covering. "Palestinians some‑ times wear that getup to conceal their identity. And this guy was out there waiting for us."

The man kept waving out the window and pointing for‑ ward.

"I don't know what to do." Keith glanced in the rearview mirror. "We could be lured into a trap."

"We've got to make up our minds before we reach the next intersection," Ann said.

"I could see which way he goes at the corner by the sta‑ dium and then turn the opposite way," Keith reasoned.

"There are too many cars in our group," Judy objected. "We can't get away from him without losing someone."

"Yes," Ann agreed, "and why would an Arab wish us harm? We're nothing but a group of messianic Jews. The Orthodox Jews and the police are our problem."

"I'm not sure," Keith fretted. "I don't like any of the alternatives."

"I think we've got more to gain than to lose by following him," Judy added. "If the police were after us, they would have simply grabbed us in the parking lot. I think we should stay with the Arab."

Keith shook his head. "I don't know what else to do. Let's see where he takes us."

To Keith's surprise the Arab turned back toward the apart‑ ment, but when they entered Ramban Street, the Arab quickly turned north on Argon and drove toward East Jerusalem. He took Nablus Road and then cut through to Salah E‑Din. Gesturing frantically over the top of the Mercedes, the Arab pointed to an alley and turned in.

Keith complied and the other cars in the caravan mechanically followed. "Oh, no!" Keith exclaimed. He pointed at the end of the alley. "The exit is barricaded with a pile of junk. We have stepped into a trap."

"The others are right behind us," Ann observed. "We're caught between them and that heap of metal."

"Maybe we should try to ram it." Keith pulled the gearshift into low. "We'll clear a path."

"You could ruin the tires," Ann cautioned. "Then we'd really be stuck."

The Mercedes stopped at the edge of the barrier and its driver got out. Several men stepped from the shadows of the alley.

"Brace yourself," Keith warned. "Here comes trouble." He jumped out of the van and prepared to stand his ground.

The Arab slammed the car door and hurried toward the caravan. He quickly unwrapped the burnoose and stuffed it into his pocket. "I was afraid I might lose you."

"Ben!" Judy shouted. "Benjamin Meridor!"

The young man hugged Judy.

"What is going on?" Keith stood with his mouth open.

Ben shook Keith's hand. "Man, I was sweating this one out."

"Benjamin," Judy said, "I thought you were at Petra getting ready for our arrival. How did you get here?"

"We got a tip that some sort of treachery was afoot. An anonymous caller sent a message that somebody in your congregation was setting you up. Arab friends smuggled my three associates and me across the border. While I was locating the Mercedes—" Ben pointed to one of the men standing by the barricade—"Odah came to your meeting place by bus trying to locate Judy. No one noticed he was in the corridor when your congregation left. Odah overheard your plans to gather at the Shrine. He got in touch with me, and we came to head you off."

"But what's the barricade for?" Keith asked.

"We piled up that junk to keep anyone from coming in the other end of the alley," Benjamin explained. "Remember, someone is selling you out."

"I don't think there's much of a mystery about the culprit's identity. Liat Collins and his people are out there somewhere. No telling what they've done. You can bet the police are looking for us."

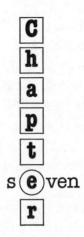

chapter

s(e)ven

KEITH'S FRIGHTENED CONGREGATION crowded around Ben and Judy, complaining and agitated, their anxiety level continuing to escalate. The warehouse's shadow swallowed the alley as the sun went down. From the edge of the group an old man called out, "What's happening to us? Night is coming."

Keith motioned for everyone to pull in. "I want you to meet Benjamin Meridor, a friend who has come to help get us out of the city. Benjamin has discovered that we've already been betrayed."

The circle exploded again, fear sweeping from person to person in a wildfire of panic. Members pressed forward like bewildered quail, scurrying for cover.

"Listen!" Keith yelled sharply. "Pay attention. Don't panic. Everything is under control. Benjamin has instructions for us. Listen," he repeated. He turned to Meridor.

"We're not sure exactly what is going on, but we must be gentle as doves and wise as serpents," Ben began. "We cannot take chances. Obviously, anyone who knows your group well can identify your automobiles. We must make adjustments. This building is empty. Please come inside to talk in private."

Keith and his friends followed Ben into an old warehouse. The Arabs switched on lights. Stucco and large chunks of plaster littered the floor. Long cracks ran down the exposed beams in the roof. The building smelled stale and dusty. Judy and Jim brought up the rear and closed the door behind them.

"Use of this place goes clear back to the British occupation," Ben explained. "Not much has happened here in a couple of decades, so it serves our purposes well. We can thank my friends Salim, Abu, and Odah for finding this place. These men are Arab Christians. Say hello to the boys."

Keith's congregation nodded politely. Though quiet, the group still appeared agitated and edgy.

"Salim and Abu know East Jerusalem like the back of their hands. They have a cousin on every street corner." Ben exchanged a knowing smile with the two men. "They're going to help us do a little horse trading. We'll spend the night here while the boys swap your vehicles for other cars. Only then will it be safe for us to leave together."

Questions shot around the room like shrapnel.

"How are they going to find so many cars?"

"Whose vehicles?"

"Do we have enough time?"

"Please!" Keith again yelled above the hubbub. "You are worse than the mob Moses tried to corral at Mount Sinai! Settle down and listen."

Benjamin held up his hand. "Since we don't know what

we're really up against, it makes more sense not to take any chances. Abu and Salim will simply switch the cars for us. They've got connections everywhere. Relatives. Friends. Car lots. Odah will drive our cars away. We'll take whatever they come up with, leave our vehicles behind for their friends, and we'll all get out of town. If our prediction of an attack is wrong, we'll just come back and swap again. Simple?"

Some people grumbled but most nodded their heads. A few smiled in appreciation.

"We'll stay in here through the evening," Ben continued, "and then start out at dawn tomorrow. We can send out for supper and bed down on the floor. Agreed?"

People nodded soberly and began spreading out around the large room. Families claimed individual spaces against the crumbling walls.

Ben took Judy's hand. "Looks like Lawrence of Arabia was the last guy to stay here. It's a little on the primitive side."

Judy laughed. "I still can't believe it's you, Ben. The burnoose totally fooled me. This ruse is simply too wild for words."

"Without those three, I'd have never made it back into the country. The boys had quite a time getting me across the border, but we persevered because we were terrified you were about to be snared by the police or maybe even Mossad."

"Ben, who called you?"

"I honestly don't know. But somehow he had to gain access to Keith's confidential information. I mean, who could have known where to reach me? And how?"

"Remember Liat Collins from our last visit? It looks like he's the Judas."

"Are you serious?" Ben pointed to a table and three

dusty chairs. "Sure I remember him . . . Not much to sit on, but looks like we don't have many choices. Fill me in on the details. Why would someone like Liat want to betray the whole congregation?"

LIAT COLLINS sat across the table from Nahum Admoni, a Mossad operative assigned to internal security. The Israeli intelligence agent took a long drag off his cigarette and blew a big puff in the air. A lean, muscular man, Admoni's face and skin had the tone and dark tan of a man who ran five miles every day. His eyes were hard, penetrating. The agent's lips were thin and taunt. A receding hairline made him appear older than he probably was.

"You are sure these people believe an atomic bomb explosion is imminent?" the Mossad agent repeated.

"Want to listen to the tape again?" Collins retorted.

"Don't get mouthy, Collins. You signed on as an informer to make yourself a hero. Besides, you're paid well."

"I told you all I know." Liat sulked.

"Your job is to keep us abreast of what the fanatical fringe is up to and to do what you can to subvert their efforts." Admoni flipped the cigarette into a dirty ashtray. "I didn't expect this bunch to be into anything quite so heavy."

"I don't have any idea what is going on with them," Collins added, "beyond what I've told you."

"Now, when is this bomb suppose to go off?"

Collins sighed. "Like I said, they believe Av 9 is D day. Beyond that date, I don't have a clue. They just wanted to get out of town."

"No idea about a time of day or where?"

"None."

Admoni looked down at the file on his desk, spreading the papers out in front of him. "We know about the American woman," the Mossad agent shrugged. "I am surprised she was able to come in the front door at Ben Gurion Airport. Bad slip-up. Judy Bithell was deported along with a man about her age. Have you seen or heard from a Benjamin Meridor?"

Collins shook his head.

"Well, one of your buddies gave Meridor a phone call two days ago."

"What?" Collins came out of his chair.

"We intercepted a call into Jordan from one Harrison Levy. He tipped off Meridor about your plans to turn the group in. I believe Harrison Levy is one of your boys."

"No!" Liat shook his head. "He couldn't have."

"We don't make mistakes on this level," Nahum growled. "If Levy is some kind of double agent, that's one thing; if you're stringing us along, Collins, that's another."

"Honest, I don't know anything about a phone call to Jordan."

The Mossad agent took another deep drag and blew the smoke in Collins's face. "Look, when you mention the word atomic, we tend to get serious. I'm sure you know what I mean. Why don't we go downstairs and have a quiet conversation with your buddy?"

"Sure." Liat fumbled for his coat. "I just don't understand. Harrison is no double agent. He's just a member of the church, a stooge."

"We'll take the elevator." Admoni ignored Liat's statement and walked out, leaving Collins to hurry behind him. He hesitated at the metal doors for Liat to enter the elevator first and then silently started their descent.

When the elevator reached the basement and the door opened, Admoni pointed toward the end of a dark corridor. He took out keys as they walked and unlocked a large fire door at the back. With a gentle shove, the Mossad agent pushed Collins ahead of him.

In the center of the dark room under a spotlight, Harrison Levy sat in a wooden chair. Duct tape bound his hands behind his back. He moaned when he saw his friend, but a strip of the silver tape sealed his lips. Levy's eyes widened in terror. Several men stood in the shadows, watching him squirm.

"Came back for a little talk, Harrison," Admoni commanded. "Brought one of your friends with me." With one quick jerk, the agent pulled the tape from Levy's mouth. Levy gasped in pain.

"Harrison, what have you done?" Liat shook his hands in his friend's face. "They say you tipped off Yaakov's contacts in Jordan. This guy Meridor. Don't you know that makes all of us look like traitors?"

Admoni pushed Collins aside. "I'll ask the questions."

"You can make this simple or hard." Admoni pulled up a chair in front of Levy and sat down. "Cooperate and you're out of here in a few minutes. Be difficult and I'll hook up electrodes to every sensitive area on your body and give you a buzz you won't forget for the rest of your life—if you survive. Understand?"

Levy nodded frantically and looked helplessly at Collins.
"Where were Yaakov's friends staying in Jordan?"

"I—I don't know. All I found was a phone number."

"Found?" Admoni leaned closer to Levy. "Tell me how you
stumbled on to this number. Was it just lying there on the
floor staring at you?"

"I saw Keith Yaakov's personal address book open on his
desk yesterday, before the meeting with Judy Bithell. I knew
something was coming down." Levy trembled. "I had seen
him write that number when he got a phone call from his
friend in America. I just acted on a wild hunch and wrote it
down. At the meeting yesterday, I thought Yaakov was way
over the line. But Liat was so angry when we left. I didn't
want anyone to get hurt, so I called in a warning."

"Wild hunch? My, my, are you ever an adventuresome
soul, Harrison. Just full of little surprises." The Mossad
agent suddenly grabbed Levy's lower lip, twisting it like a
piece of bread. "In twenty-five words or less I want to know
why you tipped off Yaakov's friends."

Levy struggled in pain and groaned. A trickle of blood ran
down the corner of his mouth. A long, low moan rolled up
from the back of his throat.

"Make it snappy," Admoni insisted.

"Keith was good to me," Levy gurgled. "I thought we were
just going to harass him, not get him and his people into deep
trouble. I didn't want Liat to hurt Keith or his wife."

"What do you know about an atomic bomb?"

"Nothing. Nothing at all. I swear. Today was the first I
heard anything about a bomb."

Admoni grabbed the man's lip again and twisted it in the opposite direction. Levy stomped his feet on the floor and thrashed against the chair until Admoni stopped.

Levy could barely speak. Tears rolled down his cheek. "I swear, I don't know anything about any bombs."

Admoni beckoned to the two agents standing in the shadows. "Hold these two for further interrogation. I want to know every thought they ever had."

"Wait a minute," Collins protested. "I'm on your team!"

"We'll find out," Admoni snapped.

"But why?" Liat protested as one of the agents grabbed his arm. "I didn't have anything to do with Levy's screwup."

"Like I told you. You said the magic word, *atomic.* After that everything went up for grabs. Collins, you better be straighter than a stick and cleaner than soap. For openers, you're going to help us find these people *quickly.* Now, get out of here."

Admoni waited until Collins and Levy were gone before he dialed his cellular phone.

"Yes." The voice on the other end was flat, emotionless.

"I'm not sure what we've got," Admoni said. "I don't think Collins is lying, but I'm not sure about Levy. Sounds like these two Americans traveling with Yaakov are still pushing a story about an atomic attack on Av 9, just like last time, before we kicked them out."

"But the whole incident coincides with current intelligence coming out of Egypt and Iran," the voice continued. "I don't like it. We've got to have confirmation. More information. We have a new tip from the Monterey Institute of International Studies. These people track nuclear smuggling out of the former Soviet Union. They say about three kilos of HEU is missing. I'm worried. Ring what you can out of those two buffoons you've got down there and then pull out the stops to find the Americans and the people from that cult. Eliminate anyone who gets in your way."

DAY TWO
AV 6 5766

"And then many will be offended,

will betray one another, and will hate one another."

Matthew 24:10

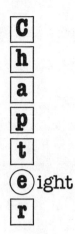

Chapter eight

Jerusalem
July 31, 2006

A BEAM OF SUNLIGHT burst through a crack in the roof and settled on Benjamin's face. The light crawled down his forehead and finally into his eyes. Ben turned away, but morning would not be denied. He dozed for a few minutes before his eyes finally focused on a mop of frazzled black hair only a few feet away.

Wrapped up tightly in her bedroll, Judy looked like a mummy in a black wig. Ben pictured her long, light brown hair that usually hung past her shoulders. When Judy was in a hurry or playful, she often tossed her head, sending the almost golden waves around her thin neck in a swirl. Ben studied the smooth line of her profile, curving around her finely chiseled nose and rosebud lips. *I barely recognized her with the dye job, but she's still gorgeous no matter what.*

Ben looked around the large warehouse at the families, still sleeping huddled together. *These people resemble refugees running from the Pharaoh. Like history's repeating itself ... except I'm sure no Moses.*

He sat up on his pallet and ran his fingers through his hair. He rubbed his eyes and stretched, then his gaze returned to Judy. Judy looked so vulnerable and small. Ben wanted to protect her, care for her. Judy had enough intelligence and audacity to take care of herself, he knew, but Ben thought she needed someone like him to make sure she never found out how dangerous things could be. *I hope she never, ever realizes just how big the world is.*

Ben thought about when he and Judy first met. Having Judy as a lab partner in first-year chemistry had been nothing but an endless hassle. Judy hadn't been afraid to try anything. *She wouldn't listen to me. Always the free spirit,* Ben recalled. At first, they had clashed and argued. And yet, she had been good for him, Ben thought, and had added some fun to his very serious approach to his studies. By the end of the semester, he was absolutely fascinated with Judy. And then, chemistry was over and she was off to her next adventure. Ben had plodded into his sophomore year never really expecting to see much of her again.

When Judy had called Ben that night about the code, he had been half angry, half thrilled. Suddenly, there she was, off on another wild tear but back in his life. The whole code thing had sounded a little crazy, but like everything else about her, it had fascinated him. Ben smiled at the memory. *The next thing I knew we were together on a bona fide date—something I had never thought possible.*

◻ ◯ ◻

JUDY INSISTED ON WATCHING a video before they started working on the project. She wanted to see *The Edge* because she loved Anthony Hopkins's acting and she was intrigued by survival stories. The movie turned out to be a good choice for Ben, too, because Judy kept snuggling next to him during the intense scenes. He had been much more aware of her than the movie. Afterward, they went to the student union for hamburgers. Judy couldn't stop talking about the picture.

"Wow," Judy had exclaimed as she plopped down in the padded booth, "was that a great flick or what?"

"I liked it." Ben slid in the opposite side. "A real cliffhanger."

"And that bear! He's the one that should get the academy award. I loved every minute of it. In fact, that movie was so good, I could eat two hamburgers."

Ben laughed. "Whatever you want, I'm here to provide."

"Really?" Judy looked at him slyly. "Dangerous talk."

"Well . . . I know you're here just to work on your bizarre project. So I suppose we ought to get to it."

"Hey—" Judy reached across the table and yanked on Ben's lightweight jacket. "Lighten up, Meridor. I'm here with you, and that's as important as whatever we're going to do."

Ben tried to find the right thing to say, but nothing came out.

Judy didn't wait for him to respond. "You always sell yourself short, Ben. You're a neat guy. I always thought you were fun to be around in chemistry. A little on the conservative side, but nobody's perfect." Judy laughed at her own joke. "So feed me and we'll go from there."

A few minutes later, Ben put a plate piled with four hamburgers on the table and pushed a basket full of french fries toward her. "There's enough food here for an army." He pulled a bottle of ketchup from his pocket.

Between bites, Judy prattled about her studies. Naturally talkative, she rambled across the college landscape like a sportscaster describing a football game while Ben listened, enraptured by every word. She quickly brought him up to speed on everything from her sorority sisters to her views on the latest discoveries in statistical probability.

"I'm sure you want to devote lots of time to this code thing you're into," Ben finally said. He wiped his mouth with a napkin and pushed the greasy basket away. "You really believe in this stuff?"

Judy became more thoughtful. "Ben, since we last had a truly serious conversation, a lot has happened in my life. I was never much of a spiritual type, but since I got into this Bible study thing, it has changed my life. Exploring Scripture has proven to be a major turning point for my life."

"Sure. Lots of people are into spirituality today. Channeling, contacting spirits, poetry, native American studies . . ." Ben shrugged. "I guess I'm more of a facts and figures man, myself."

Judy shook her head. "I'm not talking about a New Age exploration of inner space. Bible study is much more substantial. My friends helped me come to a genuine relationship with the God of the universe."

Ben pursed his lips. "Spirituality, I can understand. Having a 'relationship' with God sounds a little goofy."

"Come on, Ben. Bible study is far more a possibility in your world than you think. We're talking verifiable historical data. Concepts you can check out. Ideas that add up. The Bible is no hocus-pocus book. When you read the Bible, you're dealing with history and intellectual integrity." She paused and smiled. "And proving God is actually there."

Ben shifted uncomfortably. "Okay. Proof is my thing."

"I got interested in biblical prophecy because to me it's like solving complicated math problems. Thousands of years ago God inspired prophets who made predictions that are coming true in this century. What I want you to help me explore will reveal what's ahead in this and the next decade. No hocus-pocus there."

Ben shook his head. "I'm not sure I buy that."

"It's true. I'm convinced we can take the dates and indications that are hidden in the Hebrew text of the Bible and work on them until we know the exact times certain extraordinary events are going to happen."

"You have a sample of these 'predictions'?"

"Yes. Rabbi Edlow Moses' studies have page after page of examples, and I have a computer disk of the Hebrew text he studied. The problem is sorting it out."

Ben stuck the last french fry in a blob of ketchup. "I don't understand what you're suggesting."

"The Hebrew form gets more mysterious the longer you study it," Judy explained. "There are layers to the messages. Sometimes you can't recognize the right answer until after an event has occurred."

Ben frowned. "Sounds like gobbledygook. I'm not reading you."

Judy sucked mustard off her thumb. "Okay. You remember when Yitzhak Rabin was assassinated? Rabbi Moses found that predicted in the code and warned Rabin, but he didn't take it seriously. Well, after the assassination, *Amir*, the name of his killer, was found on the same page of the Torah. The murderer's name had been there for centuries, but no one realized it until after he was captured."

Ben pushed back from the table. "That's pretty far out."

"It's all in the Bible. The problem is getting inside the many layers hidden in the Hebrew and making sense out of them. I've come to the conclusion that any passage can be looked at from many angles. It's all a matter of the sequences and intervals between the letters."

"Hmmm," Ben rubbed his chin. "Sounds like this is more complex than simply running a computer scan. Personal recognition would be a factor." He paused and thought for a moment. "What we need is a human computer."

"What if I told you that I also have one of those?"

Ben frowned. "I don't get it."

"I've never told you about my brother, Jimmy. He's three years younger than I am."

"Is he in college here?" Ben took a drink of Coke.

"No." Judy hesitated. "Jimmy isn't in school anywhere."

"I thought you were just saying he was a brain of some sort."

Judy grimaced. "Jimmy . . . Jimmy's autistic. His world is inside his head. Sometimes he goes for days without saying anything. Or he might stand for hours like a statue, respond-ing to nothing. And yet his mind is like a sponge. Behind his seeming passiveness is a photographic memory that forgets nothing." Judy smiled, but her eyes looked pained.

"I'm not sure what to say. Is his condition like a ... disease?"

"It's hard to say. Jimmy doesn't connect with people in a normal way. People who don't know him sometimes think he's retarded. When he gets agitated, his eyes move rapidly, out of control. Sometimes he gets hooked into obsessive behaviors, but he is actually loving and gentle. And he's very spiritual."

"Does he communicate very well?"

"Under the right conditions. On the other hand, Jimmy often sounds like a runaway tape recorder going on and on. I'm about the only one who can shut him off when he gets rolling. He rattles on like someone reciting an encyclopedia."

"I don't understand how Jimmy could help."

"One of his peculiar traits is an amazing facility for numbers. Give him the date for Easter in a given year and he'll instantly calculate all the dates for Easter into infinity. Jimmy can look at a set of numbers and immediately recognize amazing patterns and connections. Jimmy spends hours listening to classical music and staring at abstract art. He can tell you mathematical relationships in Mozart's music that will boggle your mind."

"But he can't go to college?"

"Unfortunately, no. The discipline is too much for him. Structure is a problem."

"So there's not much practical use for Jimmy's abilities."

"In most things." Judy suddenly smiled. "But Jimmy is a natural for working on the Bible cryptogram. It's almost like God created Jimmy to be the ultimate code breaker."

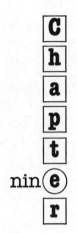

Chapter nine

DAWN'S LIGHT HAD BARELY BROKEN over the desert when six international leaders gathered in Ziad Amr's war room three stories beneath his Baghdad palace. Rich mahogany paneling and thick carpets could not keep the room from feeling dark and foreboding. Detailed road maps of Israel covered one of the large projection screens next to an enlarged city map of Jerusalem. Each man studied an identical attack report translated into his native language.

"My colleagues Orlaf Pimen and Dietrich Heinz are now positioned in Eastern Jerusalem," Anton Ketele reported. The Russian nuclear physicist pushed his stringy black hair out of his eyes and glowered at the generals from beneath bushy eyebrows. "The bomb is being assembled. We have only three days to go." He pounded his meaty fist in the palm of his hand. "The effect will be *even more* devastating than we predicted a year ago." Ketele's rumpled suit and wrinkled tie gave the appearance that he had slept in his clothes.

Ching Lin, the representative from the People's Republic of China, looked around the room at the five men listening intensely to the Russian scientist. His traditional high-collar jacket seemed strangely amiss among the military uniforms and Arab robes of the other diplomats. Squinting from behind thick glasses, Lin leaned toward his Iraqi host and whispered, "You think we can actually eradicate the Jews from the face of the earth with so small a bomb?"

"Uh-huh," Amr muttered under his breath. "Ketele is correct in his projections."

Anton Ketele turned from the large blackboard in the center of the conference room. "As Orlaf Pimen explained a year ago today, an atomic device is not difficult to conceal in a small space. Actually, we could build one in a suitcase. The van we obtained has more than enough space for a bomb powerful enough to annihilate the city of Jerusalem."

The men applauded.

Anton bounced the piece of chalk in his palm. "The United States perfected the technology decades ago. Most of what I am showing you we stole from them. The Soviet Union was quite proficient in the days before the West and our traitors gutted the KGB."

The six diplomats exchanged knowing glances across the large conference table.

The Russian cracked his knuckles and sneered. "During the last year we smuggled in the basic components for the bomb." Ketele's heavy jowls shook. "The detonating device has been hidden separately. I will pick it up after I fly in today. I'll leave immediately after this conference."

"The uranium, plutonium, the big dynamite?" Ahmed

Tibi, the general from Syria, asked. "Any problems acquiring the radioactive materials?"

Ketele grunted and smirked. "Are you kidding? I had a number of sources for enriched uranium. On October 9, 1992, one of our engineers was caught smuggling 1.53 kilos of HEU out of Moscow. The police didn't catch his accomplice, who was carrying half a kilo. In November a year later, naval officers stole HEU from a submarine reactor assembly in Murmansk. Six months later, three sailors were caught, but one got away with a beryllium rod embedded with 150 grams of HEU."

Egyptian General Wadei Abu-Nassar frowned skeptically. "Where was the atomic material stored? You make it sound like stealing chocolates from a candy store."

The Russian abruptly broke into a smile. "Never forget there is still a stockpile of seventeen thousand small, tactical nuclear warheads in Russia. Only one warhead had to disappear for our purposes."

Amr smiled at his Egyptian counterpart. "Wadei, remember the reported police bust in Bavaria in May 1994? They picked up over five grams of super-pure plutonium 239. I ended up with two grams from that heist. And I'm always glad to contribute to the cause."

The men laughed.

"I still have my eye on that little storage facility at Aktau just across the Caspian Sea in Kazakhstan," Amr continued. "Nearly three tons of plutonium is sitting there, and I've put my name on the supply. No, I never doubted Dr. Ketele would be able to assemble the necessary materials."

"You're certain such a bomb will do a minimum amount of

damage to the Temple Mount?" the Libyan delegate asked. "Colonel Khadafy remains concerned that the Mosque of Omar as well as the al-Aqsa Mosque sustain only a minimum of damage."

Anton shrugged. "Neutron bombs kill people but leave buildings intact. There will be some structural damage at ground zero, but not much." The Russian leered. "That's their beauty. We nuke the Jews, keep the shrines. Everybody wins."

Ahmed Tibi glanced up at the road map on the large overhead screen. "Is the electrical hardware for the bomb now on its way into the city for assembly in the back of the van or not?" The Syrian representative looked down at his update again. "From this report something seems to be wrong."

Using a laser pointer, Amr traced a line up the highway from Hebron to Jerusalem. "One of our vehicles was scheduled to bring the internal apparatus into Jerusalem last night, but the driver suspected Israeli security might be following. Jewish agents in Hebron watch everything. He took a detour off Highway 49 at the split in the highway near Kefar Ezyon and is currently cooling his heels on a back road at Beit Fajjar."

"This problem is serious?" Ching Lin's face betrayed no emotion but his eyes narrowed. "Someone failed us?"

"No," Amr answered bluntly. "On the contrary, our agent's acute awareness meant they avoided detection. A slight adjustment is required. A vehicle leaving Jerusalem and returning the same day will be less obvious than one now coming in from the West Bank. Our van made numerous runs to Hebron over the last month, so Israeli soldiers and security developed familiarity and a sense of false security. During those trips, the driver carried produce and merchandise." Amr cleared his throat. "I ordered our man, Mohammed Bitawi, to drive down to Beit Fajjar in the same red van. He should be underway shortly."

Lin grunted and began reading his report once more.

"Note the countdown to military intervention," Amr continued. "Once Dr. Ketele's bomb is detonated, we move instantly. Our troops sweep across the region. The nuclear explosion will instantly end Israeli military superiority."

Amr pushed a button. The map disappeared; a televised picture of an object sailing across space appeared. "Our satellite is prepared to dump plutonium across the top of the atmosphere. Electronic transmission will stop. The United States and the United Nations won't have a clue that we are on the move until it's too late. This time we will be the irresistible force, gentlemen."

"There must be no miscalculation," Lin barked. "Many Chinese harbor deep bitterness toward the West for the part capitalists played in the downfall of Communism. After the great earthquake in 2000, we were economically vulnerable. The United States and the immoral forces of capitalism swept away the Marxist foundation of the People's Republic. Our nuclear capabilities were gutted." Lin pounded on the table. "Only Japan's economic collapse caused by the great earthquake kept them from also taking advantage of us. War will return us to power and reestablish Leninist socialism."

Egyptian General Wadei Abu-Nassar spoke directly to Amr. "Have the secret negotiations with the Russians been signed and finalized? Can we count on their support?"

The Iraqi despot nodded. "We have certified agreements in hand. Our atomic attack is the signal for their army to act.

Russia's resentment toward America is as deep as China's. The old guard stands ready to strike."

"Press on," Ahmed Tibi demanded. "Bring up the area map of Israel again. I want to confirm our earlier projections." He waited for the color map to roll up before continuing. "There is no question that this region is the strategic geographic center of the world. A decisive attack here will begin the destruction of the existing international balance of power. Furthermore, the entire religious world, billions of people, will be demoralized by the destruction of Jerusalem. The time is ripe. We have only one more issue to confirm."

Tibi picked up Amr's laser pointer and shot a beam of light on Haifa, then slowly traced a line up the map in a line past Akko and Nahariya. He pinpointed the Meggido Pass and then inched down the Armageddon Valley. "This area is heavily fortified with underground hangars. In the Six-Day War, the Jews attacked Egypt by flying out of this region. We will focus special attention here. An aerial attack will follow the explosion, but additional long-range plans must be ready. A number of our generals have formulated battle plans for securing the entire valley and destroying everything in it."

Amr pulled a cigar out of his pocket. "Certainly. We can do it." He unwrapped the cigar. "Six years ago—as a matter of fact on the day the Jews call Av 9—our first attempt on the life of Benjamin Netanyahu failed. If the bomb under the manhole cover had gone off only seconds earlier, we'd have gotten him."

The dictator stopped to light the black cigar. "But the ensuing chaos still served our purposes well. Retaliatory attacks on the Palestinians and the PLO created severe disruptions that played right into our hands." He blew a cloud of smoke far out over the table. "Fighting has not stopped since that moment. Constant sniper and terrorist activity in Jerusalem and everywhere else has forced Mossad to concentrate on day-to-day problems. They've lost perspective. Gentlemen, we have our bases covered."

"Hmmm," Ching Lin mumbled. "I will not rest easy until I know that van is back in Jerusalem and all the bomb's pieces are in place for assembly."

BENJAMIN MERIDOR didn't move from his pallet until several other people stirred. Mrs. Skypanski was one of the first people to stand up. The old Polish woman struggled to her feet and rubbed her aching back. Danny Rubenstein followed. Soon others began shuffling around the empty warehouse.

"Hi, sleepyhead." Ben waved at Judy. "You going to sleep the day away?"

Judy pushed her hair out of her eyes and yawned. "Am I ever glad Keith had an extra air mattress. I still feel like I've slept on a rock slab."

"This is nothing like what a self-indulged California girl is used to, huh?"

Ben's friends Salim and Abu came in the side entrance. Abu signaled to Ben, making an O with his thumb and forefinger.

"Ah." Ben got to his feet. "The cars are here. Great. We can go as soon as everyone is ready."

"We'll need to eat something," Judy fretted.

"Abu and Salim will bring in bread and cartons of orange juice." Ben began folding up the bedroll. "I think we've got things planned so we can get out of here quickly."

"I'll have to wake Jimmy up. He could sleep through a military invasion." Judy slipped out of the bedroll. "Do I have time to get myself together?"

"Go make yourself more beautiful. I'll check things out with Keith."

Ben walked through the crowd speaking to people and patting children on the head. Some smiled and thanked him, others mumbled and only nodded. He spread the word about breakfast and encouraged everyone to hurry.

Keith and Ann Yaakov were ready to leave by the time Ben reached them. "Looks like our glorious leader is on top of the situation." Ben smiled and offered his hand.

Keith gave him a stout hug. "I'm ready for the day," he responded confidently. "I want to assemble everyone for morning prayers and then we'll try to find food."

"Way ahead of you." Ben pointed to the large door. "The boys are already setting up breakfast, and the cars are outside. Everything is in place for a leisurely drive through the city and out to the road south. We can be in Jericho by noon."

"Amazing." Ann smiled broadly. "You've really got everything under control, Ben."

Ben shrugged. "At least no one can recognize our cars. Your old buddy Liat Collins could never identify these vehicles—they belong to Arabs in East Jerusalem. I think we've shaken any tails the security people might have tried to pin on us."

"Wonderful," Ann answered.

"I knew Liat was jockeying for more control over our congregation," Keith said, "but I can't imagine him trying to destroy us. After all, he came from America. I simply can't understand what he was up to."

"The important thing is that you *did* smell a rat," Ann reassured her husband. "Your precautions protected us."

"We're safe now," Ben added. "Don't worry. In a few minutes we'll be on our way."

"I must find my Bible and start our prayers." Keith rummaged through a box sitting by his bedroll. "I know it's in here. We just threw things together."

Suddenly the sound of gunfire filled the air. People dropped to the floor of the warehouse. More shots followed.

"They've found us!" a man cried.

"We're under attack!" an old woman wailed, throwing herself over a small child.

Rapid machine gun fire exploded somewhere out in the alley.

"Quiet!" Ben yelled. "Stay down. Don't make a sound."

Bullets ripped through the sliding metal door and ricocheted across the warehouse. Ben leaped to his feet and ran toward Abu and Salim, crouched behind a support beam. He slid down beside them.

"What's going on?" Ben panted.

"I don't have any idea," Abu answered. "I'm sure we weren't followed by the police."

"Are they shooting at us?" Ben asked.

"I'm going to work my way to the back entrance." Salim got on his hands and knees. "I'll try to get a good look at what's happening in the alley. Maybe I can find out if we're surrounded."

"Okay," Ben agreed. "We need to have some idea of whether we can successfully run for it. But be careful."

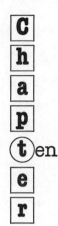

Chapter ten

SPORADIC GUNFIRE CONTINUED for another ten minutes and then ceased. Quiet settled over the alley. The back door slammed and Abu hurried in, motioning for people to gather around him.

"No one's after us," Abu explained. "Simply the local boys playing gangsters in an early morning gunfight. East Jerusalem has been a battle zone ever since the last attempt on Netanyahu's life. Everything out there will be back to normal shortly."

"That's a relief." Ben rolled his eyes. "I think we ought to get on our way immediately. The vehicles are outside with my friend Odah. He'll pass out the keys. Let's get moving."

Keith prayed a quick prayer and the messianic congregation wasted no time in hustling their gear out to the cars. Some of the neighborhood residents began returning to the deserted streets. A jeep loaded with Israeli troops whizzed by. Traffic slowly resumed on Salah E-Din Boulevard. Keith picked up the keys to a brown '92 Toyota. Ann got in the front seat; Judy and Jimmy crowded next to Ben in the back.

Keith led the caravan to the edge of the street and waited for the rest of the cars to fall in. "Salah E-Din is always busy. We'll take it nice and slow," he said to Ann, "and slide out to the old Jericho Road like American tourists out sightseeing. Keep praying until we get past Bethany."

"Look." Jimmy pointed out the backseat window. "PO 636 701."

Judy looked up in time to see a red battered van going by. "That's them! Look, Keith. There's the van that passed us yesterday in Talpiot."

Ben strained forward. "What a strange looking guy on the passenger side. No hair."

"PO 636 701," Jimmy repeated mechanically.

Keith pulled out behind the red van. "Apparently, they're going our direction."

"I know Jerusalem isn't that large, but it's strange we would see them three times in two days." Judy watched the vehicle go down the street in front of them.

"What we've got to watch out for is the police." Keith slowed at a stop sign. The red van turned right toward Hebron Road. "Since the attempt on the prime minister's life, it doesn't take much to set the cops off. The shooting this morning will have them on edge. We can't afford to accidentally break a traffic rule."

Judy snuggled close to Ben and remembered the day of the attempted assassination in 2000. She and Ben had been watching television when the special news flash announced a major explosion in Jerusalem. A number of people had been killed, and the prime minister's car seriously damaged, but Nethanyahu had survived. Judy could still see the astonished look on Ben's face.

❏ ○ ❏

BEN GRABBED JUDY'S HAND. "The code predicted an attempt on the prime minister's life. Last year we deciphered the warning."

Judy watched pictures of soldiers running down the street and smoke pouring out of a manhole cover. "Think of the implications of what we're seeing, Ben. We've been on top of this story for the last twelve months."

Ben had plopped back on the couch. "I can't believe my eyes. The assault is really happening."

"Of course. What did you expect?"

Ben turned slowly to Judy, his eyes widening in deepening consternation. He shook his head slowly. "I guess . . . I thought we were just playing a game, solving a big puzzle. I didn't really think anything would happen."

"Ben," Judy scolded, "why in the world would we have wasted our time if the code wasn't for real?"

He breathed and exhaled slowly. "I'd do anything to be around you, Judy. That's why I was into this thing."

Judy frowned but looked carefully into Ben's eyes. She started to speak but stopped and kissed him gently. "Ben, I've always been serious about what we are doing."

"Judy, I know you believe in the Bible's message, but I'm coming at this as an outsider. Even with some of my discoveries about global land mass shifts, I expected us eventually to prove the code stuff to be a fraud or maybe a coincidence.

Honestly, I never dreamed anything would come of it." He looked back at the television. "But look." He pointed at the image of the bodies lying scattered on the cement curbs and in the street. "We *knew* this was coming."

"Ben, you try to objectify everything by being scientific, but sooner or later you come to a line in the sand. God isn't a puzzle you solve. He's a reality to whom you relate."

Ben stared at the television.

"I think today is your personal turning point. The cards have been called. God is either in the Bible code or we're crazy. You don't have to be much of a mathematician to recognize how improbable any other alternative is."

"I just don't know." Ben shook his head. "I feel like I'm up against a wall. Look Judy, you're a Christian. Sure, no problem. You come from a Christian society. But I'm Jewish. Even though I never went to synagogue much, being Jewish is still the source of my identity. I don't see how I could ever fit into a Christian world. And yet—" He looked back at the television. "This is just too bizarre for words."

"Ben, I knew this crossroad would come sometime so I checked out a messianic congregation not far away in San Francisco. The members of Beth Yeshua are Jews who believe in Jesus. They understand what you're going through. I think they have answers for you."

"Beth Yeshua? The house of Jesus?" Ben rolled his eyes. "You're not serious?"

"They have a wonderful rabbi. Talking to him might help."

Ben turned back to the television and said nothing. For the next fifteen minutes they silently listened to the unfolding reports. Diplomats from across the world made statements, speculating about a state of war with the Palestinians. No one knew for sure how badly Netanyahu was injured.

"Who is this man?" Ben finally asked.

"On television?"

"No, this rabbi in San Francisco."

"Oh!" Judy smiled. "His name is Rabbi Reuven Shiloh. His people originally came out of Russia and migrated to Warsaw, Poland. He was a child when the family fled the Nazis by running to Serbia and then eventually wound up in this country."

"Well, haven't we been doing our research. You've obviously been a busy little girl."

"I wanted to do everything I could to help you," Judy said softly. "Rabbi Shiloh spent his life trying to understand how Jews can come to grips with the full truth in both the Old and New Testaments."

Ben became silent again and watched the report.

"Would you like a sandwich?" Judy finally said, hating the silence. "I have some potato chips."

"No," Ben said soberly, "but I would like to see if you could get me an appointment to see this Rabbi Shiloh tomorrow afternoon."

The next day Ben carefully watched the street signs while he cautiously turned down a San Francisco street that looked as if it might plunge into the ocean. "You're sure we're on the right street, Judy?"

"Yes." She pressed her map against the dashboard. "Rabbi Shiloh said this route was the quickest way to his place."

"I really didn't believe he would see me so soon."

"Actually," Judy said brightly, "he was extremely pleased that you wanted to come. Today fit his schedule perfectly."

"I don't know," Ben grumbled. "Maybe I've been a little hasty."

"Buck up and be the fearless scientist." Judy pointed to a narrow two-story house sandwiched between two old Victorian mansions on the steep hillside. "I think we've found it." She shaded her eyes and peered at the entrance. "Ah, yes. Looks like a mazusa on the door. That's got to be the rabbi's place. Let's go for it."

Ben knocked once and the front door swung open. A man about his own size with a white beard down to his chest peered over his round gold-rimmed glasses. "Benjamin Meridor?"

"Yes," Ben sounded hesitant. "This is my friend, Judy Bithell, and—"

"Wonderful!" the older man exploded. "*Shalom*, my children." He hugged Ben. "Come in, come in to my humble house."

Rabbi Rueven Shiloh led them down a narrow entryway past stairs leading to the second story and beckoned for them to come into his living room. The walls were lined with bookshelves crammed with books both stacked in rows and piled on top of each other. In one corner an old wooden rolltop desk was filled with sacks of papers and books lying open. An endless array of bottles, pens, scissors, and notes stuck out of the cubbyholes.

"Please sit down." Reuven pointed to a worn couch. "You must feel you have returned to your own home. Everyone is welcome here, but no one so much as a Jewish believer."

"I'm not really a believer." Ben hesitated and looked at the yellowing photographs hanging around the room. The men and women looked like European peasants of a past century. Their long beards and white aprons marked them as part of an age that had disappeared with the winds of war. Ben had seen such pictures many times. The Meridors kept their photos hidden in leather-bound albums tucked away in their closets.

"The pictures interest you," Reuven observed and wrinkled his white eyebrows. "They are my family . . . lost in Europe."

"Yes." Ben smiled. "I thought so."

The messianic rabbi sat in an overstuffed chair across from Ben and Judy. "So you are on a journey." Reuven smiled broadly. "Nothing I enjoy better than a good discussion for study. And best of all, you already know about my greatest delight, the secret code in the Torah."

"You've read the hidden messages?" Ben nearly came off the couch.

"Of course. For some time I studied this material very carefully, but I have an edge on the scholars in Jerusalem." The rabbi winked like a Santa Claus about to deliver a Christmas present. "I discovered the story of Yeshua in the Torah."

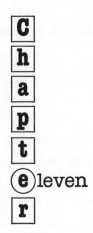

c
h
a
p
t
(**e**)leven
r

San Francisco
August 11, 2000

"SURPRISED YOU, didn't I?" Reuven Shiloh settled into his overstuffed chair with a casual air of confidence. "How can I, a Jew immersed in the Torah, believe in this person Gentiles call Jesus?" He picked up a dog-eared book from a side table. "My friend, the answer is in the Torah itself."

Ben looked at Judy and back at the rabbi. "Sir, I've never been much of a religious person but—"

"No, no," Rabbi Shiloh interrupted, waving his finger like a pointer tapping on a blackboard. "Everyone is religious. Whatever gives us meaning and purpose is our religion. The impulse drives us to make sense out of the world. Are you not a man of science, constantly asking questions? Of course you are religious. Science is your religion."

Ben blinked several times, searching to find the right words. "I never thought of it *that* way."

"Yes." Reuven continued to teach with his index finger. "What you mean is that you have never discovered how the

Holy One of Israel, blessed be His name, is the best answer to your religious quest."

Ben rubbed his chin. "I guess so."

"And you have not discovered how Jesus of Nazareth fulfills the meaning of the holy name."

"Hmmm, you might put it that way."

"Since we are both Jews, let us call Jesus by His Hebrew name, *Yeshua.*" The rabbi smiled broadly like a lawyer winning the first round in a trial. "Yes, you must discover how Yeshua connects everything the Holy One purposed in the creation of Israel to the calling of the Gentiles." He abruptly slapped the arm of his chair several times. "Edith!"

A small, bent woman shuffled into the room, her old floppy shoes softly thumping the floor. "Yes." Her voice sounded as frail as she looked. Faded pale skin and white hair made her appear almost colorless. She pulled at the edges of a crumpled apron. "Can I help?"

"Please, meet my sister." Reuven beckoned. "She has been with me for some time. Would you be so kind as to serve our guests some coffee, Edith?"

Reuven bent forward and lowered his voice. "Edith has had a difficult life. World War II was very horrendous for her. Later she met Eliezer Wolkowicz, and they immigrated to Israel." The rabbi sighed and shook his head. "Eliezer was killed by a sniper on a kibbutz. After my wife died, Edith came to live with me because she had nowhere else to go. No, life has not been easy for my sister."

Judy nodded sympathetically.

Reuven again took on the robust sound of a self-assured scholar. "Now, Benjamin, where shall we begin with you?"

"I read some Hebrew and I have been working with the hidden code in the Bible, but I don't know how to put the pieces together. One thing I have figured out is that there's a lot more to Scripture than I dreamed possible. It's hard for me to picture myself becoming a Christian, but I can't make sense out of our discoveries without thinking that God must be real."

"Ah!" the messianic rabbi beamed. "You simply need more instruction in getting to the depths of the Bible." He rubbed his hands together vigorously. "Judy has already told me what you have discovered in the code. I am sure the attempt yesterday on Netanyahu's life was rather disconcerting. Yes?"

Ben nodded. "The whole incident was a wake-up call. I know now that I'm not playing a game, but I don't know how to take the next step."

"Then let us begin in the beginning!" Shiloh exclaimed. "We must start with the *B'raisheet*, the first word in the Bible, 'in the beginning.' Benjamin, did you notice the name of the Redeemer is hidden in this first word?"

"I had no idea."

"Yes! Like the song we sometimes sing, 'Standing somewhere in the shadows you'll find Yeshua. He's a friend who always cares and understands.'" Shiloh briefly hummed the tune. "'Standing somewhere in the shadows, you will find Him,'" his craggy voice rumbled, "'and you will know Him by the nail prints in His hands.'" The rabbi leaned forward and looked over the rim of his glasses, winking as if confiding a great secret. "Yeshua is in every book of the Bible," he said in hushed tones. "Ben, you must learn not only to treasure the inspired words of the Bible but also to look behind these words and beyond the obvious meanings. Even if Yeshua is momentarily obscured, you can find Him waiting to greet you."

Edith backed through the door, carrying a tray. She placed the tray on a coffee table, pointed to the cups and accoutrements, and shuffled out of the room again.

"How can you find Yeshua in the Old Testament?" Judy asked. "I thought Jesus didn't show up until the New Testament. You must have some unique approach."

Reuven's eyes sparkled with delight. "No!" he roared. "The amazing thing is that I use the same approach every good Jew does in studying Scripture. I must teach you about the four levels of insight that build from one to the other. Only then will you be able to understand the code, the secrets of Torah."

Ben cleared his throat and started to speak but stopped. Finally he replied, "Forgive me, but I have no idea what you are talking about. I'm just a beginner. Actually, Rabbi Shiloh, I read Hebrew quite slowly. Because of the computer, I've been able to work some in the Bible code, but beyond those limitations, I know nothing."

"Hey," Judy added, "finding hidden secrets is way beyond me. I need lots of help." She reached in her purse. "If you don't mind, I want to take notes."

"Of course, of course." Reuven sipped his coffee. "Take a cup, children." He pushed the tray toward them.

"Thank you." Ben pulled a pencil from his pocket and a small notebook. "I'd like to do the same as Judy."

Reuven Shiloh smiled. "Excellent! I am pleased when I find serious students." The rabbi stretched back in his chair and opened his Bible. "Torah study has four levels. We begin with the most important level, which is the Torah's simple meaning, the *peshat*. Through the next two steps we explore the allusions and the inferences in the stories. Only then can we come to the fourth level where many great secrets are hidden. As a messianic rabbi, I spend my life looking for new insights from all four levels, including the unexpected twists in words, the treasures sprinkled throughout the many pages of the Bible."

"Can you give me an example?" Judy asked.

"Let's start with something simple. Perhaps you know the first letter of the alphabet, *aleph*, often stands for God?" Reuven pulled at his white beard, waiting for their response. "Just one letter can make an amazing difference. *Amet* is the word for truth and *met* means death. The only difference between the two is the *aleph*, the letter meaning God." Reuven winked. "What does it mean to drop this letter?" he asked rhetorically. "Take God out of the truth, and the truth brings death."

"Amazing!" Judy shook her head. "Tell us more."

"You should also know that every letter in the Hebrew alphabet has a numerical value. If we were doing the same thing with English, the letter *A* would equal one, *B* would be two, *C* three, and so on and so forth. We could make up a hidden message by sending someone a number. For example, 3–1–2 could translate into C, A, and B, or *cab*. Got it?"

"I've already discovered the *gematria*, the number system for the alphabet," Ben explained. "And I know that letters also have symbolic meaning. Like the *aleph* can also stand for an ox. A *yod* can embody the idea of a hand. Unfortunately, I don't have the slightest idea what to do with this information."

"Ah, that's where the fun begins, Ben. Once we start applying this system, exciting things happen." The rabbi opened his Bible. "Let me show you the secret meaning in the first ten names in the Jewish genealogy in Genesis. Like the letters, Hebrew names have meaning. A person's name tells us something about who he is. *Adam* meant 'man' or 'everyman.' Right? Everyone knows that."

Ben and Judy turned to each other with a blank stare.

"*Seth* stood for 'appointed.' Not so well known?" Reuven watched their look of astonishment. "*Enosh* meant 'mortal,' and *Cainan* was 'sorrow.'" He stopped and studied their faces again. "Write down what these names mean. Make a list."

Judy and Ben furiously scribbled down the information.

"You should have written the words *man, appointed, mortal,* and *sorrow,*" Reuven repeated. He took another sip of his coffee. "*Mahalaleet* meant 'blessed God.' *Jared* stood for 'shall come down,' and *Enoch* is another way of saying 'teaching.' Got those words down?"

Judy nodded but kept scribbling.

"*Methuselah* actually is a name meaning 'death brings,' and *Lamech* embodied the idea of despairing." The rabbi sat back and smiled. "Our tenth name, *Noah,* was the symbol for rest. Do you have every one of the meanings written in a line now?"

Ben looked at the page. "I think so, but I'm not sure what we're doing."

Reuven grinned. "What words seem to fit together? Look for a couple of sentences."

Ben recited slowly. "The man appointed mortal sorrow . . . The blessed God shall come down teaching . . . His death brings despairing rest." Ben stopped and looked at the page again. "What did I just say?" He read the sentences aloud again.

"Amazing." Judy looked at her notebook. "This is the story of sin, suffering, and salvation."

"Yes!" Reuven pursed his lips and poked his index finger at Ben. "You see, my fine friend, the mystery of the gospel is also hidden in the first ten names in the Bible."

"Whoa." Judy shook her head. "This stuff blows my mind. All of this insight from the genealogy?"

Reuven waved his hand, minimizing his insight. "Really rather elementary." He sipped his coffee again. "Let's go to the other end of the Hebrew alphabet to the last letter, the *tau.*" The rabbi held up a copy of the Torah and pointed to a Hebrew character. "In the earliest time, the cross on which Jesus was crucified looked more like a *t* than the *x* shape we see everywhere today. Did you notice the *tau* is shaped like a cross?"

Ben studied the letter. "The idea never occurred to me."

"I would have expected a cross to look like the jewelry I wear around my neck." Judy felt for the silver chain. "But I have seen pictures of a T-shaped cross like you are suggesting."

"You can't fully grasp the message of either the Old Testament or the New Testament unless you read with a Jewish orientation," Reuven lectured. "Late in the first century, when the Romans and Greeks gentilized the gospel story, depth was lost."

"And what does the *tau* imply?" Judy asked.

Reuven chuckled. "The human story begins with Adam and Eve's expulsion from Eden. Their sin could only be covered with an animal sacrifice, an ox. Yes?" He peered again over the top of his glasses and waited for their look of recognition.

"I think so." Judy hesitated.

"And the alphabet begins with what letter?"

"An aleph." Ben answered.

"And you, Ben, what can an aleph also stand for?" Reuven pushed.

"An ox." Ben said.

"There you have it!" Reuven exclaimed. "In the beginning human sin required the sacrifice the *aleph* suggests. In the end, transgression was redeemed only by Yeshua's offering on the cross. You can now see why the book of Revelation says, 'I am the Alpha and the Omega,' the *aleph* and the *tau*."

Ben shook his head again. "Wow. What can I say?"

"These are the amazing secrets of the Bible?" Judy asked.

"No, no. I've only given you a bit of insight from steps two and three. *Remez* and *derush* are methods of inquiry into the allusions and inferences in the Torah. I only offered you elementary insights."

"This is all way over my head." Judy turned to Ben. "I knew Rabbi Shiloh would help you, but he's opening my eyes too. If this is any indication of what the secrets are, I'm eager to push on."

Ben drank coffee and looked thoughtfully at his notepad. "Absolutely."

"Have you found the many locations of Yeshua's name during your code work?" Reuven asked with an innocence that implied volumes. "Hmmm?"

"No," Ben answered. "We haven't tried putting that name in the computer."

"Take a second look." The rabbi grinned. "And a third and a fourth. Secrets will unfold before your eyes."

"Give us a hint," Judy persisted.

"Let's start in the beginning again. In the first chapter of Genesis and the fourteenth verse, God created the seasons. Start with the *ayin* letter in *mo'adim*, the word for seasons, and count every 172 letters. The name Yeshua appears again and again, telling us that Yeshua is the fulfillment of all the seasons, the feasts, the holidays, all that the Lord established when the world was created."

Ben stared. "I can hardly grasp finding the Hebrew name of Jesus in the Torah even once."

"Everyone knows the prophecy in Isaiah fifty-three was fulfilled in the crucifixion of Yeshua," Reuven explained matter-of-factly. "The comparisons are obvious. But few people have checked into the message hidden behind this passage." Reuven quickly thumbed through his Hebrew Bible. "If you start with the sixth-to-last *yod* in the tenth verse and count every twentieth letter you will find the text spells *Yeshua Shmi*, or 'Yeshua is my name.'"

Ben blinked several times. "You're kidding."

"I never jest about the Bible." Reuven looked over the rim of his glasses. "You're the computer man. Check it out. And while you're working, take a second look in Hebrew at verse eleven. 'He shall see the labor of His soul, and be satisfied. By His knowledge My righteous Servant shall justify many, For He shall bear their iniquities.' Start with the *mem* and count every forty-second letter, and you'll find another word pops up. *Mashiach* means the consecrated and anointed one, the messiah. Encoded in this exact prophecy of the crucifixion is both the Hebrew name of Jesus and the affirmation He is the messiah. Can such be a coincidence?"

"The chances are one in billions," Judy added. "Completely impossible."

Ben closed the notepad and stuck the pencil back in his pocket. He ran his hand through his hair and rubbed his neck. "I am a Jew," he began, his voice halting. "But I can't escape such overwhelming evidence." He sunk back in the chair. "I always believed science was superior to religion. Now, my computer ends up confirming the supremacy of God." He looked anxiously at Reuven. "You are right. Science was my religion, but look at what happened. Geometry took me full circle back to the God of my people."

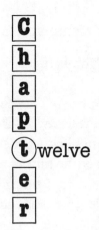

C
h
a
p
(t)welve
e
r

ANN YAAKOV WATCHED the battered red van pull away from the stoplight and disappear in the traffic. "If they'd taken better care of that Chevrolet, I would think it was ours. Come to think of it, I've seen that same vehicle driving through our area several times in the last month. You notice a car like your own."

"We saw them yesterday. It almost seems providential that we keep bumping into them," Judy answered from the backseat.

"Jerusalem is actually a rather small place." Ann turned around in the front seat. "You'd be surprised how quickly one gets to know a lot of people, especially in the Christian community."

"I suppose that's good and bad." Judy looked at the white stone buildings of East Jerusalem as they passed. "Small worlds make for big exposure."

"True," Ann answered. "Gossip flies around this town

with the speed of light. Particularly when you have our brand of minority."

"You think the powers that be don't have our number?" Keith looked in the rearview mirror as he drove. "The Hasid and Orthodox fanatics know our street address by heart. The police check us out at the hint of a complaint."

"Ben certainly did the strategic thing in swapping cars. The security people do *know* what our people drive," Ann added.

"Rabbi Shiloh told us about attempts to discredit your work," Ben said. "I know a lot of Israelis want to see you go up in smoke." As he spoke, the large stone walls of the Old City loomed before them.

"Exactly," Keith answered. "Whatever makes us look bad makes them happy. We've even had their people go through our trash looking for something to pin on us."

Ann bit her lip. "I don't want to sound like a wet blanket, but . . . Well, frankly, I have to admit I have some strong second thoughts about what we are doing today. You guys better be right. If not, we'll pay a great price."

"What do you mean?"

"If Av 9 comes and goes and nothing happens, we'll be the laughingstock of Jerusalem as well as the whole Christian community," Ann explained. "Our enemies win big."

"Ann means that our church would be finished," Keith added. "I told the others that we could just come home and resume our lives, but the truth is, this journey is either a page straight out of the Old Testament or we're on a one-way trip to the nut fringe."

Judy swallowed hard. "Rather serious set of alternatives."

She noticed the ancient Jaffa Gate to her right. "We don't want you to get any doors slammed in your face."

"I don't mean to seem ungrateful or sound like a pessimist," Ann said, fidgeting with her purse, "but I want you to understand the far reaching consequences our little exodus could have."

Ben grimaced. "I can't be *completely* certain, but we truly believe the prediction is on target."

Keith smiled at his wife. "Obviously, we hope this horrible disaster doesn't occur, but a catastrophe is ahead one way or the other." He turned left down a street lined with tall, old white buildings.

"Liat Collins would have 'proof' that my husband is incompetent. If any of the congregation is left, they may follow Liat."

"Ben and I wouldn't be here if we didn't passionately believe in what we found in the Bible." Judy squeezed Ben's hand tightly. "Honestly. We're sure an atomic bomb will explode on Av 9 this year. You can't imagine the struggle we went through to arrive at that conclusion."

"We know you're on the right track, Ben." Keith slowed as traffic piled up at the traffic light on Port Said Street. "Just wanted you to know our insecurities."

Ben raised his eyebrows and glanced nervously at Judy. Her weak smile hinted at unspoken misgivings. A sinking feeling arose in the pit of his stomach.

Delay. Ben gritted his teeth. *From the beginning I've worried about the possibility.* The word bounced around his mind like a runaway marble in a pinball machine. Warning lights lit up and bells sounded.

Reuven Shiloh's voice floated up out of the past. The old man had been explaining a fine point of the Torah and poking a long, bony finger in Ben's face.

□ ○ □

"WHY IS THE MESSIAH DELAYED in His coming?" The rabbi pulled at his beard and looked at the worn copy of the Hebrew Old Testament lying in his lap. "You've asked me a very important question, Ben. The issue of delay is profound. Did you bring me the assignment I gave you last time on Isaiah fifty-three?"

Ben opened his notebook and handed a typed page to Rabbi Shiloh. "I hope this is acceptable. I ran it off on my computer printer."

Reuven quickly read through Ben's printout. "Excellent work! I am pleased." Reuven looked over the rim of his gold glasses and spoke to Judy. "You have memorized this passage?"

"No, sir. I'm sure I should."

"Yes, of course." Rabbi Shiloh's eyes widened in mock consternation. "Everyone ought to. And you, Ben?"

"Working on it," Ben lied.

Reuven looked warily out of the corner of his eye. "You must exercise your minds! In the good old days, many Jewish boys memorized the whole Pentateuch. You're both bright enough. Get on with it."

"Absolutely." Judy's expanding grin betrayed a lack of intent.

"I need to ask about delay of a different order," Ben interjected. "Remember Edlow Moses' book on the code?"

"Of course, of course." Reuven pulled at his chin.

"Moses' study of the hidden code revealed that a great war would break out in Israel in 1996. In the same lines the code abruptly reversed direction and declared this war was delayed. It's bizarre. I couldn't tell when the war would start. Then the code implied the war was rescheduled for 2000, but again there was the word *delayed*."

"Yes, yes."

"I am very confused, Rabbi Shiloh. The code seems to say a war was scheduled twice in God's eternal plan and then suddenly delayed each time. Even more confusing, the code was written down in the Bible thousands of years ago. God seems to predict that He's going to change His own mind in the future. That's a very unstable scenario."

The rabbi looked straight ahead but said nothing.

Ben waited an uncomfortably long time for Reuven to answer. Finally he asked, "Is there an explanation?"

Reuven shook his head. "I don't know."

"I don't get it."

"Ben, the Scripture is filled with many, many things I don't understand. I have a hard enough time with what I can grasp. I can't unravel many seeming contradictions."

"But how can I believe in something I can't explain?" Ben persisted.

Reuven abruptly roared with laughter. "Mr. Science has returned to my house this afternoon."

Ben's face reddened. "I thought we were here to find answers."

"Of course, of course. But we can't possibly understand or

explain everything. Many things we must accept as true by faith. Learning to say we don't know is as important as having the right answer."

"But we're talking about a big contradiction in Scripture." Ben's voice elevated slightly. "I mean, the Bible seems to be talking out of both sides of its mouth."

"Possibly." Reuven shrugged. "And then again the passage may only be revealing a gap in our understanding."

Judy frowned. "But shouldn't we be suspicious of blank spaces."

Reuven pulled at his beard. "My children, your scientific minds need to acquire a healthy respect for mystery. Don't ever forget that the Holy One's thoughts are beyond our comprehension. What seems a contradiction to you may only be a paradox."

"A paradox?" Judy protested. "I expect everything to follow in logical order. Isn't algebra more trustworthy than philosophy?"

"You've learned how to factor love into your equations?" Reuven feigned surprise. "I'm eager to see how your work in the concept of grace is solving your calculus problems."

Judy gestured aimlessly but couldn't answer.

"Well, well," Reuven chided her, "it seems as if we've come to the end of what geometry can do for us. Logic, equations, and computers have their place, but in the end they cannot explain the mind of God. Sooner or later, we all come to the limits of our capabilities. At such moments, we stare into the darkness of a mystery that cannot be analyzed by human thought or mechanical device."

"But," Ben persisted, "how can we know what the Bible

code is actually predicting if the message has built-in delays?"

"Humbles one a bit, doesn't it?" Reuven said, tossing the question aside.

"Look, I am trying to help Judy figure out *when* a great catastrophe will destroy Jerusalem. I can't know anything with certainty if God has salted the road with delays. Insight turns into nonsense."

"I hope the Almighty who created the universe knows how important it is that *He* stay in close contact with *you*, Benjamin Meridor. The Lord is going to have a difficult time pulling things together without constant consultation."

Ben felt the color rise in his neck. He fought back irritation. "What I'm trying to articulate is—" He paused and spoke very slowly. "If God arbitrarily rearranges events, we can't tell whether an atomic bomb will explode in 2000 or 2006 . . . or ever!"

The rabbi patted Ben on the hand. "It's okay," he said gently. "We have much more work to do. The mysteries of God don't open themselves to casual observers. Don't worry, if the Lord wants us to know the full picture, He will help you find the answer."

"I'm sure you're right." Ben wrung his hands. "But the appearance of the word *delay* in the code for the years 1996 and 2000 has made everything uncertain. It means I have to be very cautious about telling anyone about a coming war or atomic explosions in 2006 even though we haven't found the word *delay* in that prophecy—yet."

"Hmmm," Rabbi Shiloh mused. "A good way to keep

from falling into presumption. Tempers all prognostications with tentativeness."

Ben shook his head. "The word *delay* has made a mess of everything."

◻ ◯ ◻

THE GLUT OF TOUR BUSES slowed traffic on the street around the Northern Wall and the Old City, but Mohammed Bitawi maneuvered around the far end of the Temple Mount and finally turned on Rohov Shivei Israel Street toward Bethlehem. Dietrich Heinz stared straight ahead. The dirty red van crossed the Mount Zion area, speeding up the valley road that leveled out in the suburbs. Just when Bitawi turned south toward Hebron, traffic stopped. Policemen and soldiers lined the curb and stood in front of a makeshift roadblock. Two cars had already stopped and police were making a quick check of license plates.

"Look—" Dietrich Heinz pointed. "We've got to get out of here."

Bitawi checked the side mirror. "I can't turn around. We are boxed in. Any quick move would be conspicuous."

Two young soldiers stepped out from behind the barrier and pointed at the van. They shouted to someone on the side of the street and hurried toward the red Chevrolet. A small police car immediately pulled into the opposite lane and advanced toward Bitawi.

"Here they come," the Arab hissed at the German. Bitawi's knuckles turned white around the wheel. "We can't run for it."

"Look natural," Heinz growled. "Smile. Don't panic. Let me do the talking."

Bitawi whispered, "Someone tipped security off. They're on to us. They'll shoot us—"

"I said smile." Dietrich tried to look pleasant. "Now!"

A young soldier hurried up to the window and pointed his gun in the Arab's face. "Get out," he commanded. "Both of you."

Heinz slipped out of the car and nodded to the soldiers. "I'm just a tourist, looking at the holy sites. Although he's an Arab, my driver is a fine man."

Bitawi stood by the open van door looking grim.

"Don't move," the soldier warned.

The small police car pulled alongside the van, and its driver called out to the soldier. "The plates don't match, but let's let our boy take a look." He turned to a young man next to him. "Collins, you know these guys?"

The man leaned over and took a hard look. "No. Never saw either one before. The Chevrolet's too dented. These guys are not with Yaakov."

The driver saluted the soldier. "Good try. Let 'em go through."

Heinz and Bitawi got back in the van and waited to pass through the barrier. The German smiled and waved politely. Within minutes they were on their way toward Hebron.

"Turn around," Dietrich demanded. "Someone's looking for a vehicle like this, and I don't like it. Get this van back to the garage at once."

Chapter (t)hirteen

NAHUM ADMONI paced restlessly across his inconspicuous office suite, waiting for a report on the sweep through Jerusalem. When the phone rang, he grabbed the receiver. "Yes."

"Nothing has turned up so far," a sober voice reported. "We found one look-alike van at Highway 3 headed south. Nothing more."

"Keep me updated. *Shalom.*"

For several minutes Admoni stared at two small erasers and drummed nervously on his desk. Nahum moved the green rubber squares back and forth, arranging and rearranging them. Finally he picked up the phone. "Nahum Admoni here. Access to internal security request."

Several moments passed. He kept shuffling the erasers around on the top of his desk. Finally someone asked, "Password please."

"Big Bang."

"Proceed."

"Nothing has come through yet on the red van." Admoni explained. "Anything on your end?"

"No."

"Any update on movement of sensitive materials?"

"Apparently the Egyptians are in on this caper," the operative at the other end reported. "Satellite reports confirm other intelligence reports of the movement of radioactive materials up from the Sinai. We think our 'friends' may have originally taken the long way around and have run a connection from Libya. We've definitely got problems. We need to find out what those Americans know as quickly as possible."

"Right." Admoni drummed on the desk with one of the erasers. "We searched the fanatics' homes and their usual meeting places. Found nothing. I can't understand why we haven't located that van. The Americans have to be someplace in the city."

"Could your informants be lying?"

"I don't think so. I've still got Levy in custody. The wimp's too terrified to lie. Collins is out trying to ID anyone suspicious."

"Keep your private line open, Admoni. We'll be in touch if anything breaks." The phone clicked silent.

Nahum lit a cigarette and settled back in his chair. After several minutes he started fiddling with the erasers again, stacking them side by side. Suddenly, he stopped and stared at the parallel green blocks. He switched them around one more time.

"That's it!" Admoni ground the cigarette into an ashtray. "They've switched cars!" He grabbed the phone, angry that he hadn't figured this out sooner, and began dialing frantically.

"Road block one," a disinterested soldier answered.

"Admoni here," the Mossad officer barked into the phone. "I'm faxing you pictures. Forget the cars and start looking for the people."

KEITH YAAKOV slowed the brown Toyota to a halt. "We're sure not getting out of town fast. Looks like everyone and his brother is sightseeing in Jerusalem today." He rolled down the window and tried to see around the line of cars. "From what I can see some tour buses have caused this congestion. Those things are impossible to get around on these narrow streets. What a mess!"

"We've got plenty of time," Ben observed from the back seat. "After all we've got four days to get out of town." He laughed. "I think we can still cover a couple of hours of driving with a little time to spare."

"Don't count on it," Keith grumbled.

"We've got faith in you even if you have doubts about us," Judy chided.

Keith smiled sheepishly but stared straight ahead. "Hey, I trust you guys completely. I'm just a little nervous about what we're doing. We're sort of out there, skating on thin ice."

"You get no arguments from me," Ben answered. "These past several years have been an adventure in living on the edge. They've pushed me further than I ever wanted to go."

Actually Reuven forced me beyond anything I would have ever dreamed possible, Ben thought. *What an unusual man.* Born in Russia, Shiloh had landed in San Francisco when he escaped to the West. He had become a believer by studying the prophecies of Isaiah. *Now, there's an expert in the fine art of driving someone out of his comfort zone!* Ben reflected. *If it weren't for him, I would never have found my way to this place.*

Ben remembered working for hours trying to figure out how the name *Yeshua* might most effectively be entered into the code. The afternoon sunlight had poured in across his desk and made it hard to concentrate. Spring had been in the air, and the warm breeze had begged him to make a quick trip to the corner store, maybe a prolonged visit to the campus café, or even a stint at the tennis court. Yet he had seemed so close to a breakthrough. Everything had been in place.

□ ○ □

"REUVEN SAID the last chapter of Genesis was really important because it contained prophetic utterances about the future of the twelve tribes," Ben said to himself as he brought up the Hebrew text on the screen. "Since there are twelve tribes, I'm going to put in a twelve space count and see what comes up."

As soon as Genesis 50 appeared, Ben punched in the number sequences for every twelfth character to appear. He hit enter and the hourglass symbol came on the screen. Several moments passed and verses twenty-two and twenty-three came up. Ben quickly referenced his English Bible.

"'And Joseph lived one hundred and ten years,'" he read aloud. "'Joseph saw Ephraim's children to the third generation. The children of Machir, the son of Manasseh, were also brought up on Joseph's knees.'" Ben put the English Bible down and looked at the screen. "I don't see how there could be much there, but I'll give it a try."

As Ben studied the Hebrew, the computer darkened several letters. With his finger he traced the characters and translated aloud. "Y . . . e . . . s . . . h . . . u . . . a." He stared. "The name is there. It's almost as if . . . as if the hidden message is suggesting that Joseph's hope for the future is fulfilled in the coming of Yeshua."

Ben put his head in his hands and stared at the screen.

What's happening to me? he thought. *I've tried to keep everything scientific. No nonsense, no superstition. And now I'm getting smacked in the face every time I turn around.*

Each of his Bible discoveries forced Ben a little deeper into shadows in his mind where he seldom traveled. And now a door near the end of the trek, an entrance into his soul, beckoned him. The place wasn't really unknown as much as the terrain unexplored and the final destination ominous.

Ben distracted himself by turning back to the computer. "I think I'll try another entry."

Reuven said Joseph was a sort of portrait of the coming Messiah, Ben remembered, *because he had the power to bless the Gentiles as well as his own people. The first five verses of Genesis 39 tell this story. Since one hundred is a number for completion, let's see what happens if I run a hundred through that chapter.*

He hit the enter key and Hebrew characters filled his screen. Every hundredth letter was shaded.

Ben stared. "I can't believe my eyes. There it is again. *Yeshua!*"

For the rest of the afternoon, Ben punched in several different combinations, passages, sections, racing through the

Old Testament until he realized the sun had set. The possibilities the spring afternoon had offered gave way to a new promise. Without ever quite knowing how, somewhere in the middle of his astonishing discoveries, Ben had reached the top of the mountain, opened the door, crossed the threshold, and entered the place he'd never been before.

For a long time, Ben stared at the pile of papers and books stacked around his computer. Finally, he clicked the button to start the printer spitting out the results of hours of work. The steady click of the pages filled his ears, but he hardly heard it.

"I can never turn back now," he said quietly.

When the printer finished, Ben took out the pages and shuffled them together. He laid the stack neatly in front of him and placed his head in his hands.

Tears ran down his cheeks, but for once Ben didn't try to fight them back. He had entered a place beyond words or figures—a place to dwell forever.

Ben had lost track of the time when Judy called.

"How are you?" she said brightly.

"A little on the thoughtful side."

"Been working on your computer?"

"Yeah. Important day."

"Me too, Ben. Remember me telling you about my brother, Jimmy? That he's kind of strange?"

"Yes, I remember."

"When I came home this afternoon, I discovered Jimmy had been reading my notes on the code. He started looking at the Hebrew text and let his mind go. Somehow or the other, Jimmy has developed a sense of how the layers in the Bible code work. I think he's found his way inside what we couldn't explain . . . I think Jimmy may be able to help us find the answers to the delay."

"Are you sure?"

"I think so. But Jimmy's discovered something else . . . something apparently very frightening. He won't talk to me. He's just sitting here staring at the wall. I don't know what to do!"

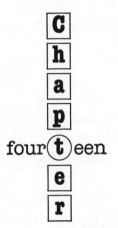

four(t)een

"HEY!" KEITH YELLED out the car window. Across the street a Hasidic boy stopped and looked inquisitively. The sober black suit and yarmulke made the young Hasid look like a little old man. *"Ha'tsee'lu!* Need a little help, kid. What's holding up the traffic? We haven't moved in five minutes."

"The road's blocked." The boy thumbed over his shoulder and tossed his head indifferently, bouncing his long side curls against his round face. "Security check or something."

"IDF troops have car checks on all the roads out of the city," Ann fretted.

"I don't like it, Ben." Keith got out of the brown Toyota and looked at the cars piling up behind them. "Maybe it's nothing . . . I don't know." He stuck his head back in the window. "I think we need to put the three of you in different cars and have an alternative plan if anything goes wrong."

"I'm staying with you, Keith," Ann insisted.

"Sure, but Ben, Jimmy, and Judy could attract attention if they're all three in the same car. Let's spread them out through the caravan."

"Everything's okay," Judy reassured Jimmy. "Ben and I are going to get out and talk with Keith. Watch for that red van to come back." She slammed the car door behind her.

Jimmy nodded.

"I think we ought to put several cars between the three of you," Keith suggested. "That way, at least, the police couldn't make a clean sweep by grabbing my car."

Ben bit his lip. "I'm not crazy about the idea, but it sounds like the right way to go. Better we have a trap door than they nab everyone in one fell swoop."

"Maybe, we ought to be ready to divide up the caravan if things get tight," Judy thought out loud. "The back half of the group might be prepared to take an alternative route."

"Good thought," Keith said slowly. "If IDF detains one group, the other could detour down the back road to Jericho. Then at least they could get through to Petra."

"I can tell Jimmy we want him near the back to observe from the rear," Judy added. "He'd probably be safer back there anyway."

"Agreed." Keith pointed to the middle of the caravan. "I'll tell only the driver in the center car of our plan. It's better the others not know if we're caught."

"I'll stay in your car, Keith," Ben suggested. "No one's looking for me. Judy should be at least a couple of cars behind us since she's their big target."

"Definitely. I'll spread the word." Keith trotted back to speak with the other drivers.

"Come on, Jimmy." Judy spoke through the open car window. "I want you to ride closer to the end where you can watch what happens behind us. Keep a sharp eye. Okay?"

Mechanically Jimmy got out of the car without changing expressions. "I will watch carefully." He walked stiffly toward the last car.

Ben stopped Judy. "I don't want you too far away. You never can tell what might happen in this wild mess."

"Hey, you're talking to the original liberated woman, remember? I can take care of myself."

"Doesn't anything ever frighten you, Judy?"

"Sure." Her voice softened. "The thought of something bad happening to you gets my attention. That scares me a lot."

Ben took her hand and smiled. "So if one of those cops came after me, you'd be all over him like a Bengal tiger?"

"I certainly would try."

"Be careful, Judy. I can't pull this off without you."

"Okay," Keith interrupted, "I talked with Rivka Berg in the middle car. Should we run into trouble, he knows to take an alternative route. If we run into trouble at the next checkpoint, we have a solid plan B in place." Keith hopped back in the brown Toyota. "The traffic is starting to move. Come on. Let's go."

Vehicles crawled across the junction at the Jericho Road. Keith turned right and the road swung around the Kidron Valley before gradually climbing up the Mount of Olives. In the middle of the curve, police maintained a roadblock.

"Act like tourists," Keith commanded. "I'll be your tour guide." He pulled a laminated badge out of the glove compartment. "Since I'm actually certified to guide Christian groups at archeological sites, I'll have the jump on the security inspection at the barricade. Get ready for the spiel the tour groups get. And pay attention. I'll be giving an exam at the end."

Ann pressed her face against the glass. "Police are making quick inspections. They're peering in the windows and checking license plates. Backup soldiers are keeping machine guns trained on each vehicle," she reported.

Keith pointed at the base of the steep incline and spoke loudly. "About ten feet down those stairs is the so-called Tomb of the Virgin. According to tradition, Mary's parents, Joachim and Anne, are buried in the same place." He leaned out the window and pointed with an exaggerated sweep of the hand. "The big gesture makes me look like a real tour guide, doesn't it?" he said over his shoulder.

Ben peered up the side of the Mount of Olives at a massive building rising above the trees. "I'm always taken with that massive Russian Orthodox Church. The onion-shaped domes look strangely different from everything else, so out of place."

"The Church of St. Mary Magdalene was built by some czar in the last century," Keith explained. "Members of the Russian royal family are buried up there. And that's *not* pious legend."

"Just make sure we don't end up in a tomb with them," Ben muttered. "We are only two cars away from the inspection point."

"Just leave matters in the hands of your faithful tour guide," Keith answered. "Don't worry. I know how to talk to these guys."

A boyish looking soldier motioned the brown Toyota forward. Keith pulled to a halt.

"I am a guide," Keith began before the soldier could speak. "Several of the cars behind me are part of a private tour." He held up the certification badge. "Is there some problem?"

The soldier didn't speak but stared at Keith. He beckoned for a colleague to check the opposite side of the car.

Keith smiled and stared straight ahead. Ann nodded pleasantly when the police guard passed her. Ben kept looking up the hill at the Russian Church. "I can't believe I'm really in the Holy Land seeing this place," he said in a loud, forced voice.

The IDF trooper returned to the driver's window. "Your destination?"

"Area holy sights," Keith explained. "We hope to see the Tomb of Lazarus in Bethany."

"Hmmm." The young man pushed his head inside the car and looked around, then returned to the blockade and talked with an officer. After a moment, the young soldier waved the brown Toyota through.

"So far so good. They bought the tourist line and didn't look at us too closely." Keith inched the car forward. "Just ahead is the Basilica of the Agony, the Church of All Nations. Beyond the site of Gethsemane, the road forks toward Jericho. We'll pull over and wait for the others to get through the checkpoint. Our big hurdle will be getting Judy across."

"I'm not fond of Judy's black hair," Ben said, "but right now I'm glad she dyed it. It'll throw the security people off."

"The ponytail she added this morning will help too," Ann

said. "The big problem is us. We still look like that crazy messianic Jewish couple."

"We're just being nervous and taking the car check personally," Keith retorted. "We don't look like the types they're chasing. Truth is the security people are constantly on the alert. The Netanyahu assassination attempt made them all crazy. We're only small fish. They're after the big barracudas."

Let's hope so." Ben looked over his shoulder. "Hey, Judy's car is through. We can go."

"Super." Keith started the Toyota. "We'll start slow and let the others catch up."

The caravan gradually reassembled, wound around the far end of the Mount of Olives, and turned toward the outskirts of Bethany. Roadside signs changed from Hebrew to Arabic. Billboards advertised distinctly Palestinian products. Dark-skinned children ran beside the road, chasing each other in a fierce game of kick the can. The brightly colored dresses of the Palestinian women dotted the drab terrain with greens, reds, and yellows. White bearded men in their traditional black-and-white checkered head scarves and black rope headbands sat outside hole-in-the-wall cafés sipping bitter Turkish coffee.

"So is this area controlled by the Palestinian Authority?" Ben asked.

"Yes and no," Keith answered. "Bethany is an Arab village and its sympathies are with the Palestinian Authority. But if security becomes a big issue, the IDF forces won't hesitate to act in this locale. We're a long way from being home free."

"Then we ought to observe the speed limits and not make any of my American-style California stops."

"Look—" Ann pointed to the far edge of town. "Another roadblock!"

"That's unusual." Keith peered out the window. "I've never seen two barricades so close together. They've *got* to be after someone more significant than we are. I'll flash my badge again, and we'll be on our way double quick."

Ben leaned over the front seat. "Maybe . . . but I don't like the looks of any of this. These blockades weren't here when we came by yesterday."

"Traffic is going through much faster at this one." Keith shifted into second. "Maybe it's just a quick screen to catch anyone slipping by the big checkpoint in the Kidron Valley."

He slowed at the wooden barrier. On the other side of the bottleneck, soldiers waiting in a jeep kept a mounted machine gun aimed at the narrow passage.

"Bo'ker tov," Keith said, greeting the large sentinel. "I'm a registered guide taking tourists down to Masada. Any problem?"

"Let me see your credentials."

"Sure." Keith handed his badge through the window. "You'll note everything is current."

The overweight guard took the badge to a man with a clipboard. They exchanged comments, and the smaller official made several notations before the soldier returned.

"Go on through," the burly man said unceremoniously as he pushed the badge back through the window.

"Thank you." Keith saluted and drove past. "What did I tell you? A piece of cake." He squeezed his wife's hand. "Honey, *now* we're home free."

The soldier made a quick survey of his clipboard. For a moment he studied carefully the name he had just written down.

"Come here," he called to the much larger guard. "I've got a match against the fax that just came through."

"Really?" The older guard looked at the list. "Samuel, what do we do next?"

"Instructions on the communiqué say to call this special security number."

"Do it!" the burly soldier barked.

Laying the clipboard on the wooden barricade, the guard punched a series of numbers into his mobile phone and waited.

"Nahum Admoni here," the voice answered.

"Bethany checkpoint reporting, sir. We have a match on one of the names sent us a few minutes ago."

"What?" Excitement crackled through the receiver. "Are you sure?"

"The driver of a brown Toyota carried a tour guide certification badge, so we didn't check his driver's license, but it's the same name listed in your recent fax. The guide's name is Keith Yaakov."

"Excellent! Where are they going?"

"Highway 36. Said they were going to Masada."

"Your name?"

"Samuel Barei."

"Very good work, Barei. You will not be forgotten."

"You want us to give chase, sir?"

"Yes. Stop them. Fire if necessary, but don't kill anyone. We need these people alive. Those rotten little insects have crawled into my spider web. I will be there shortly to have them for lunch."

chapter

fif(t)een

REUVEN SHILOH tossed restlessly in his bed until he finally pulled back the covers and sat up in the darkness. For a few fuzzy moments, the old man fumbled for the switch on the lamp stand next to his bed. When he found it, the burst of light stung his eyes. The insensitive hands of an old brass alarm clock pointed to three o'clock.

"Ah," Reuven yawned and rubbed his eyes. "What a horrible hour to wake up. I feel so unsettled, so troubled."

The rabbi slowly got out of bed and slipped on an old tattered bathrobe. The worn and faded leather of his evening slippers settled warmly around his feet. He cautiously padded his way toward the kitchen. "Something's wrong. Something's out of place."

Reuven started to turn the lights on in the living room when he saw a silhouette slumped in his overstuffed chair. A jumbled mass of gray static still buzzed across the television screen.

"Oh my," he said to himself. "Edith, will you ever stay in bed at night?"

Reuven switched off the television but didn't wake his sister. He quietly tiptoed into the kitchen. "She wanders all night," the rabbi grumbled, "and snores all day." Reuven shook his head and reached for a red coffee tin in the cupboard. He ran water into a pot.

"Four days to go," he mumbled. "I wonder where they are at this moment." The old man pulled on his beard and sighed. "They are young, and have no idea how dangerous it can be to wander around in a battlefield." He plopped down at the kitchen table.

Reuven stared at the coffee tin in front of him, the shape slowly changing before his drowsy eyes. The red tin seemed to shrink and reform into a battered red porcelain coffee cup. The sound of gunfire filled his memory and the roar of approaching bombers drowned out the present. A voice echoed from the past.

❏ ○ ❏

"SHILOH! We don't have much time left." The bearded young man yanked at Reuven's heavy winter coat. "The Germans are advancing. If we don't leave now, the panzers will soon have the town surrounded. The Nazis will blow everything to pieces." Flickering candles threw eerie shadows across the small room. The youth's face was filled with anguish.

"I can't leave until I know Edith got through the lines, Model," Reuven protested. "I must know she's not caught in the cross fire or left behind." He pounded the red cup on the wooden kitchen table. The candle bounced.

"Sure. She's your sister." Model Potok wrung his hands. "But Edith's gone. Either she got through by now or she's . . . well, there's no way to know." A bomb exploded off in the distance, and the house shook.

"Edith needs me to tell her what to do," Reuven pleaded. "She's little, afraid, so helpless. My mother charged me to care for her."

Another bomb exploded, much closer, shaking the farmhouse to its foundation. Plaster fell from the ceiling and the last two candles went out.

"We either run or die," Potok screamed. "I'd rather be blown up than fall into the Germans' hands. You know the stories. Come now or I leave without you."

Reuven struggled to his feet. He rubbed the sparse stubble on his chin. "I'm so afraid for Edith. I'd gladly die in her place if only—"

A blast of fire swept through the window, shattering its glass into a million pieces. In a split second of brilliant illumination, Reuven saw Model fly backward as if lifted by an overpowering gust of wind. Shards of glass pricked his face, his eyes filling more with astonishment than terror. Reuven's mind slid into slow motion.

The invisible force picked Reuven up by the back of his neck and sent him flying. Like a ghostly specter, he sailed through what should have been the kitchen wall, landing somewhere in the vast darkness. The sweet smell of hay filled his nose. Pieces of straw stuck in his mouth.

For a long time Reuven lay in peaceful silence, thinking he

was dead. Only as pain returned did he realize that the explosion had shattered his eardrums. The silence became his enemy. He could not hear the sound of hoof, footstep, or tank.

His hair singed, Reuven realized the back of his thick coat was only shredded, smoldering rags. He smelled of smoke. When he sat up, Reuven could see burning houses and barns. The ground trembled. Terrible dread swallowed his senses.

Reuven struggled to his feet and ran as hard as he could, frantically, without sense of direction or intent. Branches and other debris kept tangling in his feet. Three times he fell headlong into the dirt, but sheer panic propelled him onward. Reuven briefly felt a trickle of blood running down his leg and into his shoe, but he didn't dare stop.

Bombs kept lighting the sky and flares exploded overhead. With each burst of phosphorescent fire, Reuven made out other shapes hurrying this way and that. Whether the shapes were livestock or humans he could not tell. Although Reuven could barely hear the explosions, he felt bullets whistling past. Dirt kept exploding around his feet.

He had run a mile, maybe two, when he slammed into a low stone wall. The impact knocked him backward as if he had been smacked by an invisible baseball bat. The excruciating pain shocked Reuven back to his sense.

"Oh, God," he cried into the blackness. "Help me! I perish!" Reuven began crying like a baby, hot tears washing the dirt and dust from his face. "Edith? Edith! Where are you?"

Only the wind answered, blowing sand across his face. The dull pain in his ears offered nothing other than more empty silence. Lying flat on his back, Reuven held his hands to the black sky.

"Please, help my sister. Wherever she is at this moment, oh, merciful shepherd of Israel, keep her. Cover her with the shadow of Your wing. You are her only hope!"

❑ ○ ❑

THE SOUND OF A COFFEE CUP bouncing on the living room rug jarred Reuven out of his reflections. "Edith?"

"Going to bed," Edith answered. Her voice was barely audible through the kitchen door. "Nothing else on television."

Reuven listened to his sister shuffle off to her bedroom. The padding of her tiny feet in the hall made a forlorn sound, like a lost child not quite sure where to step in the dark. He heard her bedroom door close.

The red coffee tin momentarily seemed unfamiliar and misplaced in time. Reuven picked it up and then pushed it aside. "The young think they are immortal. They cannot believe that a bullet would have their name on it. My young friends have no inkling of how quickly the enemy strikes and the fire burns. In the twinkling of an eye what was solid turns to smoke. The living become a memory." He sighed. "Model Potok, my friend, I never saw you again. I'm sorry I didn't listen to you."

Reuven slipped out of his chair and knelt on the cold floor. "Oh, Holy One of Israel, blessed be Your name, though a thousand fall at their right hand and ten thousand on their left, please, please let no harm come to them. As You led me in my darkest night, take them through this time of terrors. Save those three righteous children for the sake of Your people."

KEITH YAAKOV flipped on the Toyota's air conditioner. "It's going to be hot today. It always gets scorching down at the Dead Sea this time of year. We should be there in about an hour."

"How long do you think it will take for us to get to Petra?" Ann asked.

"That depends on getting across the Jordan border and the Allenby Bridge," Ben answered. "If all goes well, I'd expect us to be in the canyon by the middle of the afternoon."

"Well, we're past the hard part now." Keith nodded confidently. "Now we know my tour guide badge is our ticket to 'pass go' even if we don't pick up an extra two hundred dollars."

"Great idea," Ben added. "That little piece of plastic took you from the most wanted list to VIP status."

As the highway slowly descended, the temperature steadily climbed. Trees and flowers disappeared, the barren wilderness becoming increasingly pervasive. Hills turned into rolling mounds of white limestone and gray granite rocks. Deep ravines and wadis cut through yellowish dirt and wound south toward the Dead Sea. Periodically, a Bedouin family appeared on the bleak terrain. Little herds of shaggy goats pulled at the occasional shrubs struggling to survive between rocks. Camels nibbled on sparse weeds barely surviving from the early rains of past months.

Keith glanced in the rearview mirror to check on the other cars in the caravan. "Oh, no!" he exclaimed. "Look!"

Ben and Ann strained to see out the back window.

"A jeep load of soldiers is chasing us." Ben turned on his knees to see out the back window. "They've passed Danny

Rubenstein. They don't seem to be interested in the rest of our people."

"Maybe they're going somewhere else and are just trying to pass us," Ann ventured.

"I don't think so," Ben answered. "Those are the same friendly guys we passed at the last checkpoint in Bethany. They're pointing at our car."

"What should I do?" Keith hunched forward against the wheel. "Speed up?"

"No, slow down," Ann protested. "They might go on by."

"At least they don't seem to be on the trail of anybody else in our group," Ben added.

A microphone boomed from the approaching jeep. "Brown Toyota, pull to the side! Pull to a stop immediately."

Keith grimaced. "Yeah, we're the target. I'm going to speed up and see what happens. That's better than throwing in the towel immediately."

Ann slid down in her seat. "Oh, Lord, help us."

"I said come to a halt, brown Toyota," security persisted.

"A sharp curve is just ahead and then the road splits," Keith barked. "There's a side road to the right, a back way to Jericho. Remember that wadi with an ancient monastery down in the bottom? St. George's? The road is steep and treacherous but the soldiers will have a hard time crowding us off."

A sharp blast of rapid gunfire filled the air. Bullets flew over the top of the Toyota. Ben dropped lower in the backseat. "They mean business."

"Rivka Berg knows to stay on the main road," Keith said. "Aaron Slatsky is directly behind us and will follow me when we turn. I'm sure Mrs. Skypanski and Judy will follow Aaron. Hang on. The fork is just around the corner."

Once around the bend, Keith cut sharply across the highway and down the steep road. The two cars behind Keith followed with the army jeep pursuing them and firing in the air. The road narrowed.

"What are we going to do?" Ann pulled at Keith's sleeve. "We can't outrun the police."

"At least we'll give the rest of our group time to get away," Keith snapped. "I don't know what else to do."

"Be careful, Keith. I've been on this road before." Ben leaned against the front seat. "Without blinking an eye, you can drop a hundred feet straight down on some of these turns. We're in very dangerous country."

Another burst of gunfire echoed off the canyon walls.

"Look out!" Ann pointed straight ahead at a pickup barreling straight toward them. "Somebody's got to get off the road."

Keith studied the old Arab behind the truck's wheel. "I don't think that old man can see the jeep yet. He's not budging. Hang on."

Keith watched the old Arab's eyes suddenly widen in terror. He jerked the wheel back and forth indecisively; the ancient pickup shuddered. Keith pulled left toward the shoulder of the road. "Hang on! We may roll!"

"Something's got to give!" Ben shouted. "That's a deep wadi to the right. There's no room to spare."

"Aaron isn't letting the jeep cut in, and they're not slowing down," Keith warned. "He's trying to protect us!"

The windshield of the approaching pickup shattered. The

sound of gunfire ripped through the air; instantly holes riveted across the hood and cab. The Arab fell forward but the pickup didn't swerve. Keith hit the ditch and bounced through the gravel, flying past the pickup. The terrible sound of crashing and ripping metal echoed behind them. Keith hit the brakes. The brown Toyota slid sideways to a stop, spraying gravel and dust through the air.

For a few moments, Keith couldn't see through the cloud of dust. He carefully edged across the highway and turned back toward the collision.

"Oh, good heavens!" Ann pointed at the mangled pile of vehicles. "They hit head on!"

"Aaron's car is in the middle!" Keith gasped.

Keith and Ben jumped out of the car. The pickup appeared squashed between the car and the overturned jeep. Gasoline leaked across the asphalt, and the jeep's wheels spun wildly. Mrs. Skypanski's car pulled up behind the crash. Judy and the old woman leaped out of her car.

"It looks like the soldiers pulled sideways into Aaron's car and then the pickup hit both of them," Ben shouted. "No one could have survived. Keith, you better get our car out of here!"

"What can we do?" Mrs. Skypanski shouted to Keith. Judy ran around the side of the pileup.

"Get back!" Ben waved his hands frantically. "Gasoline is everywhere. Get your car back, Mrs. Skypanski."

A huge fireball blew straight up in a massive sheet of fire. A second later, one of the wrecked vehicles burst into flames. A second blast of fire erupted, knocking Ben down. The searing explosion shot straight up in the air, sending a stifling wave of black smoke in all directions. Another deafening roar immediately followed behind the inferno of mangled cars. The greasy smell of burning metal and paint filled the air.

Ben tried to get to his feet. His face smarted, and he smelled burnt hair. The heat drove him backward to find shelter behind the brown Toyota. "Judy!" he screamed. "Judy, where are you?"

The only sound he could hear was the deafening roar of the insatiable flame devouring everything in sight. "Judy!" Ben screamed at the top of his voice. "Please answer me!"

A third explosion sent a car hood sailing over the top of the brown Toyota. A smoldering bumper bounced off the road a few feet away. "We're going to be burned alive!" Ann screamed. "We're going to die!"

Chapter sixteen

ANOTHER THUNDEROUS EXPLOSION showered smoking metal across the highway. Ben slid into the front fender of the Toyota and crouched against the door, shielding his face from the raging inferno. Another shock from the thunder of a jeep tire popping hit him with the force of a small bomb. Billowing black smoke swept over the Toyota and made it impossible to see more than a couple of feet. The fire crackled and popped; small blasts periodically sprayed sparks and pieces of smoldering rubber around him. Ben inched backward toward the rear of the car.

"Judy!" Ben yelled. The deafening noise of the crackling, roaring fire drowned him out. "Answer me, Judy," he tried again.

A sudden gust swept up from the wadi and blew the oily smoke in the opposite direction. The red hot metal carcasses of the melting vehicles glowed. Whatever had been combustible was quickly becoming white ashes.

"Keith?" Ben called. "Are you still in the car?"

"Yeah, I'm coming out. Stay inside, Ann. I don't want you to see." The door slammed. "Where are you?"

Ben stood up. "I've got to find Judy." He crept forward. Another surge of wind cleared away more smoke.

"My God!" Keith shouted. "Mrs. Skypanski's car!" He pointed to what was now another fireball behind the initial wreck.

"Judy!" Ben shouted, bolting toward the inferno. "No . . . no, NO! Judy, where are you? Oh, God! Still be alive! Judy!"

A tire on the Skypanski car exploded, jolting Ben again. He distanced himself from the booming fire but kept running. "Judy!" he screamed.

"Over here," a small voice answered from the other side of the road. A black head of hair slowly appeared above the drainage ditch. "Is it safe?"

In one leap Ben cleared the side of the road and landed in the dirt without noticing the gravel scrapping his backside. He grabbed Judy and pulled her toward him. "You're alive!" Ben hugged her. "Thank God, you're alive."

"I can hardly hear you." Judy held her hands against her ears. "The roaring won't stop."

Ben hugged her fiercely. "You're okay! Okay!" He lifted her off the ground and swung her back and forth. "What a relief." He brushed the dirt off her face. "I thought you were dead."

Judy kept shaking her head, trying to clear her ears. "What happened? I just remember a terrible boom, the searing heat." She rubbed her eyes. "Everything is a blur."

"We've got to get you to the Toyota." Ben helped Judy to her feet.

Judy took a couple of tentative steps then gasped, pointing at the crumpled figure of a soldier smashed against a pile of rocks. "Oh, no!"

Ben pulled her closer. "Don't look. He's dead. Just get out of this ditch." He helped her up the bank.

Keith ran toward them. "They're gone!" he shrieked. "Mrs. Skypanski, Aaron, all the people in his car. Dead!"

"No! No!" Judy reached out helplessly toward the smoking remains of the old Polish woman's car. "Not that sweet old lady."

"The explosion must have caught her just as she tried to move her car," Keith groaned. Tears ran down his face.

Ben caught Judy by the waist. "We've got to get back." He pointed to the Toyota. "Something in one of these cars might still explode. We've got to get away from the fire."

Keith pulled Judy's arm over his shoulder and the three struggled back to the Toyota and quickly got inside. Ann was sobbing, her face in her hands.

"They're dead." Ann could barely speak. "Gone . . . even the soldiers."

"Oh Lord!" Keith cried and lowered his face into his hands. "This has turned into a disaster. I killed them."

"No!" Ben turned to his friend and shook him. "No, you didn't! We did what we had to do, taking that cutoff. The wreck was an accident. An accident!"

"When the army finds the jeep destroyed, they'll be after us, ready to shoot on sight." Keith frantically rubbed his temples. "We're dead for sure."

"Listen to me!" Ben shook him again. "We don't have much time. We've got to get out of here. They'll be trying to make radio contact with the soldier's jeep. It won't take long before the authorities know something's happened."

"You're right." Keith turned on the ignition. "We've got to outrun them."

"No, Keith. Think." Ben put his hand firmly over Keith's. "You can't beat army jeeps and helicopters. We've got to think. Panic will destroy us."

"What else can we do?" Ann screamed. "We have to drive like maniacs or they've got us."

"I don't think so," Ben answered coolly. "We need to make them think we all died in the crash. That's the only thing that will buy us time."

"We can't *walk* to Jericho," Judy protested. "They'd run us down for sure."

"On the contrary," Ben countered. "Walking is our only hope."

"You're not serious," Judy protested.

"Believe it or not, that deep ravine is the quickest route to Jericho." Ben pointed down the steep embankment. "In ancient times, travelers took the wadi as one route to Jerusalem. St. George's Monastery at the bottom was a stop for pilgrims. If we can get down the side of this gulch, we can simply follow the valley and we'll be in Jericho in a couple of hours at the most. There's not a vehicle in the world that can wind through that narrow canyon. The police won't have any advantage over us."

"I don't know." Keith shook his head. "I've already made such terrible mistakes—"

"Snap out of it," Ben demanded. "We've got to act quickly and decisively. We must leave the car here so they'll think we're all dead."

"You're right." Judy's eyes narrowed. "We must throw the IDF off track so they quit pursuing us. We can't possibly outrun soldiers. They'll outflank us one way or the other."

"But the car?" Keith protested. "What can we do with the car?"

"Push it over the edge?" Judy ventured.

"I don't think so." Ben rubbed his chin slowly and stared at the burning vehicles. "They'd find it in the bottom and know we got away. We're going to have to destroy this Toyota . . . just like the other cars."

"What are you saying?" Keith dried his eyes and frowned.

Ben got out of the car and stared at the burning rubble. Only blackened wreckage remained. He turned and thumped on the car window to get the others' attention. "We can't tell who was in those vehicles; the police can't either. It's going to take them some time to find out what's left in that mess of smoke and fire."

"But we'd be walking," Ann protested.

"Remember," Ben said, "Jericho is the PLO's headquarters. We're not far from the territory completely controlled by the Palestinian Authority. Once we pass those boundaries, the IDF won't chase us."

"How in the world are we going to convincingly destroy this car?" Judy asked.

Ben rubbed his chin and walked slowly back and forth in front of the Toyota. Keith put his arm around Ann and held her close. Judy stared at the smoldering remains of Mrs. Skypanski's car.

"We have to burn it," Ben concluded.

Keith got out of the car. "What are you saying?"

Ben pointed to the gas tank. "We need to siphon gas to spread over the car."

"Just how do you propose to do that?" Judy asked.

"I'm sure the dead soldier has a military knife on him." Ben talked as he walked toward the ditch. "We can punch holes in the gas tanks. Let it run underneath. Put gasoline over the seats. Boom! The car's gone." He jumped into the ditch by the dead soldier. "Yes, here's a heavy field dagger. This will punch a hole in anything."

"We'll lose everything we brought," Judy lamented.

"Unless you want to carry the stuff down the canyon," Ben answered.

Ann shook her head.

"We've got an old plastic bowl with fruit in it." Keith opened the truck. "We can sling a lot of gas with that."

"Wait," Judy protested. "If there's no one behind the wheel, they'll know the car is a set up."

"I know—" Ben hesitated, then pointed to the body at his feet. "He's going to have to go in the driver's seat."

"No!" Ann recoiled.

"We don't have a choice," Ben said sharply. "And we're running out of time. Thinking of alternatives is a luxury we can't afford."

"Look." Judy took the knife from Ben. "You and Keith get that guy behind the wheel. Ann and I will clean out anything we need to take with us."

Ann covered her eyes. "I can't watch."

"Ben's right." Keith patted his wife on the shoulder. "I'm

going to swing the car around and back as close as I can to the fire. Let's do what we must *right now.*"

Ben and Keith pulled the young soldier out of the ditch and dragged him across the pavement while Ann and Judy quickly rummaged through the trunk, pulling out a bottle of water and a few personal effects.

"Did you get my Bible?" Keith asked and brushed smoke from his eyes.

"Yes." Judy said, waving the worn leather book.

Ben bent over the soldier. "Back up the car, Keith. I'll remove his metal insignias and any gear that would identify him as military." He hurled the IDF beret over his shoulder into the fire. Ben stripped off the gun belt and slung it backwards. "I think he's ready to go behind the wheel."

"I'll take care of puncturing the gas tank." Keith took the knife from Judy. "Just keep the dish handy." He slid under the bumper and began stabbing at the tank.

Ben pulled the soldier to the open door on the driver's side. "I think it's time for you and Ann to start the descent into the wadi." He looked knowingly at Judy. "Take Ann and start the climb down the hill."

Judy nodded. "I'll help her get out of here." She beckoned. "Come on, Ann. We need to get a head start on the guys."

Ann reluctantly watched her husband working under the car. "You'll hurry, won't you?"

"Absolutely." Keith answered. "Hey, pay dirt. I've got a hole started."

"Start filling the bowl." Ben pushed the green basin under the car. "We've got to be quick."

Keith kept the trickle of gasoline running while Ben

quickly doused the front and back seats. He splashed gas over the floor and on the ceiling. After a couple of trips, he leaned down under the car. "We need to put the driver in."

"Okay," Keith answered resolutely and slid out. "I've never done anything like this before." He inhaled deeply.

"I'll get his shoulders and you push the side of his body in," Ben suggested. "You will have to slide him over."

The two men slowly maneuvered the soldier behind the wheel. Gasoline continued to run under the car, pooling up next to the tires. Ben raised the hood and threw the final bowl of gas across the engine.

"Think it's a go?" Keith fretted.

"I want you to run over there where the trail starts down the wadi." Ben pointed. "I'm going to get a piece of burning wood out of the fire and toss it at the Toyota. It might take a minute or so to catch on, or it could blow in a hurry. Let's not chance something happening to both of us."

Keith hurried across the pavement and started down the steep side of the ravine. He paused behind a pile of rocks to watch.

Ben picked up a smoldering stick and swung it like a base-ball bat, letting it skitter under the car. After releasing the stick, Ben kept moving, running frantically across the highway.

The gasoline under the car caught fire with a whoosh, sending flames up the side of the vehicle. Smoke rolled out of the windows. Ben turned once to look and then hurried after Keith.

"It's going," Ben shouted to his friend. "Keep rolling."

"The girls are halfway down." Keith pointed toward the bottom. He slipped on the loose gravel and fell down.

The explosion sent a shower of loose rocks straight up and then down on the two men. Smoke shot toward the sky.

"It worked." Ben sat down next to his friend, the adrenaline of the past hour wearing off, giving way to fatigue. He looked back up the slope, then turned to Keith, weariness and pain etched on his face. "What did we just do?"

"Like you said . . . what we had to do." He laid a consoling hand on Ben's shoulder. "But our friends—" Keith smiled, tears in his eyes. "They are in a much better place now. With God. I only hope the Father is merciful with the soldiers as well.

"Let's pray before we go on, pray for all of them . . . and for us."

"And for us," Ben echoed.

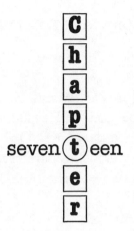

seven(t)een

JUDY AND ANN were sitting by a small stream running through the bottom of the deep ravine when Ben and Keith caught up with them. In stark contrast to the sand and chalky rocks, little shrubs and grass lined the stream. Palm trees dotted the strip, making the riverbed look like a narrow, winding oasis.

"Did you take care of—" The look on Ben's face stopped her. "Are you okay?"

"Yeah," Ben said.

"We heard the explosion." Ann looked up. "It sounded terrible."

"I'm sure the car was destroyed," Keith answered wearily.

Ben, his head down, put his hands on his hips and breathed deeply. He lifted his head, and the weariness and pain seemed to disappear into resolve. "We need to keep moving. We bought ourselves some time up there, but there's no telling how much. Feels ¹ike it's going to break a hundred degrees today." Ben dropped down by the creek. "Let's get a drink and get moving."

"Thank goodness for the stream." Keith shaded his eyes and looked down the canyon. He pointed straight ahead. "Down that way is the ancient Greek Orthodox monastery of St. George. Hermits and monks have lived there off and on for sixteen, maybe seventeen centuries. Locals consider the monastery a holy site."

"How far away?" Ann asked pensively. "I don't know how long I can make it."

"Maybe a couple of miles," Keith ventured.

"Anyone still live there?" Judy tied a scarf around her forehead.

Keith shrugged. "Five or six monks were there several years ago, but they were constantly caught between IDF raids and reprisals by the PLO. Rumor is no one lives there now."

"Will we be in Palestinian territory when we get there?" Judy asked.

"I think so," Keith answered. "We'll be fairly close to Jericho."

"Let's go," Ben said. "Stay as close to the stream as you can. It's easier to walk here."

"I hope Jimmy hasn't panicked," Judy thought aloud, picking her way among the rocks. "When he finds out we're not with the others, I know he's going to be very agitated."

"What will he do?" Ann asked.

"It's hard to say," Judy answered. "He'll probably get very quiet and withdraw. He's definitely more likely to turn into a sphinx than a raging bull."

Ann snuffled loudly and wiped tears from her dirt-streaked face. "I keep thinking about our friends back there. I loved those people, and now they're gone."

"I know, dear," Keith said, putting his arm around her shoulder and pulling her close. "Mrs. Skypanski was such a character. She brought so much life and vitality to our congregation. I can't imagine the church without her. Aaron Slatsky was equally dear to me."

"And all the others," Ann added. "To think I was worried about what people might think of us. It seems so unimportant now."

"I'm sorry." Ben glanced at his watch, then behind them. "I wish we could do something more for them, but we just can't slow down."

"I'm still worried." Judy looked overhead as she walked. "No telling what will happen when they find out soldiers have been killed. The IDF has a reputation for going crazy when that happens."

"Just don't slow down." Ben said, picking up the pace.

The terrain dipped sharply as the stream carved out a meandering, snakelike path through the narrow canyon. When the towering rock walls shut out the sun, the temperature dropped twenty degrees. But the relief from the heat was short-lived; the wadi widened as quickly as it narrowed, allowing the blistering sun renewed access to the foursome. Their clothes were completely soaked with perspiration; everyone's nose became painfully dry from the inescapable dust.

Judy stopped. "Do you hear something?"

"What?" Ben turned around.

"Off in the distance." Judy cupped her hand to her ear.

"Listen."

"Oh, no." Ben looked up to the top of the canyon. "I'm sure that's a helicopter."

"Yes!" Keith yelled. "No question about it."

"We've got to run!" Ann screamed.

"Where to?" Judy's eyes widened in consternation.

"We can hide in the rocks," Keith offered.

"Yes." Ben rubbed his chin. "If we have to, we can inch under some of these boulders . . . But what about St. George's Monastery? There should be plenty of places to hide there."

Keith grabbed Ann's hand. "Let's go! We've got to get out of here. Now!"

A BROWN-AND-GREEN camouflaged military helicopter slowly swung over Highway 36 and followed the meandering road, dropping as low as possible over the traffic.

"The road splits," the pilot advised over the radio system. "Two different routes south."

Nahum Admoni nudged the man at his side. "Collins, is there any way you could identify these people from the air?"

"I don't think so," the young man answered. "I'd need a closer look."

The Mossad agent looked away in disgust. "Get as high as you can right now," he ordered the pilot. "Let's look at as much territory as possible." The helicopter immediately went straight up.

Liat Collins pressed his face against the window. "I'm doing my best," he said into the mouthpiece of his headset.

Admoni looked in the opposite direction, toward the Dead Sea.

"Look!" Collins pounded on the side of the plastic bubble. "Smoke! Beyond the ridge. Something's burning."

"Fly over that high ridge," the Mossad officer ordered the pilot. "Take a look at the back road to Jericho."

The helicopter cut across the rugged hills and settled into the ravine. After sailing past the waterfall, the chopper cut around a high precipice and flew up the valley. A low-lying black cloud abruptly arose in front of them. The pilot slowed.

"Smoke has settled in the bottom of the valley," Admoni barked. "Lots of smoke. Something big happened down there."

"We need to be careful," the pilot advised. "I've got to go up a notch to see the source of the fire." The craft slowly rose.

"Over there!" Collins jerked on Admoni's sleeve. "Look at all those cars!"

The security agent cursed. "That's an army vehicle down there in the middle of that mess. Take us down!" he roared.

"I'll have to get on the back side of the smoke," the pilot answered. "A substantial draft is still coming up out of the wadi, blowing the smoke in a lateral direction. We don't want to go against the flow." He maneuvered the helicopter in a sweeping circle and settled down on the back side of the smoldering pileup. The pilot cut the engine and unbuckled his belt. "Let's see what we've got."

Nahum Admoni hurried out the door, shielding his eyes against the blowing sand and motioning for the other two to follow. The blades slowed and the roaring of the engine died out. Admoni got as close to the ashes as the heat allowed.

"Wow!" Collins stopped at the agent's side.

Liat Collins walked around the edge of the flames, looking at the automobiles. He covered his nose and stared at the charred human remains. Shaking his head, he backed away.

"What do you make of it, Collins?" Nahum Admoni pressed.

"I just don't know what to say."

"Recognize anything?"

"No, not really."

"What about the people?"

Collins turned and looked disgusted. "Are you kidding? I can't even make out the models of the cars."

The Mossad officer worked over to the one car not mashed into the pile up. He bent to study the blackened hood. "Look at the emblem. Here's the Toyota the blockade guards spotted." Admoni stood up and looked around. "The Toyota was the lead car. It must have been the stalking horse for the ambush." He cursed.

Collins shook his head. "Listen to me. That messianic congregation is the nut fringe but they are not international terrorists. I don't know what's going on here, but I do know Keith Yaakov isn't capable of involvement with a military action of this scale."

Admoni's arm suddenly shot out, his fist catching Liat in the chest, knocking the wind out of the informant and bending him double. "Collins, you're an idiot. You don't even have the slightest idea what you're into." The agent then shoved Liat hard, sending him sprawling in the dirt. "You know just enough to be dangerous but not enough to help." He gave a swift kick that barely missed the young man's groin. "Now get back in that helicopter before I throw you into the fire."

Liat stumbled to his feet, still gasping for breath. "What did . . . I do wrong?"

"You were born," Admoni growled. "Now get in the chopper and stay there or I'll shoot holes in your face."

Collins limped back to the helicopter and slammed the door.

Admoni and the pilot walked carefully around the fire sev eral times, staring into the ashes.

"Looks like a man behind the wheel of the Toyota," the pilot concluded. "Can't tell the sex of the person in that other car at the rear."

"Whoever was driving the pickup was waiting to complete a suicide mission," Admoni grumbled. "We're obviously dealing with Islamic fundamentalists. This confirms my worst fears."

"What do we do now?" the pilot asked.

"Not much we can do until the backup teams get here." Admoni walked away. "I have to make a phone call."

The agent walked beyond earshot and dialed another number on his portable phone. "I want internal security," he said. Thirty seconds passed before a voice answered. Admoni inhaled deeply. "I've found our missing people, and they're all dead. Lured into a trap. We made the mistake of thinking our enemies are trying to get *out* of the country. They're intentionally misleading us so our attention won't be on what they are bringing *into* the country. We need to change our strategy immediately."

The wind shifted and blew smoke over Admoni. He closed his eyes tightly and turned his back to the smoke as he listened. Once the cloud went over, he looked around and watched Collins sitting in the helicopter.

"Yeah," Admoni answered. "Collins and Levy could be part of the setup. Double agents maybe. Time to clamp a lid on both of them. They've already done enough damage. You take care of Levy, and I'll fix Collins. Who knows? Maybe I'll push him out of the helicopter on the way back to Jerusalem."

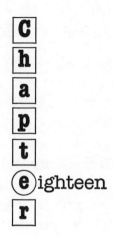

Chapter eighteen

THE VOICES SOUNDED FAR AWAY, disconnected, like people calling from the far end of a dark cave. Jimmy knew they were talking about something bad, but the only thing he could hear clearly was Judy's instruction echoing through his mind.

"Watch for the red van," she had said. "Make sure we are protected from the rear."

Jimmy turned again and again, staring behind the car. Numbers danced in front of his eyes like a hypnotic charm. *PO 636 701 . . . PO 636 701 . . . PO 636 701 . . .* Again and again the tag numbers flashed across his mind like urgent injunctions demanding his total attention. He stared at the last two cars in the caravan. No sign of PO 636 701. No road signs to Ramallah.

The faraway cacophony of voices intruded, deflecting Jimmy's resolutely fixed attention. Their anxiety distracted him. Jimmy felt their fears more than he grasped the words.

Their apprehension slowly pulled Jimmy away from the task Judy had given him.

"I'm terrified," an anonymous women in the front seat said. "I think splitting up the group was dangerous."

"How will we get back together?" the man next to Jimmy fretted. "If we don't find Keith, we're doomed."

"We've got to rendezvous in Jericho," the driver answered. "I just hope the Americans know what they are doing."

"Judy seems like such a nice person," the young woman said. "God help her if she falls into the hands of the authorities."

The mention of Judy's name jerked Jimmy up short with the force of a leash corralling a dog. Pain reverberated through his body like an electric shock. He could no longer concentrate on the license tag. He had to listen.

"But *where* will we meet up with them?" the man next to Jimmy persisted.

"I don't really know," the driver answered.

"Oh, God help us," the woman in the front seat lamented.

"Judy?" Jimmy moaned more than spoke. "Gone?"

"It's okay, son." The man next to him patted him on the hand. "Don't worry."

But fear rolled in like a blizzard. Jimmy couldn't pay attention. Nothing focused. He felt as if he were being slung back and forth in a violent thrashing. Images popped in his mind and then whizzed away like the headlights of cars speeding past in the night. Road signs leaped out and formed patterns that shaped and reshaped themselves into hexagons and other geometric shapes before dissolving into a kaleidoscope of colors.

Jimmy closed his eyes tightly to force the myriad of whirling forms to disappear in the blackness. He squinted as hard as possible, trying to squeeze the distractions from his mind. Like a blackboard being slowly erased, the compulsive urges dissolved.

"Where is Judy?" Jimmy asked with his eyes closed.

"On the other road," a male voice answered from the front seat. "The first three cars turned west."

"Why?" Jimmy persisted.

"The army appeared to be tailing them," the man next to Jimmy answered. "Don't worry. I am sure they are all right." His strained tone of voice contradicted the reassuring words.

The image of a red warning light appeared before Jimmy's eyes. Flashing on and off, giant red letters spelling danger blinked incessantly like a neon sign at a roadside diner. Jimmy felt hopelessly confused. He tried to cover his head.

"Now, now, young man." The woman in the front seat reached over and stroked Jimmy's hair. *"Ata levad?"* She tried to pull his hands down. *"A'tsuv?"*

Her Hebrew intonations rolled around like a simple lyrical melody. Jimmy intuitively knew what she had asked: "Are you alone? So sad?"

He remembered finding *Shalom Aleichem*, Judy's Hebrew grammar book. He read the primer one time and knew the alphabet and the words. After two more readings, he knew how to pronounce the words and sing the songs. A melody came back to him, and he began to hum softly. *"Shalom alaykhem malakhay hasharayt."*

"Oh, bless this fine young man," the women in the front seat said. "He's praying in Hebrew."

Letters from the Hebrew alphabet danced across Jimmy's mind, the characters looking like animals and people.

Keeping his eyes tightly closed, he watched the whirl of shapes buzz through his thoughts. Other words and phrases slipped into the parade, turning the individual characters into a train of letters.

"Mee—me—lekh ma-l-khay ha—mia—kheem," he hummed and settled back to enjoy the sound and the feel of the words. *"Ha-ka-dosh b-rookh hoo."*

Jimmy no longer heard the people around him. They had vanished. The world inside his head was so much safer and more enjoyable. The shape of the letters and the string of words brought a comforting order to the disconcerting chaos. Words led him from song to song until they brought him again to the Bible code he had discovered on Judy's computer six years ago.

Nothing had fascinated him like the code. Looking at the Hebrew letters and counting the intervals between characters was like directing an orchestra, a symphony of shapes. He could sail up, down, sideways, and vertically across the boundless sea of characters. As Jimmy's knowledge of the language had expanded, his capacity to recognize and find words grew. Every time a combination made sense and turned into an identifiable word or phrase, the discovery had filled Jimmy with ecstasy.

After several moments of reveling in the order and stability of the shapes and forms, Jimmy remembered the afternoon one particular section came together for him. Just as the Hebrew characters could be seen as geometric shapes or an alphabet or even as stick figures of animals or people, the lines could be seen in many different ways. A message began to surface. Word fit next to word. Months and days appeared. And then a complete message came together.

He knew the date of the destruction of Jerusalem! For a

few minutes the sense of meaning had been exhilarating. Then the significance of the discovery sunk in. What should he do? What *could* he do about the coming calamity? His anxiety had exploded. Retreat was the only possibility. He had reached out once more for darkness, like a frightened child pulls a sheet over his head.

The memory of that fateful afternoon once more tripped the alarm switches. Red lights flashed again. Jimmy squeezed his eyes tightly and put his hands to his ears.

MAKING THEIR WAY DOWN THE WADI, Judy and Ann struggled to keep pace with Ben and Keith.

"Listen!" Ben stopped at the edge of the stream, trying to determine from which direction the sound came.

"How much further?" Ann bent over and panted. "We're running too . . . hard. Can't . . . keep up . . . this pace."

"We're just about to the monastery." Keith mopped his wet forehead. "Hang on, dear."

Ben motioned for them to be quiet. He tilted his head.

"I hear it," Ann pointed behind them. "Sounds like more helicopters."

"The IDF is flying in reinforcements," Ben concluded. "That didn't take them long."

Ann swallowed hard and grimaced. "I'm sorry. I'll run as fast as I can."

They dashed along the edge of the streambed, leaping over rocks and shrubs. Ann tripped and fell a couple of times but didn't stop. Five minutes later they turned the corner around a steep embankment and saw the imposing building just ahead.

"Look at the size of that thing!" Judy gasped. "It comes out of the canyon wall like a fortress."

Keith pointed up the many stories to the top. "Hundreds of monks and hermits once lived in this area. The wilderness was a magnet for pilgrims."

"Anybody there?" Ann yelled.

Keith clamped his hand over his wife's mouth. "Quiet. If anyone is around, we don't want to alert them. We've just got to hide long enough to make sure the troops aren't looking in this direction."

"Get inside," Ben ordered. "Just find a door, a window."

Judy jumped from rock to rock until she was on the other side of the stream. The young woman scrambled up the bank toward the front of the monastery. "Looks like this place has been here since 'in the beginning' was pronounced." She ran her hand down the rough stone foundation. "Wow."

Keith walked past them. "I was here once," he said over his shoulder. "I know where the entrance is. Follow me."

Ann brought up the rear as they inched their way around the foundation. The sound of helicopter rotors got louder.

"These places always have massive wooden doors that a battering ram couldn't break down." Keith pointed up. "One story above us is a small plaza or veranda attached to the first floor. That might be a better place to get in than the front door.

"Let's see what I can do." Ben crammed his foot into the space between the rocks and pushed himself up high enough to get a handhold well above his head. "If I don't slip, I think I can make it." He laboriously inched his way from rock to rock until he was able to get a grip on the ledge. Even though the cement rubbed painfully against his chest, he rolled over the top and dropped a couple of feet to the floor.

"Made it!" Ben called down.

"What's up there?" Ann asked.

Ben looked around the large porch. "Looks like the monks used this place for an observation deck or a place of meditation." He walked toward the building and looked up. "Must be three more stories above me," he called back. "Bad news. There's no glass but the windows have iron bars."

"Can we get in?" Keith asked.

"I'm not sure." Ben pulled hard on the handle of a very large door, but nothing budged. "Looks like we're not in a tourist-friendly neighborhood."

Ann looked toward the sound of the helicopters. "We don't have much time," she called frantically.

Ben looked back and forth between the door and the barred windows. "The spaces between the bars are too narrow for me to crawl through, and the door's too heavy for a football team to break down." He scratched his head and returned to the ledge. "Obviously, the monks were acquainted with attacks through the centuries. They created a real bastion of male supremacy. I bet it's the same on all sides."

"The choppers are coming!" Judy hollered back. "We've got do something, Ben."

Ben sat down on the ledge and studied the monastery again. "Wait a minute!" He leaned over. "I've got an idea! Get Ann up here as quickly as you can!"

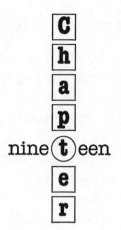

nineteen

KEITH YAAKOV leaned into the monastery wall and hoisted his wife's feet upward, rising on his tiptoes to get the last possible inch. "I'm pushing as hard as I can," he groaned. "I can't lift her any higher." The blistering sun beat down on his head, and sweat ran down his neck.

"I'm trying," Ann whispered. She clung to a stone jutting out of the wall and frantically waved her other hand over her head. "Help me."

"Okay." From above her Ben groped wildly for Ann's hand. "Just grab my fingers."

"Just . . . about . . . got you," Ann gasped.

"All right!" Ben caught her wrist and pulled up. "You're almost here. Don't stop now."

Ann grabbed the edge of the veranda and swung her leg over the side. Ben helped her land on the plaza.

"I'm right behind you." Judy immediately started up the

wall, scrambling for a handhold in the rocks. She quickly reached halfway up the wall. "This won't take long."

"I'll wait down here until you get in," Keith called to Ben. "If whatever you have in mind doesn't work, everyone will be coming back down anyway."

"What *did* you have in mind?" Ann stared at the bars across the window. Five rusted steel bands ran from the top to the bottom. A single bar crossed the middle and tied the vertical pieces together. "Bending steel bars?"

"No. It occurred to me that the monks were trying to keep men out." Ben pointed between the steel bars. "They weren't looking for the likes of you, Ann. I believe you can slip through. Then, perhaps, you'll be able to open the door."

Judy poked her head above the ledge. "Hey." She pulled herself over the top. "Need some help?"

"We're going to slide Ann through the bars." Ben beckoned to her. "You can help me push."

Ann peered into the hole. "It looks awfully murky in there."

"It's bound to be cooler than it is out here," Ben reassured her. "Come on. We don't have a lot of time."

Ann perched tentatively on the window ledge and stuck one arm between the bars. She felt into the darkness. "I guess I'm ready."

"Judy, help me balance her. We need to fit her through a pretty narrow space."

"I'm ready." Ann repeated hesitantly. "Looks a little scary."

"Careful." Ben held her arm. "When you get through, try to set one leg down so you can slide to the floor."

Ann slowly slid between two of the iron bands. Ben steadied her legs to keep her balanced. The fit was tight, but she quickly squeezed through.

"I'm in." Ann's voice echoed around the empty room. "Give me a minute to adjust to the darkness."

"What do you see?" Judy called after her.

"Looks like a big post is blocking the door." Ann sounded far away.

"How?" Ben called.

"The monks wedged a huge timber into metal brackets behind the door," Ann explained. "I can't budge it."

"Bad news." Judy stuck her head in. "What are we going to do?"

"Think you can make it through?" Ben asked.

Judy measured the space between the bars. "I don't know. Ann's pretty small. That could be a very tight squeeze for me."

"This is our only hope."

"What if I get halfway through and can't budge?"

Ben smiled wryly. "In a few days, the atomic blast will slim you down enough to slide through without any trouble."

"Very funny." Judy started working between the bars. "I might get stuck *inside* if we can't open the door."

"Our lives are in your hands, chubby," Ben teased, helping her work her feet up on the window ledge.

Judy exhaled as deeply as possible and squeezed between the bars. "Ow," she moaned. "I don't know . . . this sorta hurts. There's got to be an easier way."

"You're doing it," he encouraged. "Almost there."

"Ah!" Judy exclaimed. Her feet hit the floor with a thud. "Made it."

"What's happening up there?" Keith called from the ground.

"I think we're about to solve our problem," Ben answered. "I'll update you in a minute."

"It's wonderfully refreshing in here," Judy called out. "Too bad you're too big for the admission requirements."

"Get on with it, Judy." Ben looked between the bars. "I'm not getting any younger or cooler out here." He listened to the sound of the women straining to move the barricade. He walked back to the edge of the veranda. "The girls are trying to get the door open. I think they'll make it. Come on up."

A dull thud echoed under the wooden door followed by the sound of the heavy beam bouncing a second time. "You okay in there?" Ben called out.

"We did it," Ann chirped. "Another blow to male supremacy."

Ben pushed on the door, which creaked open enough for him to slip inside. "Hurry, Keith. The guided tour is about to begin."

The large room looked like a dining hall. Long wooden tables and benches stood in silent, regimented rows. A musty smell hung in the air and a thick layer of dust covered the floor. Blank whitewashed walls added to the austere atmosphere.

Keith edged his way around the slightly ajar door. "Great job, gang. Sure is more pleasant in here."

"Let's get the door shut again," Ben suggested. "We don't want to leave any clues for the IDF."

Ben and Keith hoisted the beam up against the door then swung it up into the metal brackets.

"Where do we go from here?" Ann asked.

"Let's just explore." Judy ambled toward the black shape of an entryway in the middle of the room. "Let's see what's in here." Judy led the group into an adjoining hall that appeared to stretch the length of the monastery. Light from small windows at each end hinted at the span of the passage and the enormous size of the building. Pitch-black openings at regular intervals suggested adjacent rooms or corridors.

"Maybe we ought to find our way to the top floor," Keith said. "We need to see if anyone's coming."

"Yeah," Ben answered thoughtfully. "In this deep valley we need to be able to see as much as possible."

"Wow!" Judy shouted. "You won't believe this room I've found."

Ben stepped in beside her. "Looks like a chapel. Melted candles everywhere. And it smells like smoke and incense."

"Can you see the fresco in the front?" Judy pointed. "It's hard to see in this light, but it's magnificent."

"It's a Madonna and child." Ben ran his hands over the little pieces of colored tile. "Who knows how old this work is."

"I think I've found a back way to the top." Keith's voice sounded far away. "Come straight down the hall and start up a spiral staircase."

"We're right behind you," Ben answered. "Don't wait for us."

Small windows along the top of the corridor let in enough light to reveal white walls as Ben, Judy, and Ann hurried down the long passageway. Their heels clicked a rapid staccato cadence of urgency against the stone floor. Above them, the clamor of Keith's shoes as he hurried up the stairs rolled down with a rhythmic padding sound. When they reached the staircase, they found the winding steps worn and slick; they had to balance themselves against the walls as they made their way up.

Keith was already trying to force the exit door open when the threesome caught up with him. "I think the hinges are rusted," he grunted. "Nothing a little oil wouldn't correct."

"Let me help you." Ben put his shoulder to the door. "Give us a hand, ladies." He pressed his full weight against the barrier. The door opened several inches and bright sunlight exploded through the crack.

"Almost," Ben grunted, leaning into the door again and gaining another foot of space. "Think we can slide through?"

"Yeah," Keith said, edging sideways out onto the roof. "We've found our perch!" he exclaimed. "You definitely get a bird's-eye view."

"No kidding." Judy looked around the area. "We must be five stories above the stream. The builders obviously selected this place because they could see around the bend in both directions. No one is going to sneak up on us if we're paying attention."

The muffled thumping of helicopter blades drifted down the valley. In the distance the gray shape of a military craft rose straight up from the site of the wreck, banked, and headed toward Jerusalem. Within seconds it was out of sight.

"If one of those things makes a sweep down the valley, we could be spotted." Ben pointed toward the door. "Let's get back inside."

As soon as everyone was settled, Ben pulled the door shut and sat down on the top step of the spiral stairs. "Helicopters will probably ignore the PLO territory boundaries. We can't chance the IDF spotting us from the air. They'd probably shoot at us."

"What'll we do?" Judy inched backward into the blackness

until she was a couple of stairs below Ben. "We can't camp out on the staircase."

"I think we ought to take shifts—one person at a time watch from the roof."

"Agreed." Keith peered out the crack in the exit. "One person could quickly get back inside unobserved if a chopper came in this direction."

"The rest of us can scout the place out," Judy added. "Maybe there's something to eat downstairs if we can find the kitchen."

"I don't mind taking the first shift up here," Keith volunteered. "Trade off every hour? Two hours?"

"How about watching in hour intervals until dark," Judy ventured. "That sun is fierce."

"Good." Ben stood up. "We'll go back down and see what we can find."

Judy led the way down the spiral stairs. "Where's the most likely place to have a kitchen? Bottom floor where we were?"

"Maybe the kitchen was somewhere around the first room we entered," Ann ventured. "It looked like a dining room."

"Good thought," Ben answered from the rear. "We might start by checking out the adjacent rooms."

Judy hit the bottom steps with a jump and bounded onto the stone floor. "Okay," she called over her shoulder, "we've already discovered there's a chapel in the middle on our left. I'm going to try the far end of the corridor."

"I'll go inside the dining area and look for other doors." Ben turned into the dark entryway.

"Judy," Ann pleaded, "don't leave me out here in the dark. I'm with you."

Ben edged his way around the dining room walls. The barred window illuminated the far end of the room and made it clear there were no exits in the back. He worked his way down the row of tables into the gloom of the opposite side of the room. A shape slowly emerged before his eyes. He could make out a door with large black metal hinges. A hand-forged pull stood out in the middle of the rough wood.

Ben held the iron handle tightly and gave it a hard shove. The door swung open so easily it flew out of his hands and banged against the wall in a vast hallway.

"Aaah!" Ann screamed.

Ben jumped backward and fell over a bench.

"Hey!" Judy scolded. "Are you trying to scare us to death?"

"Make a little noise please," Ben grumbled and rubbed the back of his knee. "You might have found a less dramatic way to let me know you were there."

"Sorry," Ann answered out of the darkness. "We didn't hear you."

"Ben, I've found a door in this hall," Judy said. "I think I can open it." A lighter shade of darkness greeted them. "Did it!"

"Pay dirt!" Ann exclaimed. "It's the kitchen"

A large open fireplace dominated the middle of the back wall from which the scant light in the room originated. Hanging irons stuck out over a mound of white ashes. Blackened iron pots were in ramshackle heaps on the floor and counters. Small utensils hung from hooks attached to the ceiling.

"Look." Ben pointed to a small door on the opposite side of a sturdy chopping block. "Perfect place for a pantry."

Judy was the first one in. "Jackpot. Look at all the cans

in here. They've got to be full of something. The Lord has provided."

Ann picked up a can and held it close to her face. "I think I've found some beans."

Ben felt his way around the shelves. "They left a considerable stash behind. I'm sure they would want us to stay for supper."

"I vote for spending the night." Ann gathered up an armload of cans. "There's plenty here for breakfast."

Judy looked up suddenly. "What's that?"

"Sound's like Keith's coming down the stairs," Ben answered, heading for the pantry door. The trio ran from the kitchen to the hall and then to the dining room and nearly collided with Keith.

"Back inside! Quick!" Keith hissed. "Soldiers outside."

Chapter twenty

BEN PRESSED HIS EAR to the kitchen door and listened to muffled voices shouting back and forth. Soldiers beat on the front door and hammered against the iron bars. Judy crouched next to him and clung to his arms. A few feet away at the back of the room, Keith and Ann huddled together in the blackness. After a few minutes the noise faded. For a long time the four of them sat on the rock floor and didn't speak. Ben felt Judy trembling. He clinched his teeth and gripped the door tightly.

Time crawled by. The silence soon became deafening, but still no one moved. The air became increasingly stale.

After an hour Judy asked, "Dare we get out?"

"I don't think so," Ben answered. "Keith saw six men, a small patrol. They could have all gone on down the wadi, or they might have left a person to watch this place."

"And even if they all left, they couldn't go too far," Keith added. "The Palestinians would shoot them. We'd know it in a hurry."

"And they obviously didn't break in or we'd hear them rummaging through the building," Judy observed.

"We don't have any way of knowing," Ann said. "So what do we do?"

Ben leaned against the door. "We can't risk making a mistake. I don't think we have any alternative except to stay in here until it's dark outside. We probably ought to spend the night and leave in the morning."

Keith pulled his wife close to him. "I agree. We don't dare travel when it's dark or we might get shot by the PLO when we get closer to Jericho."

"If we don't make a sound, the army people will give up in a couple of hours," Ann reasoned. "At least we've got food in here, and we could sleep on the tables later."

"And it's nice and cool in here," Ben added.

"I wonder how Jimmy is doing," Judy fretted. "I'm sure he's very upset."

"Our friends will take good care of him," Keith reassured her. "Don't worry."

"I get overprotective sometimes, but I've been watching out for him since he was a child. Jimmy's hard to connect with unless he feels secure. If he doesn't want to talk, you can get more out of a clam."

Ben put his arm around her shoulders. "We'll be back together in the morning. In the meantime, we need to keep ourselves entertained until it's safe to walk around."

Judy rubbed her temples and rotated her neck. "The tension is what kills you."

"I can't let my mind wander too far," Ann said, "or I start thinking about that terrible fire. All that smoke, the flames . . ." She began weeping softly.

Keith squeezed her hand. "I keep agonizing over whether we've done the right thing. What if we risked their lives for nothing? What if . . .? The possibility that we were wrong is pure agony."

"Yes, I know." Ben shifted uncomfortably. "If we hadn't spent years working on this project, I wouldn't have even come back to Israel. That said, I'm still terrified we might be wrong and those poor people died for nothing more than a wild goose chase."

"Yeah," Judy said soberly. "That would haunt me for the rest of my life."

"Tell me again—" Ann wiped her eyes. "How did you become so convinced a bomb would explode on Av 9? A little reassurance wouldn't hurt me right now."

Ben stood up to stretch. "We struggled with this problem for the past eight years. Judy and I started on the code when we were sophomores, in 1998. We graduated and got jobs in different cities, but working on the code kept us in touch. It took time for us to come to a burning conviction about our discoveries. For a long time nothing was certain."

"Rabbi Shiloh helped, but there were limits to what he could do for us. He accepted far more on uncritical faith than we could," Judy explained. "Reuven knew nothing about statistical verification and mathematical research. Some of his claims weren't easy for us to take on face value."

"Formal logic forced us to go deeper into the Hebrew text," Ben continued. "We had to deal with what seemed like contradictions and inconsistencies. Reuven didn't even want to hear about those struggles."

"For example?" Ann asked.

"Here's a simple one," Ben said. "The assassination of Prime Minister Rabin was discovered and relayed to him a year before he was shot on November 4, 1995. He paid no attention. However, if one looks carefully at the message within the text, Rabin's indifference to the warning is understandable. All the Bible code actually said was 'Yitzhak Rabin, assassin will assassinate.' This message could easily mean Rabin used assassination as a military option and he would do it again. Because Rabin was a military man and employed espionage, someone could interpret the passage to say *Rabin* was a killer. See the problem?"

"Hmmm," Ann mused. "I'm glad no one pointed that one out to me earlier. I'd be even more uneasy right now."

"We discovered another big problem Rabbi Shiloh didn't fully appreciate," Judy continued. "Most people don't realize that you can't decipher codes unless you first winnow out the ELS factor."

"What in the world is that?" Ann asked.

"Wait," Ben interrupted. "I'm going to slip into the dining room and look through the front window to see what's going on outside. At least we can determine if someone is stationed on the veranda. Judy can explain while I'm in the other room."

"ELS stands for equidistant letter sequences, the name for accidentally occurring word patterns. You can take any book in the world, count various spaces, and find names, places, and even simple sentences that just occur randomly. For example, both the words *woman* and *human* contain the word *man.* What happens if you discover that you can count every seven, fifty, or thousand spaces and come up with the word *man?* Does it mean anything? Of course not."

"I didn't dream you could do something like *that.*"

"Sure, Ann. We discovered there are all kinds of names in the Hebrew text. Not only Yeshua but Mohammed, Moon, and the names of many famous people can be discovered by simply running the equidistant letter sequences through a computer. The problem is that their occurrence means absolutely nothing."

"Wait a minute," Keith stopped her. "I know that Reuven *did find* the name of Yeshua encoded in the Bible, and it was linked to key messianic passages."

"The problem is that names like Lenin, Krishna, and Koresh can also be found in many of those same passages," Judy said. "No one would surely claim any of that crew are the true messiah."

"I've never heard any of this ELS stuff before." Keith started to pace in the small space. "It's discouraging."

"Don't let it bother you. You can find this same variety of names in any book by running a computer ELS scan. It's pure chance, statistically meaningless. Ben discovered Reverend Moon's name appears in the Torah over nineteen million times. Skipping distances of up to one thousand letters will turn up Mohammed or a ton of other names hundreds of thousands of times. You can also find Yeshua in a Hebrew translation of the Koran. It doesn't mean a thing."

"Then how do you know anything for certain from the code?" Keith fretted. "I mean, how do we know that the encoded name of Yeshua has any meaning?"

"See, now you've hit the problem Ben and I struggled with. We could not discover any principle in the Bible code to separate out the encoded names that had meaning from the names that appeared by chance and were sheer nonsense. *That* issue was our first big problem."

"You've completely lost me." Ann sounded irritated.

"Okay. Let me state the problem another way. Equidistant letter sequences have nothing to do with the authentic code phenomenon in the Old Testament. We couldn't establish any statistical or scientific evidence to demonstrate the ELS patterns were deliberately inserted into the text by God. Because of that one problem, we nearly threw up our hands and walked away several years ago."

Ben popped through the door. "Good news! Not a sign of anyone out there. I think we can safely sit at the tables in the other room. We'd certainly hear anyone trying to climb up the wall long before they got here."

"Sounds great to me." Judy got to her feet. "The fresh air sure wouldn't hurt."

"I'm hopeful the soldiers were just a single patrol simply checking the area out." Ben led them through the kitchen. "When they don't find anything maybe the IDF will leave quickly."

"Let's not stop this conversation." Keith brought up the rear. "I'm desperately trying to understand this stuff."

The two couples settled around a table in front of the window, which afforded a good look at anyone walking by the stream.

"Ben, I'm trying to explain to the Yaakovs the difference between a genuine code message and the accidental occurrence of words in the ELS patterns. I think I'm causing more problems than I'm solving."

Ben put his elbows on the table and rested his head in his hands. "Judy and I had to learn a great deal about code methodology. We discovered that the messages in genuine codes are not random or coincidentally constructed. If the message is for real, it can be statistically and mathematically verified. The messages Rabbi Edlow Moses first uncovered in his research fit this category."

"Do the passages with Yeshua hidden in them have problems?" Keith asked.

"Not at all," Ben answered. "All religious beliefs aside, Jesus has to be recognized as one of the greatest men of history and certainly in Jewish history. From that standpoint alone, you'd expect the name *Yeshua* to be encoded with important meaning. Our problem was sorting out the intentional from the accidental."

"And how did you do it?" Ann pushed.

"Some passages were easy to figure out," Judy answered. "We were careful not to be dogmatic about what we couldn't prove. We wanted to function as scientists, not theologians. When the name Yeshua appeared, we made sure it wasn't a random occurrence but fit the genuine pattern of a code, making it a true expression of inspiration."

"But we slowly began to find another important component in the authentic encoded messages," Ben continued. "The appearance of dates or verifiable phenomenon gave us the anchor we were looking for."

"Come on," Ann protested. "Speak English. What do you mean?"

"In 1992 code investigators discovered a hidden prediction that a comet would collide with the planet Jupiter on Av 8. Two years later on July 16, 1994, which was Av 8 on the Jewish calendar, the biggest explosion ever seen in our solar system blew fireballs the size of Earth into space with billions of megatons of power. A comet smashed into Jupiter."

"You gotta be kidding," Ann gasped.

"When that happened, we had a way to verify the code," Ben pointed out. "Dates weren't subjective data. The predictions were tied to a calendar. Plus, the name of the comet, 'Shoemaker-Levy,' was encoded along with it."

"That's how we began our search for the right date for predicting an atomic attack on Jerusalem," Judy continued. "As we struggled to understand principles of verification, the terrible possibilities of what might occur in either 2000 or 2006 surfaced. Of course, we were dealing with the Hebrew calendar and years 5760 and 5766." She stood and looked through the bars, down into the canyon.

Ann shook her head. "Wow. This stuff is hopelessly complex. I don't even know how to sort out what you've told me in the last hour."

Ben reached across the table and put his hand over Ann's. "I believe we can trust the fact that God wants us to know we are living in the last days. He put the code in the Bible to help people in our era—the computer age—to understand His sovereignty and to give clues, the same way He used His prophets through the ages. But we have to use our heads."

"What are you getting at?" Keith asked.

"Rabbi Shiloh wouldn't let me off the hook when I was trying to understand how some things in the Bible are so certain and others seem to be tentative. I discovered the same quality in the codes, and it really confused me for a long time. Only after a great deal of effort did I begin to grasp the meaning of the fact that God stands outside of time and apart from His creation. The Creator is able to view the entire length and breadth of history at any given moment. He can see the choices we make without manipulating us to take one path or the other. Even though the heavenly Father already knows everything, He allows us complete freedom. His foreknowledge does not negate our free will."

No one spoke for several moments.

"That's profound," Keith finally commented.

Judy rapped on the table with her knuckles. "The implication is that God wants us to survive today, but we had better keep our eyes open in the future if we really hope to survive in these end times." She cast a glance past the group and out the window. "In fact, if my eyes don't deceive me, a group of soldiers is coming up the canyon *right now.*"

chapter

(t)wenty-one

LENGTHENING SHADOWS from the surrounding jagged hills
fell across the still smoldering wreckage. Nahum Admoni
watched the team of inspectors working through the ashes.
Sentinels stood around the perimeter with their weapons
aimed at the rugged wilderness terrain. Two helicopters waited
silently on each side of the smoking heap of metal. A dozen
soldiers stood by the roadside smoking cigarettes.

Admoni alternated between studying the detectives and
observing Liat Collins, sitting sullenly in the backseat of the
police helicopter. He looked up carefully at the sky and beckoned to a young lieutenant. The soldier hurried over.

"Sun's going down," Admoni grumbled. "I'm not sure how
much longer we ought to keep this many people out here.
Have you heard anything from your patrols?"

"The patrol in the valley is already back. All they found
was a Bedouin family. The hilltops behind us are being
patrolled and are clear of any ambush."

"How about the unit you sent south? Have they reported in?"

"No, sir. I was going to check in with them right now." The lieutenant flipped on his field telephone. "Exploration base to unit two, come in."

After a moment of noisy popping, a loud voice boomed over the receiver, "Base, unit two. Sergeant Sarid speaking."

"Lev, give me a situation report."

"We went down the wadi as far as we could, sir. No PLO contact. Found nothing, sir. If anyone came this way, they're already in enemy territory."

The lieutenant looked at Admoni and raised his eyebrows quizzically.

"Ask about their location," Admoni barked.

"Where are you now, Lev?"

"We're two or three miles from your position, sir. On the other side of the creek running in front of the monastery."

"Anything there?" the officer probed.

"Nothing, sir," the squad leader answered. "The cloister is abandoned and locked up tight as a drum. We left one man stationed out front while we checked out the rest of the canyon. In fact, he's coming across the valley to join us now. No sign of anything out here but lizards."

Admoni took the phone. "Come back in as quickly as you can, Sergeant. Watch out for any possible snipers. Double-time it. We're going to close it down up here." He clicked the phone off.

"We're pulling out, sir?" The lieutenant looked at the men still working in the rubble.

Nahum Admoni rubbed his chin and looked up at the sun

again. "I don't see any point of exposing the entire platoon to possible attack in the dark. We'd do better to station a squad here and stay in constant contact."

"Yes, sir, but it doesn't look like the enemy is still around."

"No. They're long gone. No point in wasting our time chasing the wind. The important thing is to figure out exactly what happened out here. As soon as that southern patrol returns send them back to headquarters."

The lieutenant saluted and hurried off to talk to the men waiting along the side of the road. Admoni strolled up to a detective working on the Toyota.

"Got any ideas, Rosen?" the Mossad agent asked.

The detective stood up and dusted ashes off his hands. "Obviously, identification isn't going to be easy. Looks like a woman might have been driving the car in the back." Rosen pointed to the pileup. "The driver of the pickup was an Arab. Apparently shot by our soldiers. The body was thrown clear of the wreck. Wounds to the head and chest typical of our rifles. You can also make out bullet holes in the hood of the truck. From their location in or near the jeep, plus weapons and gear that did not burn or melt, we know which bodies are our soldiers." He ran his hands through his black hair, then gestured toward the remains of the Toyota. "But this one throws me."

"How come?"

"Didn't you say the religious nut was supposed to be driving the lead car?"

Admoni nodded.

"Other people were in there with him?"

"Yes. The report from the checkpoint said three others."

"Big problems." Rosen squinted and scratched his head. "Problem one: no other bodies in there but the driver and no other bodies thrown clear." He rolled his eyes. "Problem two: I think the body behind the wheel is a soldier."

"What!" Admoni's jaw dropped.

"A piece of a boot wasn't entirely burned. Looks like IDF standard-issue. We'll have to have another expert come out in the morning to verify, but that's my call."

"That doesn't make any sense at all," Admoni sputtered. "What would one of our people be doing in *their* car?"

Rosen shook his head. "I'm baffled. It doesn't add up. Collusion from our men is highly unlikely. They were all young Israelis. That angle just won't fly. And we can tell the wreck was not staged, a big smashup like this. If I'm right about the body, we've got a real wild card on this one."

Nahum Admoni crossed his arms over his chest and glowered at the twisted metal. "This reinforces my suspicions that they wanted us to think they were trying to get out of the country. We need to watch for who's coming *in*." He looked at the detective out of the corner of his eye. "What's next?"

Rosen held up his hands and pursed his lips. "I think it's going to take at least another whole day of work to adequately reconstruct what actually happened here. We need to see if we can pick up tire imprints that might give a more detailed picture of vehicle movement. It's probably going to take a couple more days to make identification of all of the bodies . . . and then we may be in trouble."

Admoni shook his head. "Make sure the area is secured for the night and then fly back in here first thing in the morning. Get back to me with anything you find." He walked away from the detective and found a clearing out of earshot of the rest of the troops. The Mossad agent dialed the special number for internal security.

"Yes." The answer was flat, blunt.

"Admoni here. We've hit a brick wall. Something strange is going on."

"What's your best guess?"

Admoni licked his lips and squinted. "We need to double the surveillance of anyone trying to enter the country. I'm concerned the whole thing is a ruse to distract us from what our enemies are really up to. Maybe these messianic screwballs are just a diversion."

"What does that say about this Collins guy? And his pal, Levy?"

"Maybe they're more significant than I thought," Admoni growled. "Collins is either an idiot or a very clever spy. Either way, I think we ought to keep them both behind bars for at least a couple of weeks. Charge them with espionage so we can hold them without bail."

"Agreed," the voice answered. "Fly Collins back, and I'll have a welcoming committee waiting to greet him. Want me to rough him up?"

"Why not. See if he'll sing like a bird."

BEN AND JUDY huddled next to the windowsill and watched the patrol across the valley. A soldier suddenly trotted down the slope in front of the monastery. He darted across the stream and up the other side where six others waited.

Judy gasped. "A soldier *was* waiting out front!"

"Quiet," Ben hissed. "Just watch."

The seven men talked briefly and then continued down the trail. No one looked back.

"What do you think?" Keith asked quietly.

"Looks like they're calling off the dogs." Ben kept his eyes on the scene. "If they don't have another surprise waiting for us, looks like we're okay. How many men did you see coming down the canyon?"

"Seven," Keith answered.

"Good," Ben said. "I just counted seven going north."

"I think we need to put someone back upstairs until it's dark," Ann added. "I'm scared to death."

Ben looked out the window again. "The sun's going down fast. It should be dark in the canyon fairly quickly."

"I'll go up again until it's too dark to see," Keith volunteered. "I've already got the lay of the land."

"Sounds good to me," Judy answered. "Ann and I can figure out how to make supper with the supplies in the pantry. Maybe we'll have a nice candlelight supper after all."

"I suggest something more like a safe, secure meal in the dark," Ben quipped. "This is no time to put our light on a hill. We need to be as inconspicuous as mice."

THE MONASTERY'S OLD DINING HALL vanished in the blackness of night. Even after their eyes adjusted to the dark, the couples could only make out shapes moving around the tables. The temperature quickly dropped. Keith wrapped his arm around his wife's shoulders and pulled her close.

"You cold?"

"Heavens." Ann laughed. "As hot as it was today, I wouldn't dare complain about it cooling off."

Judy licked her fingers. "The canned peaches aren't great, but they sure beat chewing on a piece of wood."

"I'm glad we brought water with us," Ann said. "We'd be hard put to drink what we found in those rain barrels."

"The beans weren't bad." Keith wiped his hands on his pants. "At least I'll sleep like a stuffed pig tonight. The Lord has certainly provided."

"He always provides for His people," Judy answered solemnly. "Even if we can't see where things are going, He is leading."

"Look how we've survived the day," Ben added. "What started out this morning as a quiet ride in the country turned into a disaster, and yet here we are safe, sound, and well fed. In spite of the tragedy we saw today, I believe God is in control of this whole situation. If the hand of God hasn't been on us, I'll eat my napkin . . . except that I don't have one."

Keith laughed. "That reminds me of a superstitious legend that local Jews like to tell around the campfire at night." He leaned on the table and peered out the window, silhouetted by the black wall.

"After Jerusalem fell to Islam, Moslem governors were appointed. Of course, these sheikhs controlled *En Nebi Daud*, the Tomb of David, also holy to the Moslems. During the reign of Sultan Murad, a new governor wanted to break through the monument and see the actual tomb underneath. The pasha ordered a hole cut in the floor of the shrine so he could look inside. When the governor bent over, his jeweled dagger slipped out of his girdle, falling into the blackness. He immediately ordered one of his attendants to fetch the knife. Servants let the man down carefully, and the rope remained tied around his waist so he wouldn't get lost in the cave where the remains of David were kept. After some time the concerned governor ordered his servants to draw up the rope. According to the old legend, they found the lifeless body of the man dangling at the end of the rope. The pasha ordered three other men down, but each came back dead.

"When the governor inquired, he received the explanation that the prophet David didn't like Moslems entering his tomb, whereupon the sheik went to the chief rabbi and demanded that he send a Jew into the hole. The pasha left the veiled threat that either a Jew went down or the lives of the whole community were in jeopardy.

"The old man was terrified for his people and asked for a three-day period of grace. Immediately the chief rabbi called on everyone to fast and pray. They had a dual dilemma. On one hand, they did well to fear the wrath of the pasha. On the other hand, the Jews believed King David to be alive in that tomb because of a monthly prayer of blessing." Keith cleared his throat and broke into a monotone chant. *"David melekh Israel khai va kayam."* He explained, "The prayer is, 'David, King of Israel, is alive and active.'"

"You mean," Judy interrupted, "the Jews of those days really believed David was still around?"

"Indeed," Keith continued, "and they feared he would be more than a little upset with someone messing with his grave. Finally, on the third day a man volunteered in hopes of saving the Jewish community. Having purified his body and soul, he slowly disappeared into the hole as the whole Moslem community watched. Immediately he asked to be brought up again. He soon reappeared with the dagger in hand."

"What happened?" Judy leaned forward eagerly like a child listening to a fairy tale.

"The chief rabbi hugged the man and asked the same question. The Jew supposedly said that the moment his feet touched the ground he found himself face-to-face with a noble old man clad in robes like shining silver. The aristocrat handed him the knife and with a flourish bid him be gone."

Ben laughed. "My grandfather told me such stories. My parents hated them because they were embarrassed by superstition. Now, here I am just miles away from the *En Nebi Daud,* and I'd be thrilled to have King David walk down the canyon tonight."

Wind whistled through the barred window. Across the stream just above the craggy peak, the moon rose in brilliance, bathing the wooden table in shimmering yellow light. Judy and Ben turned into black outlines against the moonbeams. Ann's face reflected the glow. She looked worn out.

"I think we ought to try to sleep," Keith concluded. "Perhaps this would be a good time to ask not David, but the Son of David, to watch over us. We've only got two days left."

DAY THREE
AV 7 5766

"Then they will deliver you up to tribulation
and kill you, and you will be hated by all nations
for My name's sake."

Matthew 24:9

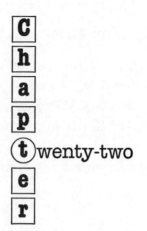

Chapter twenty-two

Tel Aviv
August 1, 2006

EVEN THOUGH THE SUMMER SUN was barely overhead, the tarmac already radiated shimmering heat when Anton Ketele stepped off the airplane at Ben Gurion Airport. He pulled his lightweight Panama hat over his eyes and hopped onto a shuttle bus. Once he reached the entrance to the terminal, the Russian immediately blended into the lines surging through passport control. After a few minutes he inched his way to the official counter. The inspector looked at his Russian passport and examined a membership certification from a Moscow synagogue stuck between the pages.

"Ha-im ata m'daber Anglit?" the Russian physicist asked.

"Sure. I speak English," the twentyish-looking man answered. "I grew up in Brooklyn." The hand-embroidered red and yellow designs on his yarmulke gave him a deceptive native look. "I'm still learning Hebrew. I volunteer to help the Israeli government during my summer vacations."

"Yesh lachem, heder panooi?" Ketele responded.

"Any vacancies left in Israel?" The young inspector smiled. "Sure, Mr. Smirnoff. We've always got room for one more person making *aliya*. Welcome home."

"*Toda raba*." Ketele tipped his hat and hurried past the counter.

"Good luck in Israel, Mr. Smirnoff," the young man called after him.

The Russian didn't stop at the luggage conveyor but hurried toward the exit. Once outside he pushed his way through the ubiquitous crowd and walked into the parking lot. He wound his way slowly through the cars, looking over his shoulder. Assured no one was following him, Ketele pulled a portable phone from his pocket, dialed, and waited for acknowledgment.

"I have arrived," Anton said tersely and clicked off the phone. He glanced at his watch and leaned against an old black Honda. Ketele lit a cigarette and kept looking up and down the rows. No one seemed to pay the slightest attention to him.

Five minutes later an old pickup pulled up across the street and double-parked. Anton Ketele rushed across two lanes of speeding cars and jumped in the front seat. The pickup immediately turned into the traffic. At the first corner the driver began a winding route through side streets.

Orlaf Pimen spoke first. "*Dobriy dehn,* Comrade Anton. I don't think we're being followed. There's no way Mossad or anyone else could pick up on our conversation in here. We've made sure nothing is bugged."

"*Xopownn Ichahroshyiy!*"

Ketele took off his straw hat and mopped his forehead.

"Excellent. The ploy worked." He laughed coarsely. *"Kahk vi zhivoteh?"*

Pimen smiled. "I'm doing very well, comrade. Things are progressing nicely."

"I understand we had problems getting equipment into Jerusalem."

Pimen nodded. "A momentary inconvenience. It proved to be nothing. Everything is now in the garage . . . except the detonation mechanism, of course."

Ketele nodded nonchalantly. "Good. I'm ready to put the finishing touches on our little warhead."

"How much money has been spent to date?" Pimen circled the same block a second time, constantly watching the rear view window.

"About five million dollars." Ketele mopped his forehead again. "Of course, that doesn't include our cut. The rest will be transferred to our account in South Africa immediately after the explosion."

"Can we trust the Arabs?"

"Yes. Only because they'll want our services in the future."

"What if we do more damage to the Old City than was projected?" Pimen pulled to a stop at an intersection. A sign pointed left to Lod, and when the light changed, he followed it.

"I guaranteed nothing but a big bang." Anton crossed his arms over his rotund chest and pushed his fat knees against the dashboard. "They'll be so thrilled with the population control measures, they won't worry about the structural damage for a while." The physicist chuckled. "Besides it will be a little too 'hot' for a stroll around the city." He leaned close to Pimen's face and asked in a low, threatening voice. "And where *is* the detonator?"

"Just ahead. The Arab village of Abu Ghosh. Everything is waiting for you. The place is only eight miles from the Jerusalem city limits. We'll load up right away."

Anton smiled. "Excellent, Orlaf. You have always been a most excellent associate. On the other hand, I'm never sure about Heinz. I don't trust Germans. They're vile."

Pimen pulled a pack of cigarettes from his pocket and flipped one into his mouth. "Don't worry. Dietrich has always been a fellow communist. He hates the Jews more than we do." He lit the cigarette and blew smoke out the window. "You can trust him."

Ketele looked sour. "They're all Nazis underneath. Swine."

The bald Russian looked straight ahead and drove without speaking, his silence signaling a reluctance to argue. After a couple of minutes, Pimen asked, "What are your calculations on the scope of the bomb's impact?"

Ketele's eyes narrowed, and he squinted at the forest whizzing past. "Of course, what we're building is really just a hydrogen bomb without the uranium-238 jacket to absorb neutrons. I'm aiming at a ten-kiloton capacity that will reach a ten-mile radius. We ought to be able to penetrate most of the metal and cement structures in Jerusalem with pure neutron radiation. That should have the desired effect."

"I believe they call that effect 'collateral damage,'" Pimen quipped. "Civilian casualties."

Pimen pointed to a road sign. "We're getting close. The road to Abu Ghosh is not far ahead."

The physicist raised his eyebrows. "Know anything about this town?"

Pimen nodded. "We have people working for us in the area. They think we are exporters sending out tourist junk. Jews and Arabs have always gotten along well in the village. No one would suspect anything bad happening there. It's a natural place to hide equipment."

"Hmmm," Anton grunted.

"The village's claim to fame is that the ark of the covenant returned there after the Philistines stole the magic box centuries ago. The town is supposed to be a place of good luck."

"Luck?" Ketele blew smoke in Pimen's direction, laughing wryly. "One of life's little ironies. Any trouble moving the device?"

"No. We moved the device here only a week ago," Pimen said, turning off the main highway and to Abu Ghosh. "From Ramallah."

ANN DROPPED DOWN by the stream and splashed water on her face. "I'm glad we started early. Every step feels like the sun gets hotter." She washed dust off her arms.

"It's going to be a scorcher today." Judy sat down beside her friend.

"We can't be far from Jericho." Keith shielded his eyes. "I'm surprised we haven't run into soldiers yet."

"Spoke too soon. Don't anyone look up," Ben said under his breath. "A man with a gun is watching from the top of that hill to our left. Just act normal and don't look."

"Is he PLO?" Judy asked.

"Got to be." Ben turned his face downstream but looked

at the hilltop out of the corner of his eye. "We've been in Palestinian territory for some time. He's probably been checking us out for several minutes."

"Let's just go on looking like—" Judy paused and looked down at her clothes. "Filthy, disheveled American tourists going to Jericho."

Ben laughed and helped her up. "Ready to travel on?"

"I am now."

Keith offered his hand. "Maybe there isn't a checkpoint in this area of the wilderness. Just open territory."

Ben took the lead, picking his way between the rocks. Judy jumped over a small bush. "I can't stop worrying about Jimmy," she said. "He wasn't prepared for this long a separation."

"I just hope he doesn't panic," Ben said.

"I'm sure our people settled in somewhere for the night when we didn't show up," Keith offered. "Of course, they'll take good care of Jim. He'll have a roof over his head and be well fed."

"How will we find them?" Judy took Ben's arm. "Did we set a place to rendezvous?"

"In the center of Jericho is a great sycamore tree." Keith glanced up toward the hills as he talked. "It's the tree Zacchaeus supposedly climbed when Jesus came by. Of course, the actual tree became firewood centuries ago. We agreed to meet in that area."

Ben pointed. "Look. We're coming to the end of the canyon. Jericho is just ahead. Let's hurry."

The wadi opened into a broad plain and gently sloped toward flat-roofed buildings. Palm trees dotted the skyline. The ancient city of Jericho spread out across the horizon.

Green-and-red Palestinian flags waved over the town. Cars and trucks rolled down the side streets, sending clouds of dust across the flat plain. The two couples headed toward the nearest road. The closer they came to the edge of town, the more military vehicles they encountered.

"Looks like we're walking into an armed camp." Ben stopped and scratched his head. "Something's popping here."

"We didn't lose the guard back there until we got out of the wadi." Keith looked back over his shoulder. "Did you notice he kept his gun trained on us?"

"Let's keep this pace." Ben lengthened his stride. "The sooner we get into town the better."

The high mountains of the wilderness loomed behind them as the foursome crossed the grassy field. The monastery built on the traditional site of the temptation of Christ dotted the top ridge of the highest peak. Far off in the distance the desert and hill country of Jordan arose like shimmering shapes in a mirage. As the couples approached the city limits, they found a razor-wire fence blocking their path.

"We don't dare try to crawl under or through this one." Ben felt the edge of one of the razor blades attached to the rolls of wire. "This stuff would cut us to pieces."

"Yes." Judy cupped her hand above her eyes and looked down the fence. "We're probably under surveillance right now by someone with binoculars. Crawling under would be an invitation for target practice."

"We don't have any choice but to walk the perimeter until we find an official entry," Keith said. "I suggest we go left. Looks like there's a guard tower down that way."

After five minutes of walking, they spotted the opening.

Several soldiers stood by the gateway; others aimed guns down from the observation platform.

"Just tourists out on a hike." Keith smiled and handed his American passport to the guard.

The young Palestinian pushed his black-and-white-checked burnoose back out of his face and nodded pleasantly. His black eyes snapped. "Enjoying our country?"

"Certainly." Ben offered his passport. "It's incredibly beautiful."

The PLO guard reached for the women's passports. "It's a little warm this time of the year for most of our American tourists," he chatted. "But they find our countryside fascinating."

"You speak excellent English," Judy said.

"English is the language of money," the Palestinian quipped as he handed their passports back. "Have a good time in Jericho."

"Looks like a lot of military activity." Ben tried to sound casual. "Something going on?"

"Just chasing the peddlers away from the tourists." The Palestinian flashed white teeth and smiled.

"Thanks." Ben walked through.

The two couples hurried past the officer and waved over their shoulders. No one spoke until they were a hundred yards away.

"That was surprisingly little hassle," Judy observed.

"They're tourist-friendly down here," Keith answered. "And they like to make the Israelis look paranoid. But something is clearly going on in town."

"How far to the sycamore tree?" Ann asked.

"It's in the center of town. Actually, we've got a long way to walk. We still have to climb the walls of Jericho."

"Really?" Judy looked startled.

"Just joking." Keith grinned.

"I hope the others are there waiting." Ben picked up the pace. "They may not have found it as easy to get through as we did."

"I just hope Jimmy is okay."

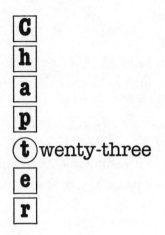

chapter twenty-three

AN UNEASY TENSION hung in the air like the thick red dust of summer. Military trucks and convoys of soldiers buzzed down nearly every side street. The red-and-green PLO flag waved from almost every residence. People on street corners worked as if preparing for an attack on the city. No one seemed the least bit interested in the two couples walking toward the center of Jericho.

The Americans said little, attempting to be as inconspicuous as possible. After a half hour they found their way to Jericho's center thoroughfare. "Look at the size of that tree." Judy pointed to a massive spread of branches shading the entire corner. "That's got to be the famous sycamore."

"You got it." Keith beckoned them to follow him across the street. "You can't come into Jericho from the Dead Sea without passing this corner."

"Do tourists really swallow the story that this is the tree from which Zacchaeus watched Jesus?" Ann asked.

Keith laughed. "Groups wander around here like they've died and gone to biblical Disneyland. They believe just about anything."

"I don't see any of our group." Judy looked up and down the street. "They should have been here by now ... or at least left someone behind as a contact person."

Ben wiped his forehead with his arm and shaded his eyes. "Not a good sign."

"They wouldn't have a clue where to go next without talking to us," Keith added. "Once they arrived in the city, this was their only rendezvous point."

"We don't have a choice but to wait here and see what happens," Ben added. "But they should have been here yesterday afternoon."

"Unless the police caught them," Ann added grimly.

"Don't even *think* such a thought!" Judy answered. "I'm really concerned about Jimmy."

Keith pointed to a couple of benches under the towering tree. "I think it's time for me to attempt a little conversation with the locals. Why don't you sit down, and I'll see what I can find out. Maybe I can get a traffic cop to talk."

"Be careful," Ann cautioned. "We can't afford for you to get thrown in jail."

Two old men sat at a rickety rusting table under the Zacchaeus tree, drinking coffee from small, thick porcelain cups. Each wore the traditional white robes that hung down to the tops of their shoes. Burnooses kept the sun out of their eyes and off their necks.

"*Samahni,*" Keith began in Arabic. "*Kahm Saah?*"

The toothless old man smiled and shrugged. He pointed at his wrist. "No watch. No time."

"Aywah," Keith answered. "Yes. I see. Well, speak any English?"

Both men shook their heads and went back to their coffees. At that moment a young policeman came out of the café. *"Keef halak?"* Keith immediately asked.

"Fine," he answered in excellent English, "and how are you?"

"A little confused." Keith pointed to another table shaded by an overhead awning. "I'm just a tourist. I could use some help."

The Arab twitched his mustache and eyed the table for a moment. "Maybe I can help." He tossed his head indifferently and sat down.

"My name is Keith." He offered his hand. "I'm from America."

"Khalil." The policeman shook Keith's hand. "I live here in Jericho."

"I was expecting some friends to meet us here," Keith began, "and they should have arrived long before now."

"Where were they coming from?"

"The Dead Sea."

"Oh!" The policeman rolled his dark brown eyes and nodded. "That's your trouble."

"I don't understand."

"Things have become quite tense since yesterday afternoon. The Israelis went nuts again." Khalil chuckled. "But the situation is becoming serious since they've gone to saber rattling this morning."

"What started the problem?" Keith said.

"Some kind of incident on the back road to Jerusalem. The IDF is claiming an attack by Moslem extremists killed a truckload of their troops. They think a suicide bomber set a trap."

"Really?" Keith's palms began to sweat, his heart pounding.

With some effort he forced his body to relax and his voice not to break. "Now that is amazing news."

"Your friends probably got caught in the resulting border shutdown," Khalil explained. "Yesterday afternoon the Israelis got excited and threw up roadblocks throughout the West Bank. They are checking everything with wheels."

"No one has come in from the West?"

"Not since last night," Khalil explained. "Cars are bottled up way out toward Ein Gedi and the resorts on the water. Your friends probably spent the night along the road or in one of those tourist traps."

"But you implied threats have been made?"

Khalil nodded. "For some reason the Israelis think we are preparing for war. Everything has become very intense in a matter of hours. You should really get out of here."

"How?"

"Right now the Israelis show virtually no interest in anyone wanting to leave the country. Truckloads of Arabs go into Jordan very easily. The problem is getting back *in* the country. The IDF is making it very hard to return."

"Just hitchhike out of town with the locals?" Keith pointed toward the desert.

"You would not have much of a problem." The policeman shaded his eyes and looked across the square. "Someone is summoning me. I must go. Good luck with your journey." He hurried away.

Keith quickly found his friends under the tree and gave them a complete report. "Sounds like our car wreck at the pass has turned into an international incident," he concluded, noticing the policeman talking to a soldier on the other side of the square. Keith watched for a moment and then suggested, "Let's sit out in front of that little fruit store and have a Coke while we talk."

"Strange how that cop took off while you were talking to him," Ben observed as they crossed the street. "Are you sure everything was okay?"

"It seemed all right." Keith sat down on a wooden bench in front of a small table. Ann went inside to buy the drinks. "He was an easygoing guy."

"We have no alternative but to wait right here," Judy announced dogmatically. "I've got to locate Jimmy as quickly as possible."

Ann returned with the drinks. "Time is running out," she fretted. "Surely the authorities can't hold them much longer. These complications make me very, very nervous." She handed out the Cokes.

Ben sighed. "After all we have been through, I've learned that often you can't do much more than roll with the punches—and remember who's *really* in charge. That's been a tough trip for me. I'm the scientist in control of the test results, remember? Mr. Computer. Well, I learned life doesn't fit anybody's set of formulas."

Judy put her face in her hands and shook her head. "I'm still learning, but what a ride this experience has been. Actually, the Bible code forced me to recognize that God has plans I'll never understand and that I simply have to learn to trust Him for the results."

Ben took a long drink. "Boy, *I* can relate. The Bible code crammed these convictions down my throat. Very early on I came to the conclusion that the Torah concealed two amazing predictions: a 'fire-earthquake' that proved to be the atomic blast and quake a few years ago in the U.S. and the collapse of the Communist system in China soon after. I almost went crazy trying to make sense out of all that."

Keith's eyes widened. "The Bible code predicted that? You must have been very upset."

"For a quasi-agnostic, the issues pushed me to the end of my self-confidence and presumption, forcing me to turn to God in ways I hadn't yet learned." Ben took another sip of the cold drink. "The knowledge of the atomic bomb and earthquake was the worst."

"Ben got into a real blue funk over that one," Judy added. "Unfortunately, I tended to think of the whole thing as a big game or a puzzle to solve. I guess I just didn't think the explosion would really happen."

"Then the terrorists set off the bomb—" Ben trailed off. "You know the results. The earthquake injured people and destroyed buildings. Then radioactive fallout, billions of dollars in damage. Nothing ever affected the national morale like that terrorist assault in the middle of a metropolitan area. But the bomb hit Judy and me with a double whammy! For months we had been wrestling with and studying the code's prediction of such a disaster. We knew it was coming, but said nothing."

"Another disturbing point was that no one would have given us the time of day if we'd tried to tell them we had a clue of what was coming," Judy added. "But the bombing shook the daylights out of me. The game was over—I knew we were involved in deadly serious business. I grew up in hurry."

Ben looked out across the street, watching the trucks and

cars pass. "I had to shift gears and start thinking in terms of the will of God for my entire life. After the bomb and earthquake, I knew I was responsible for sharing the messages we were discovering hidden in the code."

"Then Communism collapsed in China just like the code said it would," Judy said.

"I can feel what a heavy sense of responsibility this knowledge placed on you," Ann said. "The first time you came to Israel trying to warn the people, I knew you had a divine sense of mission about your discoveries. I can't imagine you living with anything other than a conviction that God had a call on your life."

"Well," Ben paused and smiled, "things were very different back then . . . very different."

Judy watched the two old Arabs still drinking coffee at the adjacent café. The policeman and the soldier kept talking on the other side of the square. Her attention returned to Ben. "You really can't imagine just how much the code has affected both of our lives . . . but Ben *really* changed."

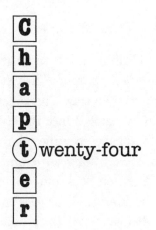

chapter twenty-four

San Francisco
March 12, 2004

THE TERRORIST ATTACK was eating away at Ben. The joy had gone out of his work, and even months after the bomb and quake, he was apprehensive about studying the code. Finally, after several weeks of badgering, Judy convinced Ben to call Rabbi Shiloh. Reuven invited them over immediately.

"Come in, come in." The bent old man waved the couple into his San Francisco home. "You've been away much too long. I have missed you."

The musty smell of the closed, stuffy homes of the elderly lingered in the hall. Reuven led the way toward the living room. "Edith!" he bellowed. "Our friends are here. Fix the coffee."

He ambled into the large comfortable room that also housed his office. "Sit down, sit down." Reuven pointed to their usual places and then plopped down in his own over-stuffed chair. "Edith!" he called again. "We're in the living room now."

For a few minutes, Ben and Judy exchanged pleasantries

and updated Rabbi Shiloh on what they had been doing. The old man listened politely. Edith eventually came in carrying her familiar kitchen tray. Uncharacteristically, she smiled and called them by name. Once the coffee cups were passed out, Edith shuffled away to some other corner of the house.

Reuven took a long sip from his steaming coffee cup, smiled, and settled back into the chair. "You're upset, Ben," the rabbi said kindly. "Your eyes show it. How can I help?"

Ben rubbed his chin for a moment. "I really don't know where to begin. I suppose the code project that began with fun and excitement has become an unbearable burden. Thinking you know the future is intriguing until you find some horrible secret about what lies ahead. Then you can no longer be a disinterested bystander. You're compelled to get into the action and try to stop the inevitable from happening."

"It's the bomb and earthquake, isn't it?" Reuven's kind voice filled with compassion. "You feel responsible for not being able to stop the explosion."

"And for not saving all of those people who died. I should have done, well, something . . . anything."

"Now you have an idea of the awful burden divine foreknowledge imposes on the Holy One, blessed be His name." The messianic rabbi stirred his coffee. "I often wonder how the heavenly Father bears the weight of knowing everything."

Ben rubbed his neck. "I never thought of my problem in that way—" He was silent for a moment and then responded forcefully. "But why *didn't* God do something?"

"Maybe He has," Reuven answered. "Possibly the Holy One of Israel gave us the Bible code so the human race would have the necessary clues to avert some of these disasters."

"Then *I* should have done something," Ben retorted.

"What would that have been?" Reuven shrugged. "You must remember you weren't the only person working on the code. Others also discovered the warning but didn't know what to do with the information or chose not to do anything with it."

Ben exhaled deeply. "I just can't let this go so easily. I feel . . . I don't know . . . that there's some sort of mission for me here. I've got to do more than just unravel mysteries and observe from the sidelines."

The rabbi suddenly broke into a big smile. "I am glad to see you so agitated. I believe the *Ruach Ha kodesh,* the Holy Spirit, is behind your discomfort." He chuckled. "Yes, your natural curiosity has possibilities for the development of personal holiness."

"What are you suggesting?" Judy asked.

Reuven pursed his lips and looked out the window. "I shall never forget the first time you came here. So young. So innocent." The rabbi suddenly shook his finger as if delivering a lecture. "But I saw significant promise in both of you. It was as if the Spirit was quickening in me an awareness that a great assignment was ahead for each of you. God has surely called you to do His work."

"But Ben didn't even believe," Judy protested.

"Oh, the Lord's work begins long before we have any awareness of our place in it. We think we have made a great decision when we open our lives to Him. In truth, we only say yes to the big yes He has already spoken to our existence."

"Then I've already failed," Ben interrupted. "I didn't do one thing about the bomb and quake."

"Ben, these matters must be worked out on a step-by-step basis. You and Judy are gaining new awareness at every turn. Remember the night you invited Christ into your life?"

Ben nodded.

"That was step one," Reuven instructed. "Now, the bomb attack has prepared you to take step two. This event forced you to consider surrendering your life to follow completely the will of God—wherever it takes you.

"Benjamin, our heavenly Father has a very important task for you to complete in the near future. He is using the code and this atomic attack to get your full attention. Your task is to be ready for whatever comes."

Ben scooted to the edge of his chair. "What's next?"

"None of us can see the backs of our heads." Reuven winked at Judy. "We all have blind spots, and the same is true in our commitment to Christ. Moments of crisis force the blinders from the eyes of our heart, and we realize how limited our dedication truly is. You have come to such a time."

"I don't understand!" Ben protested. "I've already committed my life to Yeshua. What more is there?"

"Would you be willing to be a fool for Christ's sake?" Reuven asked nonchalantly as he stirred his coffee.

"You mean make an idiot of myself?" Ben's voice rose.

"No, not at all." The rabbi smiled. "But would you be willing to be put in places where you are misunderstood and under suspicion? Could you stand up for the truth when everyone doubts you and, perhaps, thinks you a fool?"

Ben blinked, tilting his ear toward Reuven as if he didn't clearly understand what he had said.

"Scientists deal in hard, cold facts," Judy said, frowning.

"We don't like those gray areas that create misunderstanding. You're talking about going way out on a limb."

"Yes, for the sake of Christ," Reuven retorted. "Just how high, deep, and wide is your commitment to the Messiah?"

"You ask a great deal," Ben finally answered.

"Oh no!" The rabbi's eyes twinkled. "I ask nothing—but Yeshua calls for your entire life, which now includes your reputation as a scholar, a scientist, and what people would think of you if you appeared to be something of a fanatic, running around talking about bombs and the end of the world. Most of us are willing to dedicate our lives while we sit in the quiet security of a church sanctuary. It's another matter to step forward and stand on the hard, unforgiving pavement of Main Street, the place where people get stoned for their opinions."

Ben nodded his head slowly. "You are very sly, Reuven. You're quite gentle on the surface, but there's an iron fist inside the glove you use to get to the truth.

"You're right. I didn't do anything with what I knew about the bomb attack because I didn't want to be misunderstood or thought a fool. I kept my mouth shut for the sake of my reputation."

Reuven widened his eyes as if he were surprised, but the exaggeration betrayed his intent. "I suppose the issue is what are you willing to do in the future?" He looked down in his coffee cup and stirred.

Ben ran his hand nervously through his hair. "I really didn't plan to get in this deep." He shifted uncomfortably in his chair. "Obviously, if we discover the date that an atomic bomb is going to be detonated in Jerusalem, personal commitment means we will have to do everything possible to warn the citizens. That's right, isn't it?"

Reuven smiled kindly. "When Yeshua invites a person to follow Him, He invites them to come and die."

A WEEK LATER Judy had brought Jim with her when she dropped in at Ben's apartment. He had invited them in to his small place, which looked more like a research library and computer lab than a home. Jimmy sat erect on the edge of a kitchen table chair, staring at the Hebrew characters covering Ben's computer screen.

"I haven't heard much from you since we went to see Reuven," Judy said. "Have you been avoiding me?" She grinned.

"I've sorta been shunning everyone. Reuven really turned me upside down spiritually. I've been trying to process the conversation ever since."

Judy nodded. "You're a careful thinker, Ben. Don't rush into anything . . . with anyone. I know you're struggling to come to terms with the challenge Rabbi Shiloh gave you."

He shook his head. "We could be getting ourselves in deep on this one." Ben pointed to a pile of printouts. "I am convinced an atomic bomb will be detonated in Jerusalem in 2006, but I don't know the day. What does a sold-out believer do with this incomplete information?"

"You're totally committed to finding out?"

Ben rubbed his forehead thoughtfully. "I've come a long way since that day in the student cafeteria when you started me down this road. I've gone from agnostic Jew to messianic believer, and now it sounds like I'm turning into a freako evangelist-nuclear-ecologist-activist." He rolled his eyes. "But, yes, I must be true to Yeshua and to myself. I am dedicated to living out the implications of our findings."

"Praise God!" Judy clapped. "I'm proud of you. All we need now is the date, and then we're on our way to Oz and the Emerald City."

"I can't seem to get beyond the year." Ben pointed over his shoulder at the computer. "I'm stuck."

Jimmy blurted out. "Av 9."

Ben and Judy turned around. Jimmy continued to stare at the screen as if he were hypnotized. "Av 9," he said again and pointed at the Hebrew letters.

"What are you saying?" Judy stood up and reached for her brother's hand.

"The day of disasters." Jimmy's voice sounded strained. "What has been true in the past will continue to be in the future. The plan of God swings on the hinges of the holy days. This day is the axis of destiny."

Judy and Ben gawked at Jimmy. He looked like a machine waiting for a coin to start the mechanism whirling again. Judy moved to his side. "What are you suggesting?"

Jimmy's face reddened. He squinted his eyes. "I don't want to be a bad boy," he blurted out.

"Of course not," Judy comforted him. "Just help me understand what you are saying."

Jimmy turned slowly toward his sister. "I read the books. I understood what they said." He squinted his eyes tightly.

"Are you talking about the Hebrew textbooks? And *The Eternal Code* book? You studied them?"

Jimmy nodded his head emphatically.

"You understand what those books said?" Ben asked.

"I was frightened." Jimmy shook his sister's arm. "I knew when the bad things would happen."

Ben dropped down on one knee in front of Jimmy. *"Ha im ata m'daber iv 'reet?"*

Jimmy nodded his head mechanically. "Yes, I can understand Hebrew."

Ben's mouth dropped open.

"I told you, he remembers everything he pays attention to," Judy said.

"I can't believe my ears. *'Y 'hyeh b'seder?'*"

"No," Jimmy answered. "It will *not* be okay."

Ben shook his head in disbelief.

"Tell me slowly what is wrong." Judy looked straight into Jimmy's eyes. "You will not be a bad boy."

"I read the words. I could see the truth. The terrible bomb is going to explode in Jerusalem on Av 9. We must tell the people."

"Av 9?" Ben barked.

Jimmy squinted his eyes closed and clenched his jaw.

"Ben's not scolding you," Judy intervened. "It is not your fault. You haven't done anything wrong. Just tell us what you learned."

"I . . . I heard you . . . struggling to understand the sign or the closing of the age . . . the desolating sacrilege . . . the delivering up to tribulation." Jimmy put his hands over his eyes. "I read in the Hebrew Torah code, '9th Av is the day of the Third.' I knew it was the third world war, the time of the atomic attack in Jerusalem." He clinched his fist.

"It's okay, Jimmy," Judy comforted him. "None of this is your fault. You are not responsible."

"I found atomic holocaust in the code," Jimmy had continued. "It said, 'Ramallah fulfilled a prophecy.' I knew how everything fit together." He gripped his sister's hand tightly. "Judy, we must go to Israel. *I* must go to Israel and warn the people." He slowly turned to Ben. "Will you go with me?"

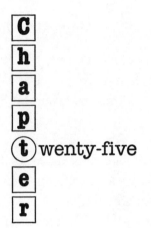

chapter twenty-five

KEITH GLANCED AT HIS WATCH. "It's well past lunchtime. I can't sit here much longer. My people ought to be here."

"Hey, look." Judy nodded toward the street. "Here comes your old buddy the traffic cop. Maybe he's got an update for us."

"He's picked up a couple of soldiers." Keith finished off the Coke. "Maybe the warm war's getting a little hotter."

Judy grimaced. "They don't look like happy campers."

Keith stood up and waved. "Khalil . . . I believe that's the name."

The three men marched toward the café. The Palestinian policeman didn't smile as he approached the table. The two PLO soldiers lowered their rifles.

"Hey—" Keith smiled as he spoke. "We're on your side, remember?"

"Do you have passports?" the policeman asked.

"Sure." Keith turned toward the table. "This is my wife, Ann, and—"

"You will come with us," the policeman said, cutting him off. "Please do not give us reason to deal with you with force."

"I . . . I don't understand." Ben stood up. "We're just tourists."

"Do not make any fast or rash movements," the policeman warned. "We will shoot instantly if necessary."

"Now, just wait a minute!" Ben protested. "I don't see any reason for tough talk."

The two soldiers immediately circled the two couples, nudging them with the barrels of their guns. Khalil stepped in front and motioned for everyone to follow him. He paraded them down several blocks until they came to a large stucco building with barred windows. Once inside, he led them down two long corridors to a large detention cell. The policeman gestured for them to sit on the other side of an old, marred table. The room was hot and stuffy.

"Why did you try to strike up a conversation with me?" Khalil leaned over the table and spoke into Keith's face.

"Just like I told you . . . I was trying to find the friends we were supposed to meet in the center of town."

"Don't lie to me," the policeman snapped. "Further deception will only make matters worse."

"I have no idea what you're talking about," Keith pleaded.

"Honest," Judy intervened, "we're just Americans trying to see the Holy Land."

Khalil looked knowingly at the two soldiers. He pulled out a packet of cigarettes and offered one to each man before lighting his own. The smell of smoke made the unpleasant room almost unbearable.

"What have we done wrong?" Ben pleaded.

Khalil nodded in the direction of one of the soldiers. "Shkaki has been following you down the wadi since this morning. Yesterday afternoon, we picked up the IDF patrol that crossed into our territory and were prepared to fire when they retreated. Obviously, they knew where the lines were drawn. Next, they sent you people down as bait. What are you? American Jews doing volunteer work for Mossad?" He blew smoke in their faces.

Judy and Ann coughed and tried to fan the fumes away. "Now just a minute," Keith protested. "That's absolute nonsense."

"You were trying to pump me for information," Khalil persisted. "No one could have walked down the wadi without passing that wreck the Israelis are so upset about. You people already knew all about the incident. You came in here pretending to be tourists while collecting information on our state of readiness."

"Do I look like a spy?" Ben scoffed.

Khalil shot Ben a hateful look. "We want to know what you are after, and we want to know right now." He turned to the soldier. "Shkaki, did you ever rough up a woman?"

Keith threw his arm around Ann. "Don't you *dare* touch my wife," he threatened.

Shkaki suddenly swung the butt of his rifle into Keith's stomach. Keith buckled immediately and slumped to the floor. Ann screamed and grabbed for her husband. Keith lay on the floor, gasping for breath.

Ben grabbed Ann's hand. "Listen. We are Americans. Look

at our passports. We came here as tourists. We haven't even been here long enough to get in trouble with the Israeli government."

"Think we mean business?" Khalil asked coolly.

"Absolutely," Ben answered.

Ann slowly helped Keith back up into his chair. His face was white, and his hands were shaking.

"We want to know what the Israelis are up to," the policeman demanded. "We're sitting down here minding our own business when these maniacs start screaming war and staging a fake incident up the valley. We know none of our people attempted any suicide forays up there. Obviously, this is a ploy, and they're up to something." He leaned to within an inch of Ben's nose. "I want to know what it is."

"Honest," Ben pleaded. "You can check us out. We are expecting to meet several carloads of friends, fellow tourists. They should have been here long ago."

"We're Christians," Keith groaned. "We belong to a messianic fellowship in Jerusalem. The Israeli government doesn't like us any better than you do."

"Now that's a truly wild story." Khalil turned to Shkaki. "Give these people high marks for creativity. Not much on credibility, but they are amusing."

"Please," Ann begged, "we lead Christians on tours all the time. My husband has a guide badge."

"Where?" the Palestinian office demanded.

"Oh no," Keith moaned. "I left it on the dashboard of the car."

"Which car?" Khalil demanded.

The two couples looked at each other. Keith shut his eyes tightly.

"Where's the car?" Khalil shouted.

The four young people stared at each other. Keith shook his head. "I blew it."

"Be straightforward," Ann urged. "That's always best."

"We were in the wreck," Keith admitted grudgingly. "It wasn't any sort of military operation. A truckload of soldiers just ran into an old man driving a pickup."

"What?" Shkaki grabbed Keith by the shirt. "Say that again."

"Honest. We saw the smashup, but it was just a bizarre wreck. Nothing more."

"But your car?" Khalil pressed.

"Got caught up in the explosion," Ben answered. "We were nothing more than victims . . . but we were afraid because the IDF was involved in the crash. The Israelis wouldn't have believed us."

Shkaki shoved Keith down in the chair and began speaking rapid-fire in Arabic. Khalil listened and kept shaking his head. After a minute, he picked up a phone. He talked in Arabic for several minutes before he put the phone down.

"You could have saved yourself a considerable amount of trouble if you'd told us the truth in the first place," Khalil snapped. "Now we have no idea what's *really* going on. You're waiting for friends who never come? Just out for a little stroll, yet you're involved in an international incident? You are a very interesting bunch for sure."

"Now that you know the facts, can we go?" Judy begged.

"Everything is so simple for Americans," Shkaki snarled. "Our hit-and-run suspects just want to walk on down the street as if nothing ever happened."

"You're not going anywhere," Khalil barked, "until we have all the facts and get this mess sorted out. If it takes until next Christmas, you're going to be in the cells down the hall."

"No! No!" Ben begged. "We've got to get on our way today."

"Today?" Khalil laughed. "You'll be lucky to be out of Jericho in a month."

Before his suspects could lodge another protest, the policeman stomped out of the room and the two soldiers marched the couples out of the detention room and down the corridor. At the end of the dark hall, the foursome were ushered into a large cell and locked in.

NAHUM ADMONI sat at the end of the long conference table in the Mossad headquarters on King Saul Boulevard in Tel Aviv. He stared at the other Mossad officers sitting around the table. "Let me get this straight," he growled. "The PLO is claiming the pileup was just an accident? How stupid do they think we are?"

At the other end of the table the tall man with graying hair crossed his arms over his chest and stared out the window. "The whole thing doesn't add up," Yehuda Gill said. "There's a piece missing in this whole scenario. That's what bothers me most," the head of the intelligence agency concluded.

Admoni was seldom asked to sit in on meetings with the head of the Mossad. He liked being considered an insider but was uneasy with his own lack of insight into this situation. Perhaps the immediate conference was contrived to expose his limitations.

"Where would these messianic Christians have picked up the atomic bomb talk?" a second agent to Adomni's right asked. "People don't bounce those warnings around by accident, particularly when we're getting alerts at the same time of the movement of critical atomic materials into our country."

"The data is clear." The agency head held up a report. "I trust LAKAM, our section for scientific relations," Gill said firmly. "They sit right under the prime minister's office and do a good job of gathering intelligence in the United States. Yes, there's enough unaccounted for enriched uranium and plutonium floating around the Middle East to destroy several nations. But why would a Christian group be talking about it? Bizarre."

"Our people have cross-checked every aspect of what we have learned from this Collins character," Admoni added. "The woman identified as Judy Bithell was ejected from the country a year ago with a young man named Benjamin Meridor. Meridor is an American Jew; Bithell a born-again Christian type. Neither fits the profile of political operatives."

"These are the same people the army was chasing when the wrecks occurred?" the agency head asked.

"We believe so," Admoni answered. "Initially we thought the pair perished in the fire. Now the issue is clouded. They may have escaped."

"Where could they have gone?" Yehuda Gill's eyes narrowed. "Isn't Jericho the only possibility?"

Admoni nodded his head soberly. "They would have had to run like deer immediately after the wreck . . . but it's possible."

"We've run these questions through Sayfanim, our department dedicated to PLO activity," the second agent added.

"We can't find any connection between the Americans and the Palestinians."

"Couldn't all of this activity be nothing but a smoke screen?" Admoni ventured. "Maybe they are simply trying to divert our attention from the real action. Could we be looking for the wrong people?"

Yehuda Gill stared at Nahum with cold, calculating eyes. "Where are you keeping Collins and Levy?"

"They're in a jail in Jerusalem, being held without bail. I can keep them tucked away for at least a week."

"The calendar is running against us, gentlemen," the agency head concluded. "Av 9 is the day after tomorrow. Never a good day for Jews."

"You believe in that superstitious nonsense," Admoni scoffed.

"I believe in everything—angels, devils, goblins, spooks, coincidence, fate, and God." Gill's voice sounded harsh. "I believe that since the beginning of time something has been trying to destroy the Jewish people, and I never underestimate any of the possibilities." He stood up and pushed his chair back. "And I believe you better have more satisfactory answers for me within the next twenty-four hours or face the possibility that all of us might be out of business because of the high probability that we all will have been blown to the moon."

twenty-six

ORLAF PIMEN carefully steered the old pickup through the erratic traffic on East Jerusalem's Salah E-Din Boulevard. Near St. George's Anglican Church, he slowly pulled into the auto repair shop. Pimen drove through the large metal door, and Arab workmen in dirty overalls immediately pushed the door shut. The Russian exhaled slowly. "Good. No trouble with the police."

Anton Ketele grunted and hopped out of the truck.

The Russians didn't speak to the Arabs but walked directly to the back room. Workmen immediately began unloading the crates tied in the back of the pickup.

Ketele stopped at the door for a moment and glared at the men lugging the heavy boxes from the back. *"Beperncb beereegees!"* he screamed at the men.

"He is telling you to be careful," Pimen explained to the Arabs. "We wouldn't want to blow any of you boys to pieces."

The men's eyes widened in horror. They bobbed up and down in agreement. *"Aywah, aywah.* Yes. Yes."

"Skolkayy vrehmeenee aighmot reemont?" Ketele asked.

"Not long," Pimen answered. "It shouldn't take but a few minutes to move the equipment into the back. Let's greet our colleagues." He opened a metal fire door and led Ketele into the hidden inner laboratory.

Dietrich Heinz leaped to his feet. "Comrade!" He rushed across the room and kissed Ketele on both cheeks. "Welcome to the great experiment."

Ketele smiled mechanically and shook his hand. "Good to see you."

"Please meet Abdul." Pimen presented the Arab in charge of the assembly area. "Our friend has been most helpful in installing the basic equipment in the van."

The Arab bowed politely.

"And this is Mohammed Bitawi." Pimen beckoned the driver and his accomplice forward. "He and this fine young man have the great honor of driving the van."

Anton Ketele shook Bitawi's hand with great solemnity and patted him on the shoulder. "A glorious task, indeed! You will be richly rewarded in eternity and remembered on earth."

Bitawi grinned from ear to ear. The teenager stared straight ahead.

"We begin at once," Ketele instructed the group. "The bomb must be completely assembled by tomorrow afternoon at the latest. The technical demands are significant, and we have no time to spare. The work is tedious. We must be ready to begin the final installations in less than thirty minutes."

"We are ready even as we speak." Dietrich Heinz snapped

his fingers and pointed beyond the room where the red van waited. "I made sure everything is in place." He hurried out the door into the large hidden assembly area, barking instructions like a general charging into battle.

Orlaf Pimen peered out from under the hairless bony ridge that almost concealed his eyes. "Where are we in the countdown?" The dark shadows around his eyes made his low rumbling voice sound even more ominous. "When do you and I leave this doomed and forsaken place?"

Anton Ketele cracked his knuckles and smiled. "The bomb assembly should be completed by late tomorrow afternoon. At six o'clock we will receive an emergency communiqué from Baghdad instructing the two of us to proceed to Tel Aviv immediately. Specially arranged tickets will be waiting for us at the airport. By 8:30 we will be on our way to Rome."

"And Dietrich?"

"He will be sent south to Egypt as soon as he has everything in place. Heinz will throw the final switches after we are gone. The driver will not know that once the van is started, there is no way to prevent the bomb from exploding.

"The two Arabs will leave this garage just before midnight. As soon as they reach the Old City, park, and turn off the ignition, the bomb will detonate. The timer is essentially a backup mechanism. Once the Arabs are in the truck, the doors will automatically lock with no possibility of their escape. The system is foolproof. Those two idiots will be vaporized even if they get cold feet."

Pimen rolled his tongue around the front of his mouth and pursed his lips. "Will Heinz make it out?"

Anton laughed loudly. "Why Orlaf, what a devious mind

you have! Let's just see how well our German friend functions during the next twenty-four hours."

"Dietrich is a valuable scientist," Pimen said sourly. "We might need him again."

Anton laughed. "My, my, what a sentimentalist you have become, Orlaf. Maybe the religious atmosphere around here is affecting you." He laughed again. "Let's get to work."

CHING LIN LISTENED CAREFULLY, waiting for the military call to be decoded as he spoke. The delay in the top secret transmission from China made the conversation somewhat disjointed. "Yes, yes," he replied. "But are our troops now positioned for immediate deployment across the borders of India as well as sweeping south to join with the Iraqi army's assault on the northern borders of Israel?"

The Chinese leader drummed on the table with his fingers for several seconds. "Good. Good. And there is no problem with the Russians?" After several more seconds he hung up.

Ahmed Tibi walked briskly into the command room. Aides snapped to attention. Tibi laid a pile of computer reports on the conference table. "It will soon be dark in Jerusalem. Have we heard from Ketele? Did he arrive without incident?"

An aide saluted. "We have received confirmation that Pimen and Ketele have joined Heinz in Jerusalem and are at work. The final phase is underway."

"Excellent." Tibi smiled. "The Syrian army is fully armed and ready to move. Regardless of any intelligence reports the Israelis receive, they can do nothing to resist the one-two punch the bomb and our instantaneous attack will deliver. The next two days will forever change the course of world history. Moslems can now reclaim their sovereignty in the Middle East."

Ziad Amr abruptly entered through the side door from the communications center and smiled at the other leaders. "Our satellite is now fully armed," he announced definitely. "We push the button and intercontinental communication stops. Gentlemen, centuries from now our ancestors will not speak of world conquest in terms of Alexander the Great or the Caesars. *Our* names will be on their lips and in the pages of history, spoken with unending praise and admiration."

"Here! Here!" Ahmed Tibi applauded.

ON THE OTHER SIDE OF THE WORLD, the workday had just begun. Two National Security Council advisers met in the corridor outside the conference room in the White House. "We have only a few minutes before the president calls the meeting to order." The gray-haired man spoke softly. "What's your opinion?"

The army general shook his head soberly. "Adrian, everything about the current international scenario is bad. The Israelis just sent confirmation that the Egyptians are currently on a military standby basis. Countries don't assume such a posture unless they're looking for big trouble."

"There's no question the Chinese have started south with full-scale troop movements. Ed, what in blue blazes would they be doing in concert with the Egyptians?"

General Davis scowled. "Beats me. And we've picked up satellite pictures of the same rumblings going on in Iraq. Of course, Amr always has his people ready to attack somebody somewhere, but no question the Iraqis are also on a full alert.

If I was putting together a battle plan for a major war, that's how I'd be lining up the players."

Adrian Randolph nodded. "I agree, but the whole thing doesn't make any sense. Those people know the Israelis have nuclear capability. If they get their troops too close, the Jews will bite big-time."

"Yes," the general rubbed his chin. "But Israel needs our approval to pull the trigger on the big bomb. They are probably hoping we'll issue some sort of ultimatum for everyone to call off the dogs and things will quiet down."

Randolph leaned closer to the general's ear. "I don't think the president is going to stand with Israel this time. You know his every decision is based on public opinion polls. He can't decide whether to take a bath or a shower without finding out what the majority of Americans favor. A potential confrontation is just too controversial for his nervous system."

"So, what's your bottom line, Adrian? What's going to happen in there in a few minutes?"

"Two factors are paramount." The adviser abruptly sounded factual and objective. "The attack within our shores was too overwhelming for Americans. Turned everyone inward. Isolationist thinking followed. Reactionary behavior. Voters are totally preoccupied with their own backyards.

"Second, people blame the Jews for creating the climate that resulted in the terrorist attack finally occurring here. Support for Israel is zero. Anti-Semitism is growing. We're not going to get mixed up in a war in the Middle East right now. The Security Council is about to take a hike."

"Agreed." General Davis shrugged. "The Israelis aren't going to start slinging nukes unless we support them. If we signal resistance, they'll think twice about initiating a pre-emptive strike."

Adrian Randolph rose to his full height and looked the general straight in the eye. "They'd better! Any more nuclear explosions and we'll have World War III on our hands!"

YEHUDA GILL looked at his watch. Even though it was still quite light outside, sundown was not far away. He shifted his weight uncomfortably from one foot to the other and looked at his watch again.

The large mahogany door opened and a secretary stepped out. "The prime minister will see you now," she announced. "Please go in."

The Mossad's chief officer walked briskly into the spacious office and stood at attention in front of a long desk. The prime minister looked up and waved but kept talking on the phone. "You are sure of the size of troop movements." He spoke with intensity. "No question of the figures?" He waited. "I see."

Yehuda looked at the pictures on the wall. The prime minister stood in a friendly pose with the president of the United States and the prime minister of England in front of a rose garden. In another picture, he was wearing military fatigues, standing with a new group of IDF inductees on top of Masada. Gill recognized one of the new soldiers as the prime minister's youngest son.

The prime minister hung up the phone. "I appreciate your coming at once. I was getting final confirmations from the IDF." He pointed at a chair in front of his desk. "Sit down, Gill. I need the best information Mossad can give me."

Yehuda Gill sat but remained militarily erect in his chair. "Yes, sir," he began. "I am ready with a full report."

"Just the bottom line," the prime minister answered. "I have a general picture of what the Egyptians and Iraqis are up to. We know the Chinese and Russians are doing strange things." He leaned back in his chair. "I'm not a superstitious man, Gill—or particularly religious either. But I keep thinking about the Yom Kippur War. Golda and the boys didn't pay attention to how inviting a religious holiday is for an attack."

"Yes, sir." Gill nodded. "I am aware that Av 9 is also a problematic date on our calendar. We have factored the significance of history into our thinking."

"And?" the prime minister pushed. "What do you come up with?"

Yehuda Gill cleared his throat and inhaled deeply. "Although we don't have all the pieces fully sorted out, we are getting strange, disturbing reports and warnings about an atomic attack. We may be dealing with the nut fringe, but then again, we have enough intelligence data to turn on the warning lights."

The prime minister nodded his head. "Yes. I'm equally disturbed. Particularly when you have only one chance to be right. I've seen the watchdog reports from the United States' CIA people noting the number of atomic weapons unaccounted for, weapons that could be surfacing in our backyard.

"Loose nukes are no small problem. I got a memo from Bill Potter at the Monterey Institute of International Studies. Nobody knows more about the nuclear smuggling going on out of the old Soviet Union than those people. They're very worried about that three tons of plutonium sitting in storage at Aktau in Kazakhstan, just an arm's reach from Iran. Gill, we turn to your agency for the final word. What is it?"

"Mr. Prime Minister," Yehuda spoke slowly, "I want to propose very dramatic steps that could backfire and make all of us look bad. But I believe radical action is justified at this moment."

"Yes?"

"Tomorrow night after the sun goes down, we recommend that you seal off the borders and suspend all air travel in and out of the country. We should scramble our fighters and make sure all air corridors are under strict control. We propose you put the military on alert and be prepared for military action on two fronts. We must be ready to confront the Egyptians to the south and the Iraqis and Syrians from the north and east. Mossad recommends mobilization be top secret until the last possible moment in order to catch all adversaries off guard."

"Hmmm." The prime minister rubbed his temples and stared at the ceiling. "Such actions would bring commerce and transportation to a halt. The move could cost millions in tourist dollars alone."

"Correct," Gill answered.

"Then again, no one could ever claim we weren't alert. No Yom Kippur War egg on our faces. We'd be ready for any surprises."

"And we might be able to apprehend the perpetrators involved in a bomb plot."

"What's happening with the borders now?" the prime minister asked.

"We've been letting people out but carefully checking

everyone coming into the country. Security is closely watching for the arrival of any suspicious shipments. No stone goes unturned."

"You'd tighten up and not let people in or out?" the prime minister concluded. "Shut everything down until the matter is completely sorted out?" He rolled his eyes. "Rather strong medicine, isn't it?"

"Can we gamble on the possibility of an atomic attack?"

The prime minister crossed his arms over his chest. "We can't afford to be hit first. Our publicly stated policy has always been that we are willing to make a preemptive strike because our small country would not be able to sustain a direct attack. Are you suggesting we also strike?"

"No, sir. Mossad urges a defensive national posture until Av 9 passes. We propose to bottle up all travel in and out of this country for twenty-four hours. If we're wrong and nothing happens, we endure inconvenience and some financial loss, but we signal to potential adversaries that we maintain eternal vigilance. If subversion really is afoot, we call their cards. People won't like the inconvenience, but no one can say your government wasn't prepared."

The prime minister nodded his head vigorously. "No one's going to play me for a fool. What you propose is severe, but the stakes are high. I've already called a cabinet meeting for first thing in the morning. At three o'clock tomorrow afternoon, we will put the military on full alert, and three hours later we'll seal the borders. By six o'clock, it will be impossible to get in or out of the country."

**DAY FOUR
AV 8 5766**

"But he who endures to the end shall be saved."

Matthew 24:13

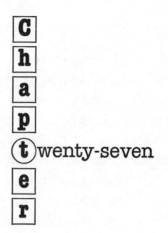

Chapter twenty-seven

Jericho
August 2, 2006

THE SOUND OF FOOTSTEPS jolted Ben awake. He opened his eyes but couldn't see anything. Except for the hint of moonlight coming through the open window, night shrouded the prison cell in opaque blackness. He listened intently as the noise trailed away into silence. The smell of the place stung his nose and made his stomach queasy. A large rat scurried in front of him and darted through the bars into the adjacent cell. Ben gritted his teeth and tried not to jump.

He shifted uneasily, trying to stretch his cramped muscles without waking Judy, who was slumped against his shoulder. The unheated jail did nothing to shield them from the bitingly cold desert night. He and Judy had huddled together against the wall while Keith and Ann slept on the only mattress in the cell. Judy's warmth helped keep his teeth from chattering.

Ben held his arm up toward the moonlight slipping

through the lone barred window. He could barely make out 5:45 on his digital watch. Ben groaned and tucked his arm more tightly around his chest.

For several minutes, he tried to go back to sleep but couldn't. The consequences of their being stuck in jail kept rushing through his mind. The rest of the caravan didn't know where to go. The Yaakovs and Judy were trapped in what would surely become a death chamber. And the whole mess was his fault. Ben remembered his distant relatives who had perished in the Holocaust and wondered if they had the same misgivings and fears during the hours before their deaths.

Judy looked deceptively small and helpless curled up in a ball next to him. Her determination and fire would never allow her to admit the apprehension Ben knew she must be feeling.

"Don't worry," her small voice abruptly whispered. "It's going to be okay, Ben." She squeezed his hand. "You're not responsible."

He pulled her closer and smiled. *Judy even reads my thoughts.* Ben hugged her even more tightly. *I don't think I could live without Judy.* Ben suddenly remembered that it was in a jail that he realized for the first time how important Judy was to him.

It happened during their first trip to warn Israel about the impending atomic attack. Immediately after landing, they had gone to the offices of *The Jerusalem Post* to get the story in print. Within five minutes of their arrival, the reporters virtually threw them out. Judy wasn't discouraged but Ben recalled their abrupt exodus had been a revelation to him. Only then had he fully realized how difficult it might be to get anyone to listen.

"I know what to do," Judy had said. "Maybe this is only a wild hunch, but let's go to the Knesset and talk to the politicians. We're talking national security here. They'll listen."

"We can't get in *there* of all places," Ben had objected. "Security has got to be tighter than a drum."

"Come on." Judy had jerked on his arm. "Let's grab a bus. Won't take long to find out."

And it didn't. Once they got a hearing with security personnel, the front door had immediately opened. Ben and Judy had been ushered into a special room that appeared to be the first step in giving them immediate access to members of Israel's parliament. Another guard came in to chat. He appeared pleasant enough until the first man suddenly jumped up and began speaking rapid-fire Hebrew into a cellular phone he carried in his inner pocket. Within seconds, six additional security personnel had charged into the room and whisked the couple out of the building to a downtown detention center. Ben and Judy had tried to explain the message they had deciphered from the Bible code. After six hours of intense scrutiny, Ben and Judy had been tossed out, apparently labeled and rejected as harmless nuts.

Ben's reflections were interrupted by the hint of dawn breaking through the cell window, turning the sleeping shapes of the Yaakovs into people once more. Ben saw again the thick layer of dust on the floor, the trash lying around the cell. At the end of the hall a PLO guard was sleeping in a chair. Ben hoped the room would warm up quickly.

Judy cuddled closer. "Try to catch a few more winks," she murmured. "It's all in the Lord's hands anyway."

Ben smiled and scooted closer. Judy had said those exact

words when they had decided to contact the scholars at the University of Jerusalem.

❑ ○ ❑

AFTER THEIR ADVENTURE at the Knesset, Ben and Judy spent two days trudging up and down stairs at the university, seeking conferences and consultations with rabbis and professors. Each time they laboriously presented the details of the Bible code, no one showed the slightest interest. The intellectual establishment seemed to be in singular agreement that they were fundamentalist cranks. After forty-eight hours of beating on doors, no one gave them the time of day. Their warnings were written off by the intelligentsia as sheer nonsense.

Ben decided to try a long shot. Perhaps a publisher would print their findings in some form that could be distributed throughout the country. Only after contacting a dozen firms did he finally face the truth. The printers agreed with the professors. No dice.

Judy reluctantly closed the phone directory. "We haven't even been in this country long enough to have developed a bad reputation. Yet you'd think we had been on television advertising that we're the latest nut crop from America. Every door has been slammed in our faces."

Ben nodded his head. "It seems like there's a conspiracy out there to keep any and everything related to prophecy, the Scriptures, and the Christian faith from seeing the light of day. Israeli society has closed up shop."

"I just don't understand it, but we are clearly shut out."

Ben pursed his lips. "I think the picture came into focus

with that professor we talked to. Once the rabbis discovered the predictions that Yeshua is the messiah in the Bible code, they threw the whole thing out as bogus. The code in the Torah is now seen as a fad, nonsense. They promoted it until then."

"What do we do next?" Judy asked.

"Rabbi Shiloh is supposed to have contacted someone named Keith Yaakov about our coming. He's a messianic rabbi from Philadelphia working in Jerusalem. Maybe his congregation will be more interested."

Judy looked through her purse and pulled out her address book. "Look—we're not that far from where they meet. The place is close to Ben Yehuda Street."

"Why don't we take a taxi and see if we can turn up anything? We really don't have any other alternatives left."

Within thirty minutes they had found the meeting place, but the building was locked and the shades pulled on the windows. A small sign promised that services would be held in two days, on the Sabbath, but the sign gave no other directions or phone numbers. Ben beat on the door several times.

"Can I help you?" a young man asked in excellent American English.

Ben turned to find a tall redhead standing behind them. "I'm looking for the people who run this place."

"Why?" the young man smiled but wasn't friendly.

"I'm trying to find Keith Yaakov. Would you know him?"

He extended his hand. "Sure. I'm Liat Collins, a colleague of Keith's. You sound like you're from the States."

"Yes. A rabbi named Reuven Shiloh wrote Keith Yaakov to expect our visit."

Collins offered his hand to Judy. "We get lots of visitors

who are here just to cause trouble. I have to check people out before we let them know where our offices are. The congregation experiences a tremendous amount of persecution."

"I can believe it," Judy answered. "We haven't exactly been treated like royalty. People in this country seem rather reactionary. Even the university people are narrow-minded."

Collins stiffened. "Political turmoil causes one to be a bit on edge," he said defensively. "We are virtually in a state of war most of the time."

"You ought to suggest that the establishment figure out how to tell their supporters from the enemies," Judy said sharply.

Liat Collins pointed down the street. "Follow me and I'll take you to Keith's office. His wife, Ann, is there right now."

They had walked for a couple of blocks when they came to a modern office building. Collins led them up two flights of stairs and pointed to a door marked only with a number. He suggested they go in. Then he disappeared back down the stairs.

Keith Yaakov jumped up from his chair when the two Americans entered the room. "Yes, I've been expecting you for days!" He walked across his spartan office with his hand extended. "My friend Rabbi Shiloh said you were coming here with an important message."

"My name is Ann." A petite young woman hurried from the opposite side of the room. "Is it ever good to see a fellow American. Do sit down."

Judy responded with a hug. "You're the first friendly faces we've seen." She sat down on the couch across from Keith's desk.

"Things aren't easy these days." Keith pulled up a couple

of chairs for his wife and himself. "We need all the help we can get."

"Please understand," Ann broke in. "Everybody in this country walks on eggshells. It's as if we live in a constant state of war."

"It's bad," Keith added. "And the security people are unbelievably paranoid. Anything sets them off. I'm surprised you haven't been followed."

Ben looked at Judy blankly. "It never occurred to me that anybody might try. Actually we've been kicked out of every place we've been."

"We'd certainly be an easy target though," Judy rolled her eyes. "The two of us are about as naive as they come."

"I'd be willing to bet someone has been on your tail," Ann added. "Probably best you came here last. We're really suspect. A messianic congregation in Jerusalem is considered to be as bad as a staph infection in a hospital."

"So what is this urgent message you traveled across the ocean to tell us?" Keith asked.

Ben looked at Judy. "I hope you won't think we're a couple of paranoid schizophrenics, but we have a sort of . . . well, a kind of end-of-the-world warning we've found in the Bible."

Keith looked at his wife and frowned. "Really? Rabbi Shiloh said to take you seriously, but he didn't hint about something that earthshaking."

Judy swallowed hard. "We have a warning. As strange as it sounds, we're sure that the Lord wants the people of Jerusalem to be aware of an impending nuclear disaster."

Ann's mouth dropped. "Are you serious?" She looked at Keith, her eyes filled with consternation.

Keith grimaced. "No wonder you've had a hard time. Anyone talking about bombs is going to get the door."

"Or a special trip downtown to the prison," Ann warned. "Terrorist talk is highly seditionist. You're really playing with fire."

A loud rap on the door rang across the office.

"Who is it?"

"Tahanat!"

Keith leaped to his feet. "It's the police." He rushed to the window. "Look. Three police cars are parked in front of this building. We're surrounded."

"We've got to open the door." Ann wrung her hands.

"We don't have anything to hide." Ben stood up. "We've been doing everything we possibly could to get somebody to listen."

"I'm sure they've been following you all along," Keith concluded. "When you came here, you went over the edge. We're considered subversive." He crossed the room and opened the door.

"Come with us," the policeman said in broken English. "Don't take anything. Just come immediately."

"Wait just a minute," Keith protested.

The policeman stuck a leather wallet with identification in Keith's face. "Resist and face the consequences."

"Please—" Ann waved her hands at the officer. "We don't want any trouble."

"Then follow me immediately," the policeman insisted.

Keith and Ann were taken away in one car, Ben and Judy in another. Once they reached the station, Ben didn't see the others again. For the next five days, he faced constant interrogation, being hustled back and forth between different cells. At night the light above his head was left on and during the day he was constantly harassed. No one would tell him anything about Judy. He found himself weeping when the guards weren't hounding him.

Finally, the guard returned Ben to a new cell that didn't have a light shining overhead. He had slumped down on the crude bed attached to the wall and stared into the shadows. Fatigue swallowed him. His emotions were like a dam about to burst under an unbearable weight. Bitter tears ran down his face; his stomach was in knots.

"Judy," he cried aloud. "Judy, what have they done to you? Please, God, protect Judy." Ben buried his face in his hands and sobbed. Suddenly a profound realization filled his mind. Judy had always been the sparkling, dancing little delight that fascinated him. But through their meandering adventure in discovering the code, Ben had not comprehended how profoundly he cared for her. She was simply always there, taken for granted. But now Judy was gone, and Ben ached for just a glimpse of her lovely face. "Judy," he cried out again, "I really do love you."

Suddenly the door opened. A guard towered over him. "Get up. Let's go," he said. "Follow me."

Ben stumbled down the long sterile corridor behind the guard. In a few minutes, they turned toward what Ben was sure was the back of the building. A door opened and the guard led Ben out into the open air. A fresh breeze blew across his face and the sunlight felt blindingly wonderful.

"Get in," the guard ordered and pointed to the open door of a small Ford. "Keep your mouth shut and sit in the backseat."

He yanked Ben's arm and pushed his head down. Ben barely slid into the backseat when the door slammed behind him. "The doors automatically lock, so there's no point in trying to get out," the guard warned.

The car immediately sped away and merged into the downtown Jerusalem traffic. The driver wore a large hat and sunglasses. He didn't speak but drove straight out of Jerusalem. For the first time in several days, Ben realized how grimy and dirty his clothes felt. His pants were wrinkled; his shirt stained. He rubbed his chin and tried to see his reflection in the rearview mirror. He needed a shave.

An hour and a half later the Ford pulled into Ben Gurion International Airport. The driver turned away from the normal arrival lane and drove into an area marked SECURITY. A policeman waved him through a gate and onto the tarmac close to the parked airplanes. The car stopped near the back of the terminal. The driver got out and opened the back door.

"Get out and follow me," the driver said, speaking for the first time. "Don't try anything funny or the price will be greater than you want to pay." He spoke surprisingly good English.

Ben slid out and nodded compliance. They walked through another door also marked SECURITY. A group of men were waiting inside. Ben eyed them apprehensively.

"You are going to be on the next airplane out of the country," the driver explained. "Your passport will be returned as you board the airplane. You have been expelled from Israel with the warning never to return. Understand?"

Ben nodded. "Where is Judy? I won't leave without her."

The guard grabbed his shirt and shook him. "You haven't got the picture yet? You'll do what we tell you."

"I won't leave without her." Ben tried not to sound confrontational; his voice trembled.

"Take our hero upstairs and get him on the airplane." The guard pointed toward a stairway. "Keep him away from other passengers until he's ready to board."

Two men hustled Ben up the back steps. They popped through a door and were suddenly in the main terminal before Gate 36. The security personnel ushered Ben into the waiting area immediately in front of the ramp down to a waiting El Al 747.

"Ben!" a woman's voice called out from across the waiting area. "I'm here. I'm okay."

"Judy!" Ben cried. "Thank God you're all right!" He bolted from the guards and reached out for her. Judy met him in the middle of the area. "Oh, Judy. I've been so afraid for you. Did they hurt you?"

"Just frightened me, that's all." Judy hugged him tightly. "I worried about you every moment."

Ben looked into her eyes but said nothing.

The security guards pulled the couple apart. "Get on the airplane and don't come back," one of the men warned. "Try it again and the next time you won't ever leave this country." The man pressed passports into their hands and pointed at the door. "Get going."

Ben grabbed Judy's hand and hurried down the ramp. "I'm so glad you're alive and okay." He suddenly stopped and held Judy close. "Thank God we survived." He took her hand again and ran for the open door of the airplane.

❏ ◯ ❏

THE MEMORY OF THEIR SURVIVAL suddenly filled Ben with new hope. They did it once, they could do it again. The sunlight coming through the cell window grew stronger and dawn fell across Judy's face. She stirred but didn't wake up. Ben hugged her once more.

"Oh, Judy. How could I live without you," he said under his breath. "If we go, we'll go together."

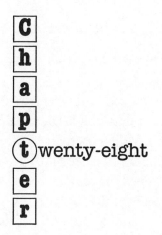

Chapter twenty-eight

"BREAKFAST." The Palestinian jailer beat on the bars. "I leave inside. Come back later." The barred doors swung open and the man sat a tray on the floor. He quickly locked the door again. "You eat now."

"Nothing like breakfast in bed." Judy sat up and rubbed her eyes. "How very thoughtful of your friend Khalil to send a little something over."

Keith rolled over in the bunk and gently shook his wife's shoulders. "Look, dear, I think our waiter brought you a croissant and tomato juice with a touch of lemon."

Ann pushed her hair out of her eyes. "Oh! My back feels like it will break in half."

Ben picked up the tray and sat it on the bed between the Yaakovs. "Sorry. Looks like the best we're getting is warm tea and chunks of stale bread. Nothing more."

"No bacon and eggs?" Judy frowned. "But since we missed supper last night, who can complain?" Judy reached for a piece of bread. "The PLO spa system can certainly help one lose weight."

Keith looked out the barred windows. "Going to be another hot day. The locals are already buzzing up and down the streets. Military activity hasn't slowed down any overnight. If anything it has picked up."

Ben sipped the tea and looked at his watch. "I guess I don't need to tell you that today is Av 8."

"We're running out of time," Keith answered.

"And I'm very, very concerned about Jimmy," Judy added.

Ben sat back down on the floor and stared at the wall. Judy gently rubbed the back of his neck. "Don't blame yourself. We've all done the best we could."

"And you came back at great risk to yourself," Ann added. "Both of you exhibited amazing courage. What more could anyone ask?"

Keith smiled. "I suppose I ought to come clean. I never told anyone about the first warning you gave us that day in my office. I felt we had enough credibility problems without disseminating such a terrible message. We didn't think you were crazy, but I guess we didn't really believe it."

Ann nodded. "Ironically, the truth is quite the opposite of what Liat Collins accused us of. Keith agonized over frightening the Holocaust refugees. We decided to err on the side of caution. In fact, we didn't make any plans ourselves until we got Reuven Shiloh's last warning just before you came back."

"I know we must have sounded like creatures from another planet." Judy munched on the bread.

"Collins went through every possible gyration trying to

find out what you told us." Keith laughed. "He even implied you might be from the CIA. I think that was when I first became suspicious of him."

"You know what I think," Ann added. "I think Liat was responsible for the police coming to arrest you."

"Us," Judy added. "We all got a free guided tour of the Jerusalem pokey, remember?"

"We never did find out what happened to you," Ben said. "They whipped us out of the country without giving us a clue about your fate."

"Actually, the authorities sent us home a couple of days before they deported you," Keith explained. "Apparently, the police decided we weren't much more significant than any of the other people you talked with. Of course, the arrest added to our already dubious reputation."

"But why all the drama?" Judy asked. "I mean, running us out of town on a rail. You'd think we were first-class terrorists."

"When you mention atomic bombs, you get everybody's attention," Keith explained. "Those words started the ball rolling. Then, your appearance at the Knesset threw all their switches. You were simply too straightforward, too candid. As best I can tell, the government followed you from that moment on."

"I think your use of the code book was also a big red light," Ann added. "Rabbi Edlow Moses' writing is too controversial even to discuss in public. Orthodox Jews are very upset about the way in which the code has been used. The repeated appearance of Yeshua's name blew all their fuses. You can't even bring the subject up without a major confrontation."

Keith shrugged. "Put all that together and the result is

deportation. The government just didn't want to mess with you. They pulled the plug."

"And now the Palestinians have done the same thing at the other end." Ben paced up and down in the cell. "It feels like they've thrown the key away. I don't see how we'll get out of here in time."

Judy hugged him. "It's all in the Lord's hands anyway," she said in his ear and kissed him on the cheek.

Ben smiled weakly. "I wonder how our people at Petra are handling the delay. They must be tremendously concerned."

"Who are they?" Keith asked.

"A number of American Christian missionaries worked on end-times prophecy for decades and came to the conclusion that God had prepared a secret place in the Jordan desert to protect Jews," Ben explained. "They studied a combination of passages in Revelation 12, Isaiah 63, and the book of Obadiah that led them to believe an abandoned city in the mountains of ancient Edom was a chosen haven."

"When we looked at the Hebrew words in Micah 2:12–13," Judy added, "we found confirmation of their conclusions. The prophet foresaw the Messiah gathering the surviving remnant of Israel like a shepherd gathers his flock. The Hebrew word for 'flock' is *bozrah*, which is also the ancient name for Petra."

"We anticipate that God will bring many more Jews to this place as the Tribulation begins to unfold," Ben continued. "We want to be ready to take care of the groups regardless of how large or small they are. These people will be an important component in the hope of the future."

"Of course, in the modern world we call the desert area Petra, an entire city built into the soft red rock of seven-hundred-foot cliffs, so beautiful it should be one of the wonders of the world," Judy added.

"Reuven knew these missionaries and put us in touch with them," Ben said. "They've been helping me get the place stocked with supplies to carry us through the atomic attack."

"Do you think we will ever get there?" Keith looked out the cell window again. "What an irony. We're so close and yet—"

Judy drank the last of her tea and set the chipped cup back down on the tray. "I think it's time for a morning prayer meeting. If there was ever a time we needed the direct intervention of the heavenly Father, it's this very minute."

"Absolutely," Ann said. "Paul and Silas found that a little prayer session in a jail could bring big results." Ann slipped off the bed to the floor. "I don't know why we can't expect the same thing."

"I suggest we get down our knees and plead for God's hand to open our jail cell," Keith added.

"I want to pray for Jimmy," Judy said.

"And that the entire caravan gets through." Keith knelt beside his wife.

"Maybe they'll just keep going," Ben said thoughtfully. "Perhaps they'll just go on to Amman. That's certainly better than being bottled up in Israel."

"Let's just leave it all in the Lord's hands," Judy concluded and bowed her head.

WHEN THE JAILER CAME BACK for the breakfast tray four hours later, he left a meager lunch. Another pot of tea replaced the first one. Four pieces of pita bread were stacked next to a dirty dish of falafel. A handful of raw carrots completed the offering. The hungry prisoners ate it all with little comment.

The heat of the noonday sun banished the memory of the cold night. The metal roof was quickly turning the cell into an oven. The two couples kept praying.

An hour later Khalil shouted as he came down the hall, "Everybody up. Pay attention." Another guard accompanied him.

The two couples scurried to their feet and looked expectantly through the bars.

"Come with me," Khalil demanded. The guard unlocked the cell.

"What's happening?" Ben asked.

The policeman didn't answer but stepped in front while the other guard fell in behind the Americans. They walked briskly back down the corridor to the original detention room. Khalil opened the door and pointed inside. "Go in."

Keith exploded. "Our friends are here!"

Ephraim Neuman leaped to his feet. "Thank the Holy One of Israel, you're alive!"

Rivka held out his arms. "Praise the Lord!"

Jimmy stood like a statue, looking apprehensive and stoic. Judy rushed toward her brother. Only after she hugged him did his arms mechanically reach around his sister.

"I take it that you do know each other," Khalil observed caustically.

"Yes, yes." Ephraim Neuman's voice cracked. "These are our friends, the people we have been searching for. The colleagues we told you about."

Khalil looked at the other guard and tossed his hands up indifferently. "So, it looks like their story fits."

The guard shrugged.

"You are very fortunate," Khalil said. "These people showed up at the police station looking for you. Luckily they had the same story that you told me yesterday."

"We couldn't get through," Rivka agonized. "We've been holed up out by the Dead Sea for two days." He held two fingers in the air.

"I didn't find PO 636 701," Jimmy told Judy. "I watched behind us but I didn't see the car."

"That's okay, Jimmy." She hugged him again. "You did a good job."

"These people don't know anything about the pileup on the back road." Khalil spoke directly to Ben. "And they certainly aren't Mossad operatives. They can't even find their way through town very well." He raised his eyebrows. "You are most fortunate that they got through."

"Can we leave?" Keith asked urgently.

"Why not? Your story checks out. There's no danger anymore."

Jimmy shook his head violently. "No. In A.D. 135 Simeon bar Kochba's army was completely wiped out by the Romans, ending the last Jewish uprising. It happened on Av 9. All Jews were expelled from England in 1290 on Av 9. Both Jewish temples were destroyed on Av 9. There is always danger on this day."

Khalil looked at the other guard. "What's this guy talking about?"

"When World War I began in 1914, all the Jews in Russia were immediately persecuted and thousands were killed on Av 9. This action correlated with the Jews being expelled from Spain in 1492 on Av 9." Jimmy paused to get a big breath of air.

"Thank you, Jimmy." Judy put her hand over his mouth.

"What's this Av nonsense all about?" Khalil looked menacingly at Jimmy.

"He's just got a problem." Judy smiled like a mother explaining a five-year-old boy breaking a vase in a department store. "Little things set him off. He's all right now." She again clamped her hand over Jimmy's mouth.

The PLO policeman shook his head. "Americans!" he muttered to himself. "Okay. The whole bunch of you get out of here. And keep out of trouble."

"Absolutely." Ben shook Khalil's hand. "The very best to you, sir. Merry Christmas. Happy Ramadan. Whatever." He hurried through the door. The rest of the group scurried behind Ben, racing down the hall and out of the administration building.

"Should I keep looking for PO 636 701?" Jimmy asked.

"No!" Judy hugged him. "Cross those people off your list! We're on our way somewhere else."

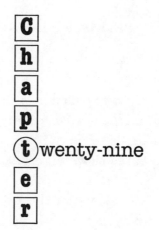

c h a p (**t**)wenty-nine **e r**

WHEN KEITH AND ANN YAAKOV burst through the front door of the police station, forty members of their congregation broke into applause. People hugged each other. Some broke into tears. Arab passersby stopped and stared at the strange family reunion.

"We were terrified for your safety," Danny Rubenstein said, slapping Ben on the back. "I thought we'd never get through the blockade. The IDF was really nasty." The little man hugged Ann.

"And the road was incredibly hot down there by the Dead Sea," his wife added. "I thought I'd melt into a sweat bucket," the overweight woman said as she fanned her face with a piece of newspaper.

"What finally broke things loose?" Ben asked.

"Strange thing." Danny shook his head. "Late this morning the IDF pulled out and started south toward the Negev. The talk up and down the line of cars was that the army was going to Egypt."

An elderly lady pulled at Keith's sleeve. "Where's Mrs. Skypanski and the others? And Aaron Slatsky's carload?"

Keith looked at Ann and back to Ben. "Let's go across the street." He called above the chatter. "We need to talk among ourselves."

"Come on," Ben said. "Please sit down on the benches under the tree. The shade will help."

The congregation gathered around Ben and Keith, pushing, pulling, and chattering. Keith signaled for silence. Ben spoke first. "We have very little time and can only give you the bare details. It is important that we get out of Jericho immediately. Understand?

"I think Keith should tell you what happened."

Keith took a deep breath. "We had a tragic accident . . . caused by the army chasing us. A pickup driven by an Arab—" Keith swallowed before continuing. "A pickup pulled out in front of the caravan and crashed into the IDF jeep. Aaron and Mrs. Skypanski's car were caught in the pileup." He cleared his throat and clinched his jaw. "There was an explosion . . . the cars caught on fire . . . everyone was killed."

Deafening silence fell over the group. People covered their mouths; some hid their eyes. Sobbing broke out. The older people sunk down on the park benches.

"Aaron, Golda, Mariam—" a woman lamented. "Gone?"

"That sweet little woman," someone groaned.

"Did we come through so much for nothing?" an older man anguished.

"What about their bodies?" Danny Rubenstein ventured.

"Everyone and everything was incinerated." Keith's voice was barely audible. "The fire was awful." He cleared his throat. "Our car was also destroyed."

"Why?" Rivka wailed. "Why *them?*"

Ben inhaled deeply. "Evil never gives up," he said bluntly. "We must run for the border this very moment because the devil's strategy is relentless. From the first day of Israel's existence, the attack has not ceased.

"Look at us. We haven't done anything wrong. Our friends just happened to be standing in the middle of the battlefield. They got caught in the cross fire."

"Exactly." Judy put her arm around Ben's waist. "In war there are casualties. We can't retreat because our friends fall. We must remember the great honor of being chosen to fight the Lord's battle."

"Aaron, Mrs. Skypanski, Golda, Mariam, and Daniel are the newest heroes in God's kingdom." Ann's voice was uncharacteristically forceful. "This is not a time to fix blame but to thank God for their courage."

"When we reach our destination tonight, we will say Kaddish," Keith continued. "The mourner's prayer will comfort us, but now the clock is ticking. We must hurry to our destination."

"Where?" Danny Rubenstein asked. "Isn't it time for us to know the place?"

"Certainly," Ben answered. "We kept the location a secret to keep from jeopardizing you. Obviously, your lack of information was vital in convincing the authorities to let us go. But that's behind us now. We are going to ancient Bozrah, now the famous city called Petra, only seventy miles southeast of

Jerusalem. Friends have stored provisions there to tide us through the impending disaster."

"But we don't have time to spare," Keith urged. "Let's get in our cars and cross the border as quickly as we can. We'll have to squeeze the four of us in somewhere."

"We can readjust," Danny answered. "Ben will need to be in the front car."

"Let's go," Ben pressed. "We've already lost more than a day here in Jericho."

The group said little as they returned to their cars. After a few minutes of reshuffling, the caravan of six cars slowly pulled away from the curb and wound through the side streets of Jericho until they found the highway to the border. Traffic limped along, stacked up, and the pace slowed unbearably. The wilderness became increasingly hot as they approached the Jordan River bottom, the dirt turning hard as cement. Ben fretted and tossed in the car seat, but there was no way to get around the bottleneck. Time dragged.

"Look," Danny pointed. "The final checkpoint is just ahead. I thought we'd never see it."

Ben leaned against the dashboard. "The Israelis sure aren't working this side of the border hard, but look at what's happening on the Jordanian side. No one is checking passports. Traffic is not coming through."

"People are stacked up as far as the eye can see." Danny shaded his eyes. "I'd hate to be over there."

"What time is it?" Judy leaned forward in the backseat.

Ben looked at his watch. "Five forty-five. The sun is going to start fading before long. I had hoped to get to Petra while we still had some light."

Danny inched forward behind a pickup full of Arab laborers. The lone guard took one long look inside the pickup and flagged the workers through the checkpoint.

At that moment two truckloads of Israeli soldiers sped over the hill behind the caravan. Without waiting for the cars to get out of their way, they passed on the road's shoulder, spraying rocks in every direction.

"Watch out," Ben warned. "The cavalry is charging up behind us. Not a hopeful sign."

The trucks flew past Rubenstein's car and pulled to a stop at the fence running along the border. Soldiers jumped out.

The border guard stared at the convoy and then stuck his head in the car. "Who are you?"

"We're a Christian tour group," Keith answered. "I'm taking the people to sightsee in Amman."

Soldiers emptied out of the trucks and began fanning across the area, holding their rifles in readiness. The young border guard turned around and looked puzzled. He scratched his head and frowned at the new troops.

"We're trying to get to the hotel before dark," Keith added.

"Any problem with us going on through?"

"I don't know." The soldier looked a second time at the troops hurrying along the perimeters of the border checkpoint station.

"The five cars directly behind us are also a part of our group," Keith urged. "We'd like to cross together. Do you want to see our passports? We're Americans."

Soldiers started yelling commands back and forth. Some of the troops positioned themselves along the rolls of barbed wire running under gun towers overlooking the road. Other men blocked the incoming side of the highway.

The border inspector took a second look inside. "No, passports aren't necessary. You're obviously American tourists. The whole group can go through." He straightened up and spoke to one of the soldiers who had just arrived. His voice carried back through the car window. "We are expecting more trouble coming in from Jordan?"

Danny Rubenstein immediately drove forward on the winding stretch of pavement that led to the Allenby Bridge. The little caravan passed the stalled traffic on the other side. Irritation and anger was etched in the faces of the waiting drivers. They snarled and glared as the messianic Jews passed.

"I know those people can't understand," Judy observed, "but thank God they can't get into Israel."

"I hope the troops make sure no one comes across tonight," Keith added. "Little do they know what they're really doing."

Danny looked in the rear mirror. "Strange. Look behind us. No one came through the checkpoint after our last car. Why didn't they let the rest of the line through?"

Judy looked out the back window. "You're right. We're the last train going south. Thank God we slipped through in the nick of time."

PUSHING PAST luggage laden tourists stacked up in the entryway, Orlaf Pimen and Anton Ketele rushed into Ben Gurion Airport. Each man wore sunglasses, carried an attaché case and one small, black bag. Pimen's black hairpiece did little to conceal his bald head.

Everywhere people were nudging and shoving and arguing.

Passengers seemed unusually agitated. The Russians ignored the chaos and barged into the ticket line. With total indifference to protests and threats, they quickly wormed through the queue to the front of the KLM ticket desk.

"I'm sorry, sir, but you must wait in line like everyone else." The ticket agent gave Ketele a haggard look, pointing to the back of the long line of seething passengers.

"Listen to me. Two tickets are reserved for O. Pimen and A. Ketele," Ketele barked as he and Pimen set their luggage down. "Make it quick. We don't have time to wait."

The man behind the counter smiled the smile of one who has been yelled at all day and shrugged. "I'd suggest you cool your heels, sir," the Israeli said in impeccable English. "You aren't going anywhere tonight."

"Don't jerk us around," Pimen snarled. "Hand us the tickets, or I will come back there and get them."

"Ease up, Ivan," the agent shot back. "I'm from Chicago. I didn't take any guff from you pushy types at O'Hare, so I sure ain't gonna take it here."

"Let's start again," Anton said, forcing a smile. "We just want to pick up reserved tickets for Pimen and Ketele for the 8:30 flight to Rome."

"And let *me* start again." The agent smiled back. "All flights are canceled until further notice. No one is going or coming. The government shut everything down a couple of hours ago."

Pimen reached across the counter and grabbed the man's coat, jerking him up against the counter. "I want those tickets now!" he shouted in the agent's face. "You got a hearing problem?"

Immediately a small man in a dark suit threw a strangle hold around Pimen's neck and jerked him backward to the floor. Pimen's black hairpiece sailed across the terrazzo floor. "Security," the plainclothes policeman hissed into Pimen's ear. "Don't make me hurt you."

Ketele turned and sent a vicious kick into the man's ribs. The officer gasped but only increased his hold on Pimen's neck. Instantly, a second, larger policeman appeared, drew his gun and delivered a sharp blow to the back of Anton's neck, sprawling the Russian on the floor beside his comrade. The beefy cop stuck his knee in Anton's back and pointed his pistol at the downed Russian's head. Passengers scattered in every direction.

"Move and I shoot!" the policeman shouted at Ketele. The ticket agent ducked behind the counter.

"And I will break your neck," the red-faced policeman wheezed in Pimen's ear. "We've been tailing you ever since you first pushed your way into the airport."

"You will pay!" Ketele threatened. "We have diplomatic passports!"

"Get up slowly," the officer with the gun demanded. "Keep your hands in the air and don't make any sudden movements."

The smaller officer released his choke hold on Pimen who shrugged the man off and stood rubbing his bruised throat, his bald head dotted with perspiration. "Our government will have your heads for this," he managed to croak out.

"We'll see." The red-faced agent picked up one of the attaché cases and slung it on the counter. "Let's just see what your kicking, diplomat buddy is all about."

"Stop," Ketele threatened. "That is a diplomatic pouch, and you can't touch it."

The officer opened the case and peered in. "Look at this." He held up two passports. "One from Russia and one from Iraq."

"Give me that—" Anton grabbed for the passports.

The policman slapped his hand aside. "You had me there for a second, friend. But Israel's not exactly on speaking terms with Iraq. If you had any sort of diplomatic immunity before, it just went down the toilet." With a flourish, he tossed the passports back in the briefcase and pulled handcuffs from his belt. "This will help you keep your hands to yourself." He twisted Ketele's arms behind his back and tightly secured his wrists.

Ketele cursed and jerked at the restraints.

"I think Mossad should have a look at these passports," the policeman said, snapping the briefcase shut. "And these two characters too. They smell like a problem for intelligence."

"Their passports said they were in Jerusalem. Maybe we'd better go back there and find out what they were up to." The larger policemen kept his gun on Pimen while tossing his cuffs to his partner. "You cuff baldy. I'll let Jerusalem know we're on our way."

"No!" Pimen screamed, trying to twist out of the cuffs already being snapped on his wrists. "Not back to Jerusalem!"

"I'll have a car meet us out front." He holstered his pistol and reached for a mobile phone on his belt. "We don't need to waste any time. Security is bad enough as it is."

"Not Jerusalem!" Pimen screamed again, his voice cracking. "No! No!"

"Shut up!" Ketele shouted back.

"What's wrong with Jerusalem, boys?" The smaller policeman glared at Pimen. He twisted Pimen's arm. "Huh? Why don't you want to go there? . . . Something's not right here."

"Not Jerusalem," Pimen pleaded. "Not Jeru—"

Ketele kicked wildly at Pimen. "Keep your mouth shut, you blubbering idiot." A kick connected with Pimen's stomach, doubling him over. Ketele took another kick at the man's lowered head, missing and nearly spinning himself to the ground.

The two policemen separated the Russians, pushing them toward the exit, while the larger officer talked in the phone. "Get a car around front immediately," he ordered.

"No! No! Anywhere but Jerusalem—" Pimen's voice faded into the uproar in the lobby.

"Guess you won't be needing these," the ticket agent called out, dropping the Russians' tickets in the trash.

FOR THE NEXT TWO HOURS the little caravan sped through the desert. Daylight lingered, but the sun slowly disappeared below the horizon. The cars finally descended into a deep canyon. The valley narrowed, sheer rock walls towering above them.

"We'll park the cars just ahead." Ben pointed to a broad flat area at the base of the rock outcropping. "The canyon gets too narrow to drive any further."

"How will the older people handle the walk?" Ann asked.

"We'll take it slow. We don't have very far to go." Ben pointed up the trail. "The path is sandy and they won't go up any steep inclines."

Lofty boulders began to shut all light out. The passageway

looked like a dark crack between two huge megaliths, each seven hundred feet tall. Ben hopped out and began directing the cars, parking them against the stone wall.

"Follow me," Ben called out to the group. "I'm going to have Keith and Ann bring up the rear. Please get behind Judy and me." He pointed toward the opening. "Stay close. Watch your step."

Judy kept smiling and encouraging the others. "I don't want you out of my sight, Ben," she said under her breath. "Tonight I'm stuck to you like glue."

Ben gave her a sly little grin. "Just try to get away." He kissed her forehead. "When this trip is over, I'm going to make sure we don't ever have this problem again."

Judy blinked twice. "Wh . . . what did you say?"

"Come on," Ben called to the group. "Don't be afraid of the canyon. It's not as bad as it looks." He dragged Judy behind him. "We're not far away from the end."

"What do you mean?" Judy pulled at his sleeve.

"It's something I've been meaning to talk to you about," he said over his shoulder. "But it'll have to wait until we get these people settled."

Danny Rubenstein interrupted them. "I've always heard about this area, but I can't believe how majestic it is. Like a hike through a miniature Grand Canyon."

"Too bad the sunlight isn't brighter," Ben answered. "The colors look like the painted desert."

"But why this place?" Danny asked. "Why would the Bible direct us to come here?"

"I don't know." Ben picked up the pace. "Maybe the rocks are so high they'll prevent shock waves or bursts of fire from hitting us. Possibly the wind currents will keep fallout from drifting in. That's just a guess. But it is the place prepared by God in the wilderness for believing Jews to hide during the Tribulation. Revelation 12:6 is just one of the biblical passages that mentions it."

"Did you know the apostle Paul lived here during the three years he was in the desert after his conversion?" Judy added. "El Khazneh, often called the Treasury, housed many famous ancient people at one time or another." She slipped her hand into Ben's. "All that history—I think it's kind of romantic." She squeezed Ben's hand.

"Danny, you won't believe your eyes," Ben said as he walked. "El Khazneh is a building carved out of the rock cliffs and nearly three stories high. No one really knows who did the work, but it was completed before the first century. Similar structures are all over the area. Thousands of beautifully carved caves wait here to provide shelter. Fresh water runs into carved cisterns. It's a miracle civilization has stayed away from filling this place up for hundreds of years now."

Judy smiled. "It's just been waiting here for God's timing," she said.

The canyon's meandering trail narrowed, but no one complained. The noise of the outside world completely dissolved in the rock valley. The group became silent, the solemnity of the vast cliffs resonating with their own awareness of the significance of the final lap of their journey.

Ben slipped out through the final cleave in the seven-hundred-foot-high canyon. "Here we are," he called over his shoulder. "Hey! We made it!" Ben shouted, his voice echoing off the rocks. "We're here."

"Oh!" Danny Rubenstein exclaimed. "I wasn't prepared for anything like *this.*"

Huge columns of polished red rock towered above the entrance to the Treasury. Polished panels of rock and carved ornate urns loomed above the vast open area in front of the ancient edifice. Light streamed from the doorway inside the rock building. Camels standing in the sandy area looked quizzically toward Ben. Dark shadows of horses loomed against the rocky backdrop.

"Ben's back," a man yelled from somewhere in the darkness. "They've arrived!"

"Get the lights on," someone called out. "Fire up the generator!"

"Our friends are waiting for us," Ben shouted back to the people following him. "Hurry."

The sound of a gas motor broke the stillness. Suddenly soft light flooded the open space, exposing the beauty of the pastel colors of the rocks.

Several people appeared from among the rocks. "Let us help you," a woman said.

"Thank God you're here," another voice called out.

An American suddenly appeared in the Treasury's doorway. He called out, "Thought you were a goner, Meridor! We've been expecting you for days."

The refugees poured out into the open area. People hugged each other. Some wept.

Ben held up his hand. "Friends, even as Moses found passage through the wilderness not far from here, God made a way for us. We have been snatched from the fire. Welcome to your new home."

The people hurried inside the building.

Ben looked at Judy for a moment and then hugged her fiercely. "We did it." Ben forced a smile. "*We* did it . . . and we came out alive." He kissed her tenderly. "We can do anything as long as we're together—and God is with us."

Chapter thirty

CANDLELIGHT cast long shadows over Keith's little tribe, huddled together in the great hall inside El Khazneh. The faint glow was hauntingly reminiscent of thousands of evenings across more than twenty centuries when travelers and sojourners from far away lands gathered in this hidden city. The missionaries served the last of the soup from the large aluminum kettle simmering over the open fire; the group quickly consumed the hot broth with delicious hard-crusted bread.

"Ah, this coffee is wonderful," Judy announced. "That junk they called tea in jail was as bad as the Turkish coffee peddled on the streets."

Rivka Berg shook his head emphatically. "Come on! A baby could be weaned on this watered down stuff." He grimaced. "Don't call this coffee."

"Well, it's not champagne," Keith said as he stood up, "but

I want to propose a toast. What an incredible job our friends have done for us." He held his porcelain coffee cup to Ben and Judy. "Here! Here!"

"Yes!" The group applauded and returned the salute.

"And especially to Jimmy." Keith smiled at the young man sitting close to his sister. "No one demonstrated greater courage and conviction than Jim Bithell. He was willing to put his life on the line for us. We owe him a very special round of applause."

Once again the congregation cheered. Keith patted Jimmy on the back several times. For the first time, Jimmy smiled. He looked embarrassed but pleased. Jimmy glanced from the corner of his eyes, watching Judy's reaction.

"Speech! Speech!" people called good-naturedly.

Jimmy squirmed but kept smiling. Finally he stood up. "You are my friends," Jim said slowly as he awkwardly crossed his arms over his chest. "Thank you for the car ride and taking care of me good." Jimmy looked down at his feet. His voice no longer had the mechanical sound of a Dictaphone, but was soft and warm. "Av 9 has been a bad day, but tomorrow I will be here with you. In this place, Av 9 will be a good day." He raised his eyebrows and looked toward the far wall, shifting his weight from one foot to the other. "And I love you." Jim quickly dropped to the ground and ducked his head.

Ben patted him on the back. "Great speech." Judy hugged her brother.

"The loss of our friends weighs heavily on all of our hearts," Keith continued. "Some of them had already lived through unspeakable horrors, but they were still willing to stand up for Yeshua and be counted. It would have been much easier to stay behind closed doors and keep their convictions to themselves. Yesterday these dear ones entered into the joy of their reward. We are the ones feeling the pain, not them."

The group murmured their agreement.

"When we gathered in the parking lot and left Jerusalem, Mrs. Skypanski led us in Kaddish prayers to begin the mourning for all those left behind," Keith continued. "Now it is time for us to say the mourner's prayer for her."

A bent little woman in the back of the circle held up her hand. "She was my good friend," Ruth Goldstein said. "Her invitation brought me to your congregation and eventually to believe in Yeshua as the Messiah. I would like to be the one to say Kaddish."

"Of course, Ruth." Keith sat back down in the circle. "In a few hours, we will have many people to mourn, but now we must remember our own dear ones. Ruth, lead us and we can join in as we remember the Hebrew words."

Men produced talliths. Some covered their heads with yarmulkes. Many of the women put scarves over their hair. Ruth Goldstein stood up.

"*Yit-gadal ve-yit-kadah shmei raba,*" Ruth began, the cares of the ages etched in every wrinkle of her face. Each word carried an unbearable cargo of woe. *"B'almas divra khir'ute ve-yamlikh mal-khutei be-hayeki-khon.*" She paused to catch her breath. Tears ran down her cheeks.

Keith leaned next to Judy. "She prayed that God's holiness would be recognized throughout the world and His sovereignty be accepted everywhere."

"Uve'yomei-khon uve-hayei di-khol beit yishrael ba-agala u-vizman kariv v'imru amen," others in the group prayed with her.

"They are asking that recovery of faith happen during our lifetime and in the life of Israel," Keith whispered.

The mournful dirge ascended like incense. Suddenly Jimmy's voice joined the chorus chanting Kaddish.

"Oseh shalom bimromav hu ya'aseh shalom aleinu v'ai kol yisrael v'imru." the congregation's fervor diminished. "Amen," they concluded together.

"Amen." The slight old woman sat down.

"I am sure you are exhausted." Alec Downs, one of the missionaries, spoke sympathetically. "We count it a great privilege to serve you." The tall, burly American pointed through the large open door into the black night. "Unfortunately we can only run the generator during emergencies. We have to conserve our fuel. I'm afraid I can only offer you accommodations of the same class they gave our Lord in Bethlehem. But it does put you in rather good company. We have prepared beds and cots in caves all over the place. They are ready whenever you wish to retire."

"How can we ever thank you enough?" Danny answered for the group. "You took us in like orphans out of the storm. We will pray fervently that God repays you endlessly for your every effort."

"Thank you," the missionary answered.

"Tonight I wouldn't know if elephants ran through my bedroom," Rivka Berg joked. "After the last night on the roadside, I'm too tired to turn down hay or straw. I'm ready to hit the sack any time the barn opens."

"Psst." Ruth Goldstein shook her finger. "I was in your car last night. You snored like a wounded water buffalo." She waved him away. "Give the rest of us a break. Keep down wind. Put him back up there in that far canyon."

Ben poked Rivka in the ribs. "You go out there with the camels.

"Seriously, I would suggest we turn in as early as possible," Ben continued. "It's already quite late. We have no idea when the bomb will explode. We believe somewhere between now and tomorrow evening the tragedy will occur. I'm sure we'll know soon enough. In the meantime, we need all the sleep we can get."

"Agreed. I'm ready," Keith added. "The Jericho jail bunk left a lot to be desired, and we weren't even sleeping on the floor like you and Judy. I'm with Rivka. Let's go."

Alec Downs passed out assignments. Some couples were billeted in caves, others in tents. Missionaries with flashlights led the people across the rocks. The pitch-black night made it difficult to walk far without artificial light. Flashlights and candles dotted the terrain.

"I've made arrangements for the four of you to stay here in caves near the great hall," Alec explained to Ben and Keith. "I felt like leadership needed to be in a central location."

"Thanks, Alec." Ben looked around the spacious rock room. "I have a hunch we'll be packed before long. People will be pouring out of Israel. Things are going to get very bleak."

Alec bit his lip. "Yeah, we don't have long to wait. I'll be with some of my friends. We'll pray through the evening and into the morning hours."

"Great. Judy and I are going to sit outside and talk a bit. We, uh, need to consider some strategy for the future."

"Sure." Alec started down the rock steps. "I'll be across the way if you need anything. Just call."

"Let's sit out under the stars." Judy pulled on Ben's arm. "Just out here with the night . . . and each other."

They walked away from the huge building and found a natural rock seat close to the camels and horses. The animals huddled together, oblivious to their presence.

"Wow," Ben said. "Look at the sky. Not a cloud up there. Must be a million stars though."

"Yes." Judy snuggled close. "Breathtaking."

The stillness deepened. Ben gazed skyward.

"To think this whole journey started because I tried to find out what the twenty-fourth chapter of Matthew meant." Judy sighed. "All I wanted to know was how to make sense out of the predictions Jesus made about the end times. I was only interested in solving a puzzle."

"And we ended up getting swept into the greatest mystery of our time." Ben laughed. "The code. Can you believe it? We were just trying to grasp the Torah code and the whole thing turned into chaos."

"But look at what it did for us."

"Yes. For us," Ben said thoughtfully.

"Us?" Judy beamed. "By the way, I didn't quite get something you said back there on the trail as we were coming in." She feigned a frown. "You were going to fix something—"

Ben held her hand tenderly. "I have a confession to make, Judy. I know I'm often distant. I don't mean to be. I was only about six or seven when I first heard the stories of what happened to my relatives during the Holocaust. I was devastated—and terrified. I realized people I loved could evaporate in a puff of smoke." Ben wrung his hands. "Without really knowing what I was doing, I disappeared into an emotional cocoon. I decided to keep a safe distance from anybody I might care about."

The wind picked up and sent a swirl of sand flying through the air. Off in the distance, the sounds of people talking broke the silence.

"The first time we were separated in Jerusalem, I realized how much I loved you." He squeezed her hand. "I was terrified they had hurt you somehow." He stopped and swallowed. "And then suddenly, there we were, back together in the airport, being thrown out of the country."

"But you never said anything. Why didn't you at least give me a hint?"

Ben hung his head. "That's what I need to confess. When I recognized how deeply I cared about you, I got scared again. Everything inside shut up like a clam. I went back to my world of computers and math formulas." He slowly turned toward her. "I'm sorry, Judy. I'm just so—"

Judy threw her arms around his neck. "Ben, I've loved you forever. Well, at least since that silly chemistry class when you wouldn't pay the slightest attention to me." She kissed him fervently.

Ben held her close and spoke softly. "When I'm with you, I'm complete, settled as never before. You add life, vitality, spontaneity. You make me what I want to be."

"Oh, Ben."

"I can't stand the thought of facing the future without you.

I want to make sure we are never separated again." He kissed her tenderly.

"In a few hours, everything is going to change," Judy said soberly. "Our world will never be the same."

"Yes." Ben sighed. "Forever altered."

"And if we've been wrong and the bomb doesn't go off, the deaths of Mrs. Skypanski, Aaron Slatsky, and the rest will hang over our heads."

Ben shook his head. "I've been afraid even to consider the possibility, but you're right. The responsibility for their lives would hang like a millstone around our necks."

"But if the bomb does explode, I shudder even more. The predictions in Matthew 24 will start unfolding with the fury of a whirlwind. The twenty-one judgments of the book of Revelation will follow not many months behind that Av 9 war around Jerusalem."

Ben held her at arm's length. "But whatever comes, we can face it together. As long as we have each other, we can bear the rest."

Judy hugged him again. "As far as I'm concerned, we can let one of those ordained missionaries take care of the technicalities before God and man first thing in the morning. I'm signed on with you for the duration."

They stared into the sky and held each other close. For a long time neither spoke. Judy finally said, "I want to remember this moment forever."

"Me too."

"I can't believe I feel so tired at a time like this," she finally said. "It's as if a spring suddenly came unwound. The last two nights, the chase, the escape . . . I'm just exhausted."

"I hate to admit it, but I'm about to crater too. Maybe we ought to turn in. We've covered a lot of territory in a few minutes." Ben laughed. "There's no telling what tomorrow will be like."

"What time is it? Can you see your watch?"

Ben held his arm up and turned it toward the moon. "I can just make out the numbers. My goodness! No wonder we're tired. It's 12:02. At least six hours into Av 9."

Judy stood up. "Maybe we ought to say a prayer right now."

"Sure." Ben took her hand. "Tonight, we pray Your kingdom come—"

Suddenly the opaque sky exploded in dazzling light, the reds, grays, blacks in the rocks instantly visible. The wave of light passed over like a squall line racing before a thunderstorm. The dazzle faded momentarily and then far off in the distance a huge fireball soared up over the top of the mountains. The explosion expanded as it went upward. Clouds of black smoke rolled out and turned underneath as if feeding the eruption. The sky turned violet and crimson. Then the brilliance slowly faded as a violent torrent of wind rolled over the top of the canyon, spraying sand and dirt in every direction. Behind the gale, a tidal wave of rumbling sounds swept down the valley like a hurricane coming ashore.

Ben and Judy buried their faces in each other's shoulders, struggling to breathe and keep sand out of their eyes. The deafening roar slowly subsided.

Judy whispered in Ben's ear. "Remember what I read so long ago in Matthew? 'When you see all these things, know that it is near—at the doors!' Remember?"

"Thank God that we ran the race to the end, Judy. We were faithful. Yes, the doors are about to open. Regardless of how bad things get, we can look toward tomorrow with hope. We can enter together."

Appendix

A SECRET BIBLE CODE REALLY EXISTS, and it predicts an atomic holocaust in Jerusalem, as happens in this novel. Is the prediction reliable? The answer is yes and no. Yes, the Hebrew Bible really does have equidistant letter sequences (ELS) that predict an Av 9 5766 (August 3, 2006) atomic explosion in Jerusalem, and the plain text of Ezekiel 38 and 39 spells out the events that follow whenever the explosion occurs. But we must also remember that if we took other books, translated them into Hebrew, and turned our computers loose looking for messages encoded by skipping a particular number of characters, we would find many words and some rare phrases printed there by pure mathematical probability. The problem is to discern the real from the random.

Here's an example of the reason the Bible code is something of an enigma. Using a very short ELS, the word *Jerusalem* is encoded along with the phrases "Atomic holocaust," "World war," and "Your city to be destroyed by an act of terrorism." These phrases are connected to Deuteronomy 5:9: "For I, the LORD your God, am a jealous God, visiting the iniquity of the fathers upon the children to the third and fourth generations of those who hate Me." It's difficult to believe that these words are occurring by mere coincidence.

Look at a longer skip sequence found in Isaiah 32. Beginning with verse 1, the letters that "fall out" spell "atomic weapon." Trace the sequence through thirty-three chapters. In Isaiah 65:18, the *m* of atomic coincides with the *m* of *Jerusalem*. A coincidence? Maybe. Yet, the code sequence ends in Isaiah 65:18, in the middle of the following paragraph:

For behold, I create new heavens and a new earth;
And the former shall not be remembered or come to mind.
But be glad and rejoice forever in what I create;
For behold, I create Jerusalem as a rejoicing,
And her people a joy.
I will rejoice in Jerusalem,
And joy in My people;
The voice of weeping shall no longer be heard in her,
Nor the voice of crying. (vv. 17–19)

Confounding!

Is the code actually predicting that a world war will break out in 2006? I don't know for sure. The message could be a warning, or the war could be delayed by God for some reason. The prediction could even be a one-in-a-billion coincidence, like winning the lottery in three states on the same weekend. We used that date in this novel because we believe it could be a valid prediction. We'll certainly find out in 2006!

Robert Wise and I knew about the secret Bible code for many years before the rest of the world found out about it. We even included a code message in our first novel together in 1993, *The Third Millennium.* We found clues in the writings of Sir Isaac Newton. Newton was, in my opinion, the most brilliant mathematician who ever lived. He made more mathematical discoveries than even Albert Einstein. Newton was a devout Christian who spent nearly half his time studying Bible prophecy. We personally studied his very profound writings.

Three hundred years ago, Sir Isaac Newton explained that Jesus' triumphal entry into Jerusalem on a young donkey happened exactly 173,880 days (69 "prophetic weeks"; each "day" of the "week" represents a Hebrew calendar year of 360 days each) after Artaxerxes Longimanus made his decree to rebuild the walls of Jerusalem on March 14, 445 B.C., exactly the day Daniel said the Messiah would appear and be "cut off." Daniel wrote that prediction seven hundred years before Jesus came to the earth (see Daniel 9:24–27).

Newton thought the rapture could occur at any time, but he didn't think Jesus would return to establish His thousand-year reign on earth until shortly after the year 2000. The solution was much too complex to be unraveled with anything less than computers. Newton spent much of his life searching for the secret Bible code, but didn't find it because modern computers weren't invented until three hundred years later. (However, I'm surprised he didn't find the codes even without a computer.)

In 1997 Michael Drosnin, a brilliant Jewish reporter with *The Wall Street Journal* and *The Washington Post*, wrote *The Bible Code*. His book quickly became a best-seller in sixteen nations.

He was originally skeptical of the existence of a genuine Bible code, as most people are when they first hear about it. Drosnin went to mathematicians at Hebrew University years ago to disprove the Bible code. Drosnin is, by his own admission, an atheist. I, too, was cautious until I studied the code in depth and personally researched the arguments posed by both Jewish and Christian scholars. When math scholars at Hebrew University showed Drosnin their amazing research, he became convinced of the validity of the code and wrote his book.

Scholars didn't find Bible doctrines, only historical facts and dates. Since I believe in the inerrancy of the original copies of the plain text of Scripture, if code sequences ever are found in the future that in any way contradict the plain text of Scripture, I would throw them out as a bad coincidence. But it hasn't happened. If the codes are all a coincidence, as some Jewish and Christian leaders claim, why are there only historical events and dates and names and no doctrinal statements in the codes?

For example, in warning of disaster the codes gave the name "Yitzhak Rabin" along with the city "Tel Aviv" and the year 1995 (actually, its equivalent on the Jewish calendar), as well as the name of Rabin's assassin, "Amir," with the phrase, "name of assassin who will assassinate." Drosnin warned Rabin a year before the fact that the prime minister was targeted. Rabin was skeptical and didn't believe the codes.

Newton and *Einstein* are both encoded in the Bible with some statements about them. In addition, *Shakespeare, Roosevelt, Churchill, Stalin, Hitler, Wright Brothers, Nixon, Clinton, Princess Diana,* and *Netanyahu* all appear in the code.

Many of earth's greatest earthquakes (including the exact dates in some cases) are there.

One of the most amazing code sequences concerns the bombing in Oklahoma City. In fact, after the bombing occurred, researchers simply put the word *Oklahoma* (in Hebrew, of course) into the Bible code computer program. (Since Robert Wise lives there, he was particularly intrigued with the result.) "Oklahoma" was only encoded once in the entire Old Testament, and surrounding it, either in the codes or in the plain text, were the following phrases: "Terrible frightening death," "Murrah building," "His name is Timothy," "McVeigh," "He ambushed", "he pounced," "Terror—two years from the death of Koresh," "Day 19," "On the 9th hour," "In the morning" and a few other related phrases. Of course, we now know Timothy McVeigh bombed the Murrah Building at 9:00 A.M. on April 19, 1995, exactly two years after David Koresh was killed in Waco, Texas.

A good friend, who is the pastor of a messianic Jewish congregation in Israel was skeptical too. I showed him the actual biblical text where these phrases are bunched together at definite skip sequences, and he was shocked to read "Timothy McVeigh" and other actual phrases in Scripture. I believe the words were put there over three thousand years ago by Almighty God, who is sovereign over all historical events past and future, when He handed stone tablets to Moses and inspired the other writers of Scripture.

Many Christian leaders are skeptical about the Bible code. Many of the doubters are my good friends. As a psychiatrist, I try to analyze why so many people deny the obvious—and why I personally refused to believe in the validity of Bible codes until I pulled out some of my own probability and statistics textbooks from graduate school and medical school. It's as though this time the emperor really is wearing clothes but everyone is laughing and saying he is naked. Bystanders are afraid to disagree with the mockers and insist, "I don't see clothes on the guy."

I don't know for sure why many people are missing out on this miraculous computer-age discovery, but here are my guesses. When I studied medical history in medical school, I was shocked to find out that many of the physicians who made the greatest discoveries—like bacteria for instance—were ostracized and sometimes even locked up in mental institutions.

People have a tendency to think that mankind already knows everything important. When a new discovery comes along, it upsets us. When Thomas Edison invented bifocals, enabling many people to see well enough to read again, many of the pastors around the world preached against them, calling them "devil eyes" and saying that if God wanted people to see He would have given them better vision naturally.

At the onset, Jewish rabbis loved the Bible code because it verified the authenticity of the Torah (Genesis through Deuteronomy) and the rest of the Old Testament. Now, most of them have become skeptical. Could it be because the Hebrew name for Jesus, *Yeshua,* is encoded along with messianic phrases in every messianic chapter in the Old Testament? Now they are saying the codes are a coincidence. As "proof," they point out that Reverend Moon can be found throughout the Old Testament if the right code sequence is used. However, remember that the Hebrew word for "Moon" is only two letters long;

of course, that two letter sequence will probably be found many times in any Hebrew book the size of the Bible if you feed those two letters into a computer and command it to search forward or backward with any sequence from two to two thousand letters apart.

We simply don't like any new information that shakes us up. I'm still skeptical about many of the techniques Drosnin used in *The Bible Code.* I think most of what he says is very valuable, but he is a reporter, not a mathematician. I have had many years of study in math and statistics (attending college, graduate school, medical school, and seminary from age eighteen to age forty), so I can see the value of the actual coded phrases, but I remain skeptical of some of Drosnin's "hidden text" messages, without necessarily ruling them all out either. (A hidden text message occurs when the letters in a verse are left in the same order, but the spaces are moved, changing the meaning of the passage.)

It may surprise you to find out that Robert Wise and I "predicted" in our first novel, *The Third Millennium,* that the war described in Ezekiel 38 and 39 between Israel and the Muslim nations (and Russia) would break out on the Av 9 in 1996. It would take many pages for me to explain to you all the reasons that I chose that date, but the date seemed to fit many prophecies in the plain text of both the Old and New Testaments. Robert and I wrote that into the novel in 1992, and it was published in 1993. But it wasn't until Drosnin's book came out in 1997 that we discovered that Av 9, 1996, *really was* encoded in the Bible. The code states that Prime Minister Benjamin Netanyahu would make a trip that day to Amman, Jordan, and there he would be "certainly assassinated," an act that would trigger the nuclear holocaust in Israel soon afterward (before the Jewish New Year). But encoded along with these phrases were the words *delayed, delayed, delayed.*

In reality, Netanyahu was scheduled to go to Amman, Jordan, on *Av 9, 1996* (though he was warned not to by Michael Drosnin through contact with Netanyahu's father). But King Hussein of Jordan got sick that day and canceled Netanyahu's trip. The trip, the assassination, and possibly World War III were all "delayed, delayed, delayed" that day by a sovereign act of God. This "atomic holocaust in Jerusalem" is also encoded for Av 9 in the year 2000, but the word *delayed* occurs once with it. Does delayed here mean "delayed from 1996 to 2000"? Or does it mean "delayed again"? I don't know. We'll find out in 2000. The next time it is "scheduled"—so to speak—is Av 9 in 2006, and the word *delay* does not appear near this date. For that reason we chose 2006 for this novel. However, Ezekiel 38 and 39 tell us that when this battle occurs, God will supernaturally destroy Israel's enemy soldiers and deliver Israel for a seven-month period. I believe the Great Tribulation will follow that seven months of peace. Most of the twenty-one judgments of Revelation will occur then, *I think*, in a 1,260-day period, and then Jesus will return to establish His millennial kingdom, hopefully around Feast of Trumpets in 2010. However, I am purely guessing, so please don't take my words as a completely reliable prediction; it is only a guess—an educated guess, but still a guess. No man knows the day or the hour, except the Father in heaven.

By the way, do you invest in Asian stocks? If the Bible code is right, you had better sell them. The codes predict huge earthquakes in China and Japan, especially in the Jewish year that occurs from the fall of 1999 to the fall (Feast of Trumpets) of the year 2000, with an "economic collapse" in Japan (no date). Drosnin revealed this possibility in his 1997 book, and the Asian markets began to fall until late that year and in early '98. The code also seems to predict that Communism will collapse in China.

The codes do not say when the rapture, the Tribulation, or the Second Coming of Christ will be. That is, we don't think they do. But probably only one-hundredth of one percent of what is buried in the codes has been discovered. They do encode a "fire-earthquake" to "destroy" the city of "L.A., Calif." in the year 2010, a year that is encoded for the world as a year of "gloom," "darkness," and "days of horror." Robert Wise and I are using many hundreds of passages of prophetic Scripture from the Old and New Testaments and combining them with our own Bible code research to make some educated guesses about how things could *theoretically* unfold. Our conclusions are reflected in the next novel, picking up on what happens right after the atomic holocaust in Jerusalem. We will guess about the end-time events in the sequel to *The Secret Code*, which should come out in the year 2000.

I hope the rapture of 1 Thessalonians, chapter 4 (and 1 Corinthians 15:51–52) will happen some time between now and the Great Tribulation. I studied at Trinity Seminary in Chicago (Deerfield, Illinois) and finished my seminary degree at Dallas Theological Seminary, so I hope DTS is right about the rapture occurring seven or more years before the Second Coming of Christ. That scenario would put the rapture prior to 2004 if the Bible code events of 2010 are describing the end of the Great Tribulation.

The more I study Bible prophecy, the *less* dogmatic I become. There are many Bible-believing Christians who believe the rapture will occur prior to the signing of a peace treaty between the Antichrist and Israel seven years before the Lord's return, which is the *pretribulation* position; it is the one that I personally believe is probably true. But only God knows. Other Christians believe in a *midtribulation* rapture, just prior to the nasty events of the Great Tribulation, which we know will last 1,260 days (three and a half years). Our next novel will take that position just for the sake of open-mindedness, even though I prefer the "pre-trib" position. Many other godly men and women believe in a *post-tribulation* rapture occurring as the Lord is descending to earth. There are other positions other believers hold as well.

Our hope and prayer is that, whatever your beliefs may be, you'll read our entire series of novels: *The Third Millennium, The Fourth Millennium, Beyond the Millennium, The Secret Code,* and the sequel that follows, with predictions for the years 2006 to 2010. We trust that you will be inspired to visualize how the prophetic events in Scripture can come to life, because they *will* come to life. They are *already* coming to life in our own lifetimes!

If you are merely biding time in the foolish rat-race of life, living for sex, power, and money, "get real!" Ask Jesus, the Son of God, the Messiah, to forgive your sins and to become part of your daily life. Develop a *relationship* with Yeshua, the God-man, the Jewish carpenter who died on the cross to pay for your sins and will come back soon to end the Battle of

Armageddon at the end of the Great Tribulation to begin His Kingdom—His millennial kingdom.

Your kingdom come, Your will be done on earth as it is in heaven. Amen.

Sincerely, from a fellow soldier on His Kingdom Team,

—PAUL MEIER, M.D.
Dallas, Texas
Fall, 1998

About the Authors

Paul Meier, M.D., is the cofounder and medical director of the New Life clinics, the largest provider of psychiatric services in the United States. He is the author of more than forty books including the best-sellers *The Third Millennium, The Fourth Millennium, Beyond the Millennium, Love Is a Choice,* and *Happiness Is a Choice for Teens.*

Robert L. Wise, Ph.D., is a noted teacher, lecturer, and author of twenty books including *Quest for the Soul, The Fall of Jerusalem,* and *All That Remains.* He and Meier are the authors of *Windows of the Soul, The Third Millennium, The Fourth Millennium,* and *Beyond the Millennium.* His classic, *When There Is No Miracle,* recently has been re-released.